Longlisted for the Miles Franklin Award

"America please meet Omar Musa, a writer with the attuned ear of a great poet, the narrative gifts of a seasoned novelist, and no slight exposure to the beautiful struggle. This book is like one of those hip-hop songs that forevermore becomes an anthem—this time for the disenfranchised aspirants of Australia. Read him now or suffer for it."

—Mitchell S. Jackson, author of *The Residue Years*

"Omar Musa's writing is tough and tender, harsh and poetic, raw and beautiful; it speaks to how we live and dream now. This novel broke my heart a little, but it also made me ecstatic at the possibilities of what the best writing can do. His voice is genuine, new, and exciting; his voice roars."

—Christos Tsiolkas, author of *The Slap*

"The streets are alive with the sound of Omar Musa! Blood and fire, destruction and generation, nightmares and dreams, all converge in this breathtaking rendering of the forever-journey of masculine coming-of-age. Musa is a sterling stylist, and the combination of poetry and prose, literary narrative and hip-hop verse in *Here Come the Dogs* does that impossible thing: creates a work unlike any other."

—Porochista Khakpour, author *of The Last Illusion*
and *Sons and Other Flammable Objects*

"A beautiful and angry book. Musa is a poet, and every page of this book speaks to his ferocious talent."

—Fatima Bhutto, author of *The Shadow of the Crescent Moon*

Omar Musa is a Malaysian-Australian rapper and poet from Queanbeyan, Australia. He has opened for Gil Scott Heron, Dead Prez, and Pharoahe Monch and performed at the Nuyorican Poets Café in New York City. He attended University of California, Santa Cruz. He has released three hip-hop albums, two poetry books, and received a standing ovation at TEDx Sydney at the Sydney Opera House. He lives in Australia.

HERE COME THE DOGS

HERE COME THE DOGS

OMAR MUSA

THE NEW PRESS

NEW YORK
LONDON

Page 339 constitutes an extension of this copyright page.

Requests for permission to reproduce selections from this book should be mailed to:
Permissions Department, The New Press, 120 Wall Street, 31st floor, New York, NY 10005.

First published in Australia by the Penguin Group (Australia), 2014
Published in the United States by The New Press, New York, 2016
Distributed by Perseus Distribution

LIBRARY OF CONGRESS CATALOGING-IN-PUBLICATION DATA

Musa, Omar.
Here come the dogs / Omar Musa.
pages cm
ISBN 978-1-62097-117-8 (pbk. : alk. paper) — ISBN 978-1-62097-119-2 (e-book)
I. Title.
PR9619.4.M874H48   2015
823'.92—dc23   2015008416

The New Press publishes books that promote and enrich public discussion
and understanding of the issues vital to our democracy and to a more equitable
world. These books are made possible by the enthusiasm of our readers; the support
of a committed group of donors, large and small; the collaboration of our many
partners in the independent media and the not-for-profit sector; booksellers, who
often hand-sell New Press books; librarians; and above all by our authors.

www.thenewpress.com

Book design by Laura Thomas
This book was set in Adobe Garamond Pro

Printed in the United States of America

2   4   6   8   10   9   7   5   3   1

For my mother, Helen

The true subject of poetry is the loss of the beloved
— Faiz Ahmed Faiz

Face the fire
— Jimblah

HERE COME THE DOGS

PROLOGUE

This has always been a land of fire.

Once a year, the Ancients would go into the mountains in search of bogong moths. They carried burning branches and thrust them into rents in the rock, stunning the congregated moths, then catching them in fibrous nets or kangaroo skin. The moths were roasted on fine embers and the Ancients feasted, vomiting for the first few days but then growing accustomed to the rich, fatty food. The Ancients would return from the mountains with glossy skin, glistening like shadow.

Afterwards, fires would burn on the mountains for days.

PART ONE

1

Where are these cunts?

Too hot, bro,
        too fucken long without rain.
Two by two they troop in,
           the madness of summer in the brain.

In the dying light,
the crowd looks like hundreds of bobbling balloons,
waiting to be unfastened.

      Sweating tinnies and foreheads –
            sadcunts and sorrowdrowners the lot of them.

I stand up,
six-foot-two and shining,
     yawn,
twist side to side on my hinges
     and survey the crowd.

It's not like the boys to be late,
especially on a day like today.

Summer,
      the deepest season,
      throbbing with danger and promise,
      every scallywag, seedthief and skatepark
         wrapped up in a white hot skin.

And here come the dogs . . .

Strange, smiling creatures,
lean-flanked and
         ready to race.

An old bloke turns around and grins
with opalised eyes.

'Nothing like the ole dishlickers, eh?'

I smile and flick a fly from my knuckle.

'Fuck noath.'

The dogs' barks detonate across the track.

The trainers are gruff people,
but now they coo to the hounds,
straightening their racing silks,
crouching to check and bend their ankles.
            (one says a prayer and kisses
            his dog on its narrow head)

A dry wind scythes across
the stands and I reach up
to keep my hat on.

'Bushfire weather, ay?'

The old timer is right.

The Town is a powderkeg,
a perfect altar for a bushfire –
                                    the sole god of a combustible summer.

B-Boy Fresh

But I'm crisp tee fresh –
black on black, snapback,
toothbrush on sneaker,
        throwback fresh.

But fark me dead,
the joints and muscles ache nowadays.

Sign of the times, ay?

I look at the old timer
and immediately touch the
muscles under my shirt
just to make sure.

I grin –
Solomon Amosa, you vain, vain bastard.

The big news

Jimmy ain't hard to spot in a crowd.

With all the grace of jangling keys,
my half-brother lurches
through the mass of drinkers and gamblers,
sharp Adam's apple visible even from here.
His eyes cut left to right,
paranoid and grim.
Walking behind him is Aleks,
smiling and nodding at people that he passes.

What a crew –
a Samoan, a Maco and my half-brother, a *something*.

        The only ethnics at the dog races.

When Jimmy sits down I smack him
across the back of the head,
            harder than I mean to.
'Oi, what took you so fucken long?' I say, taking my cap off and pass-
ing my hand over my dreds.
'I had shit to do, bra.'
Aleks looks away and checks his bet,
        already bored of the bickering.
'Like what?'
'I don't fucken have to tell you everything, do I? Jesus.'
Jimmy looks like he's gonna say something else
but instead he conjures two ciggies from behind his ear,
lights one and passes the other to me.
We smoke for a minute
and listen to the announcements.

'Conditions are ideal tonight, ladies and gentlemen.
We have a perfect track for racing.
Good luck and good punting –
may the racing gods be in your favour.'

Jimmy ashes his durry
and then looks sidelong at me,
lips expanding into a frog-like grin.
'Oi, guess what?'
I'm watching some lads on a stag's night stumble along.
They're dressed in a bright-yellow uniform, wearing wigs.
Jimmy and Aleks look at each other and grin.
They're already wasted,
sour bourbon vapours practically hissing off them.

'What?'

Jimmy clears his throat, then announces, 'Sin One's gonna do a come-
back show. With the DJ Exit on the decks.'
My eyes cut back. 'Sin One? You serious?'
'He's moved back, brother,' nods Aleks.
I blow out smoke. 'Ohh, man. When?'
'After Chrissie.'

Sin One is almost universally recognised
in the underground
        as the greatest rapper Australia has produced –
        a prophet, nah, a god.

And he comes from our Town.

Can you imagine how fucken proud we are?

Drinks

When I bring back the tinnies,
Aleks and Jimmy are embroiled in an age-old argument –
    who the best Australian MC is.

I take a black marker from my pocket
and begin to draw on a five-dollar note as I listen.
Jimmy, who loves lists,
    reminds us yet again of the five main criteria
    you judge an MC by.

1) Flow: how do they ride, bounce off, play with, sound on a beat?
2) Lyrics: how do they play with words, use metaphors, create memorable images, tell stories?
3) Voice: were they naturally gifted with a voice that just *cuts through* and gives you shivers, that booms or rasps or honeys?
4) Consistency: have they produced quality work over an extended period of time?
5) Live show: can they rock the fuck out of a crowd of people, big or small?

Added to this are more nebulous criteria based on online rumours, freestyle abilities, face-to-face encounters and gut feelings.

Jimmy and Aleks prefer grimier, old school Melbourne stuff,
    samples and dusty loops.

    I'm more into synths and instruments,
        newer, smoother Sydney shit.

    'All right, then. Top five best MCs,' says Jimmy, who reels off his list
immediately. 'Brad Strut, Trem, Geko, Lazy Grey, Bias B.'
    Aleks, too, is ready. 'Trem, Strut, Pegz, Delta, Vents.'

'Hm. Fucken hard one.' I think for a second. 'All right, um . . . Solo, Mantra, Suffa, Tuka, Hau, Joelistics . . . That new Briggs shit is heavy, too. And that dude One Sixth from Melbourne.'

'I said top five, bro,' snaps Jimmy.

'Oi, relax.'

'Storytelling, mate, *lyrics*, that's what it's about,' announces Jimmy.

'Yeah, yeah, you always say that. Then Solo from Horrorshow or Mantra's number one,' I say. 'Deep shit. Mad flows, too.'

Aleks and Jimmy shake their heads in unison. 'Nah, that shit's gay as, always singing and shit. That's not true school. Plus, Solo looks like a tennis instructor,' says Jimmy.

'You're one to talk, you preppy cunt! You're stuck in the nineties, bro. Music moves on,' I say.

'Now, Trem. That's an MC. Tells it how it is – graff, crime, darkness. Voice is like a fucken . . . like a diamond cutter,' says Aleks. 'Strut too – apocalyptic.'

'You can't dance to it, but,' I counter. 'That shit's too serious for me. When it started, hip hop was about getting a party goin'. Sydney shit does that better.'

Jimmy is getting heated. 'Sydney shit is weird. Their accents sound American. They say "days" like "deez" and "mic" like "mark". Hate that.'

We laugh.

'What about a chick?' I venture. 'None of us even put one in there.'

'*Tsk.* Ya PC cunt. Been hanging with that femmo girlfriend of yours too much. When chicks rap, I just don't *feel* it.'

'What 'bout Lauryn Hill? Jean Grae?'

'Aussies, I mean'

'Layla. Class A.'

The boys shrug. As Aleks leans forward, a blue bead swings on a leather strap around his neck. 'The Hoods sold more than anyone else,' he says.

'Fuck sales. It's not about sales; it's about impact and the quality. If you use that argument, you could say Bliss n Eso are more important than Def Wish Cast.'

'Or Vanilla Ice is better than Kool G Rap.'

Jimmy turns his glittering eyes on me. 'Those private school boys must've taught you about hip hop, ay. That's why you're not into the hard shit.'

Cunt.

The private school thing is always Jimmy's trump card,
                 no matter what the argument,
                 and it always works.
Aleks frowns.

'Fuck . . . I went for basketball, you know that.' I say, lamely. Then I return to the name that kicked off the debate – 'Sin One. *Orphan Slang. Fire and Redemption.*'

The others nod.

'Yeah, goes without saying. Should be top of every list. Pity it's been so long since he released an album,' says Aleks regretfully.

I look at the five-buck note –
Queen Elizabeth now has a crown of thorns
and a timebomb on her shoulder.

'You seen our dog yet?' asks Aleks.

Mercury Fire

Tonight is Mercury Fire's last race.

He's our favourite,
the reason we still come to the greyhounds.

It began as a joke –
        'Oi, wanna see bogans in their natural habitat?'

But then we saw him race.

Blind in one eye with a kinked back leg,
he's smaller than the other dogs,
but somehow he beats all comers.
Every time, he starts slow
but ends with power,
                hunger.

                We've heard that in training
                he's thrown real rabbits and possums to chase
                so that he keeps the blood lust up.

An ageing warrior,
        close to the end.

We all sit silently,
drinking.

Aleks

We never get to see Aleks.
He's got a missus, a young daughter
and a house he built himself.

Still, even after all this time,

he has that pirouette of smoke
         in his eyes.

At age five he moved here from Macedonia
and despite limited English
quickly established himself
as king of the kids
with his fast, big fists.

At age thirteen he knocked out an English teacher
who tried to make him
spell his name with an 'x',
not a 'ks'.

It was around this time he found
another use for his hands.

One day, when a graff crew from Sydney
painted a wildstyle piece under the bridge
        over the river,
Aleks discovered a love
to replace the sweet science

                (though if lessons needed to be taught,
                cunts needed to learn).

From then on it was burners/
boltcutters/
blackbooks
and
guerilla expeditions to Bunnings
to rack paint cans/

            And don't forget
            that rush that makes your dick hard.

The Old Timer

'When I was in England,
I visited Old TRAFFORD,
the home of MANCHESTER UNITED.'

'We can hear you, mate –
we're right here.'

The old timer's been talking frog shit for nearly
fifteen minutes now.

Sad bastard –
           desiccated look of a dedicated drinker.
           Threads from a cheap Western –
           ten-gallon hat, bolo tie,
           spurs on boots.

'Johnny No-Cash,' says Aleks in my ear.

I stifle a smile.

'The coach told me I had the BEST LEFT BOOT
he had ever seen.'

Bullshit artists
come a dime a dozen in this town –

                  it takes one to know one, ay?

A message from Georgie

Good afternoon, beautiful boy.
In boring lecture having naughty thoughts about u.
Can't wait 2 c u 2nite. Luv, Porge x

Love?

I pocket the phone.

When's this race gonna start?

A little something to rev things up

I wipe the top of the cistern
and bring up my hand –
there's white powder on my palm.

I love doing that.

It's almost like I've busted someone in the act.

Aleks takes out a marker
and writes his tag on the cubicle wall
with a flourish.

JAKEL

Meanwhile, Jimmy racks up
three lines
with a seasoned hand
and his keycard.
            My brother Jimmy, who could never

even handle his beer back in the day.

Aleks does a line and blinks.

'Dearo fucken me! This is good shit, bro. Aryan white.'

I roll up the drawn-on five-buck note
and hoover a line.
The cocaine hits immediately –
a cold zoom in the guts,
a perfectly timed tackle.

I backflip
into a glacial crevasse.

The track

The track smoulders.

Thick lights shine down
holding within them insects
and motes of dust.

The dogs' feet articulate
                         on the soil of the holding pen.
In part dieted on honey, vegetable oil and eggs,
        their coats glow.

Tinny announcements over the loudspeakers.

The trainers are hand slipping the dogs now,
one hand on the collar
the other arm hooked at the base of

their undercarriages
shuffling them forward into the traps.

Like everyone else,
        we riffle and check our betslips.

In the stands,
we can hear the dogs' high-pitched
whimpers and yelps
as they scrape in the traps.

We begin to cheer.

The race

Bang goes the gun,
            zoom goes the artificial rabbit,
                        off go the hounds
                                like water out a
                                    sluice.

They are a rumbling mass at first
but as they round the corner
they separate into surreal, spear-headed things
that lope and arch through the air –
                        feet, dust, sound.

The crowd rises
and we do too,
ten-feet tall and charged with powder,
seeing the race in jittering frames.

Here comes Mercury Fire!

                                   A grey streak of
                                   ribs/
                                   sinew-lashed muscle/
                                   light.
Right down the straight
he looks like a young dog again,
propelled by furious, otherworldly energy.

He's neck and neck for the lead with
two black hounds,
            loping forward, urging/
            and we're screaming, screaming/
'Come on, boy. COME ON!'
and Mercury Fire is straining onwards
every muscle working for the one goal,
courage and conviction in the blood,
launching over the track for the last time.

He comes in third.

I realise that I've been holding my breath
the whole race.

What happens to a racing dog past its prime?

Jimmy says they find them homes
where they get retrained as house pets.

Aleks says he's heard of a bloke
in Wollongong who's killed over five thousand
healthy hounds with a captive bolt gun
once they lose speed.

I say they get their ears cut off
(cos of the ID tattoo)
then let go in the bush
cos owners don't have the heart to kill them.

Jimmy

Jimmy is arguing with me about money again.

'Jimmy, it's five fucken bucks, mate. I'll pay ya back tomorrow.'

'That's what you always say.'

Jimmy –
catfood-hearted,
jelly-spined motherfucker.
Cheap-deodorant, call-centre Jimmy.
No good with his fists
                    but uses rumours like napalm.

He's family but,
so what the fuck can you do?

Outside the racecourse

Eyes tick like a stopwatch/
People head home or out/
A cop car smears by/
Then a Ninja Turtle-green Supra
with two chicks hanging from one window/
techno pumping/
'Ay, boys, show us where ya piss from!'/

We're cracking up
and our middle fingers go straight in the air/

This is good shit/

'Oi, I'm tilted.'

'Me too.'

I'm trying to keep it together but
Jimmy and Aleks not so much.
Chewing like mastodons,
they must've taken pills, too,
the sly cunts.

People are milling around the entrance.
The old timer is rabbiting on to someone
and we swerve to avoid him.

     ' . . . the best left boot he'd EVER seen.'

Gladys

I chase her down in the carpark.

Red, wary face,
god-awful turquoise windcheater
and a cockney accent.

But there's something about the old duck
that chokes me up.

I introduce myself,

squat down and pat Mercury Fire.

'He did good, yeah? Especially for his last race.
I trained him since he was a pup,' she says.

Mercury Fire studies me with
his one good eye, grinning and panting.

'I know, I know. Me and my mates have
been watching him race for the last year.
The best there was, seriously. I mean is. Was.'

I'm talking too fast. Slow your roll, Solomon.

She's looking away now –
'Yeh. Probably gonna send him to a new home, or . . .
I'm moving back to England in a few weeks.'

Why at that age? Are those tears?

She keeps talking –
'They like it, you know. The dogs. They like racing.
People reckon it's cruel but we treat em better
than most owners treat their dogs.'

She's looking directly at me now.
I wonder if she can tell I'm out of it
but then she looks past me.

I shake her hand awkwardly. 'Best of luck, ay.'

'Yer, you too.'

She smiles and I smile back.

'Hey, can I ask you something?' I say.

A phone call

Georgie's busting my balls
and it's ruining my high.

'It's cruel, Solomon.
They exploit those poor animals.'

Hasn't she got something better to do?
I thought she was studying.

'Can we talk about this later? Please.'

I hear Jimmy behind me
singing 'My Cherie Amour'
        like Stevie Wonder.

I throw a crushed tinnie at him.

'I'll be back at yours a bit later, all right, babe?
Don't wait up for me.'

The cypher

On the way to get chips and gravy
we see a cypher –
        a circle of youngsters rapping.
Seven kids, seven heads bobbing,
some of them sipping on longies
as they wait for their turn to rap.

The lad beatboxing is a Koori fulla –
I used to play ball with his older brother.
He's supplying a steady, boombap beat.

A few of them nod at us
and we observe from outside the circle.

I always thought that, from above,
the circle of heads
would look like bullets loaded in a chamber,
each MC ready with his percussive, weaponised voice,
some rapid fire,
some jamming.

A pretty brunette is up first.
She's got a dope flow
but it's obviously a written verse.
Next is an African cat
who's using an American accent –
we all wince.
Someone else takes over the beatboxing
and the Koori fulla starts freestyling,
clowning on people in the circle.
He's a cocky cunt, just like his bro.
His flow is a bit off
but his punchlines are hitting
          and soon we're all laughing.

I make a mental note
to keep an eye out for him.

I look up and for a second
I swear I can see skulls swinging

from the trees above us
but then I realise it's a trick of the light.

Jimmy and I step forward
and rap for a bit
but we're rusty.
All it takes is a week off
to lose the edge.

Plus neither of us were ever MCs.

But it's part of the game –
        gotta give it a go.

Afterwards, we smoke a joint with the youngsters.

'You lads aren't going out tonight? Heaps going on, uce.'

The Koori lad and the brunette are arm in arm
and he says, 'Nah, brus. Can't get in anywhere, ay.'

The brunette pipes up, 'Would rather be doin this anyway.'

We laugh.

'True.'

Fights are freight trains

You can see em coming a mile off,
        and if not,
            make em happen.

The line for chips and gravy is rowdy.

This shardhead behind us is
gnashing and doing a weird jig
on the spot.

Jimmy blows kisses
at his methed-up, cue-ball eyes,
                    taunting him.

Aleks places
a hand on Jimmy's shoulder –
'Leave it, bro. Leave it.'

My bro cocks his head,
as if trying to hear a faint noise.
He looks at me,
then back at Aleks.
Then he turns to the shardhead
and spits in his face.

When the meth head lashes out,
it's wild but somehow finds its mark –
a savage kiss on the end of a whip.

Jimmy drops straight away.

Before he even lands Aleks and I
are on the shardhead and
there are no words,
just the sound of rockmelons
dropped onto asphalt from a bridge
and soon blood mixes with chicken salt
and footsteps are everywhere and a chick is on her mobile

and Aleks is grimacing as he punches
and the methhead is shrieking like a berserker now
and some of our punches are landing on each other
and one of us is yelling same team, same team
and Jimmy is on his feet unsteadily
smiling eagerly,
and he says 'white cunt' but we all know
it's not about that well it may be
and he starts to kick the shardhead in his face
but that's not cool so Aleks edges back and is shaking his great head
and the chick is screaming
the cops are on their way fuckheads
so we wrestle Jimmy out the door
and into the early morning darkness.

What's got into him?

These swings are too small for us.

Aleks is throwing tanbark into the dark –
he hasn't said a word since the fight.
I roll a joint and pass it round,
        Pete Rock playing from my iPhone.

Jimmy won't shut the fuck up
about the fight,
reliving it over and over,
        as he always does.

Without warning, Aleks stands up,
walks to Jimmy and stops in front of him,
faces centimetres apart.

Jimmy looks confused at first
then stares back,
face hardening.

Aleks searches Jimmy's face,
holding him squarely with his stare,
breathing, searching.

'I'm off, brother.'

Jimmy starts after him but I grab his forearm.

'Leave him alone, bro. Jimmy. James, leave him alone,' I say.

Aleks is now a slash of ink,
　　　　darkening into the crosshatch of trees.

Jimmy sits back down –
'What's got into him?'

Wish we had a white person with us

Ten empty cabs have passed us by.

The cabbie

His breath smells of cardamom tea
and a twelve-hour shift.

He eyes us warily –
'If you need to vomit you tell me, yeah? I'll pull over.'

'Nah, nah. No worries. We're big boys, mate.'

There is a diamond-shaped,
gold-tasselled passage from the Qur'an
hanging from the rear-view mirror.

The cabbie smiles tightly. 'Big night?'

'Bro, you don't know the half of it. Fucken hektikkk.
Ay. AY! Turn this song up!' slurs Jimmy.

'Where you from, mate?' I say.

'Here.'

'Nah, nah, I mean originally.'

'. . . Pakistan.'

'*Assalamu-alaikum,* brother.' The words sound strange coming out of
my mouth.

His eyes, framed by the rear-view mirror, widen with surprise.
'*Wa-alaikum salam.* You Muslim?'

'Yeah, once. Um, I mean, yeah.'

'His name was Sulaiman,' Jimmy crows. 'Now it's Solomon again.'

'Sulaiman? Ah, a good name. A wise man.' The man nods.

I wind down the window
and blow my breath out subtly,
hoping he won't smell the alcohol.

Too late, probably.

When I get out at Georgie's college,
I shake the cabbie's hand –
'*Assalamu-alaikum.*'

He turns to smile
and I see for the first time
the right side of his face is
                    scabbed and bruised.

'*Wa-alaikum salam.*'

Drunk sex

The arch of her foot
on my teeth,
her thighs move apart.
Erykah Badu's voice curls
around us.

The heat unbearable.

'Fuck.'

One of her heels is digging
into my flank
and in a shudder of moonlight,
I realise she has cut her hair
into an ashen wedge
She holds my face close,
and I try to smile

but her presence is crushing,
    it almost makes me scream.

Instead I keep moving,
deep, shallow, deep, shallow,
and I'm relieved when she closes her eyes.

I watch her eyelids,
and notice for the first time a crooked lower tooth.

Afterwards,
watching a dreamcatcher spin on the ceiling,
my skin sticking to hers,
I say, 'I bought a dog tonight.'

'A dog?'

'Yeh. A greyhound.'

She pauses before laughing uncertainly
    and kissing me.

'You mad bastard. You've got nowhere to keep it.'

A dream about Georgie

I'm the only passenger on a plane –
the sky is the colour of Turkish delight
or suicide bathwater.

Shirtless,
tattoos alive, swarming,
jostling down my forearms.

There's a gin and juice on the tray –
       strong.

I hear a sound
akin to birds chirping,
but can't tell where it's coming from.

Georgie appears –
stepping down the aisle solemnly,
as if at the head of a procession,
carrying something heavy and square.
She's wearing weighted pendants in her lobes
and a headdress of feather flowers.

She looks beautiful and sad.

The plane starts its descent.

I can see rivers, lakes and dams,
holding within them braided veins of light.
The land looks both rich and barren.

The plane is low now, about to land.

In a glance I observe an extraordinary scene
in Munro Park.

A man is kneeling on the kick-off line with
his arms behind him.
Another man is standing close, one arm outstretched,
and a sudden flash leaps from his hand.
The kneeling man jumps backwards
and lies with his arms outflung as if crucified.

It takes a second to see this.

I try to scream to Georgie
but I make no sound
and I see that I am tied to the seat
and can't move so I bang
my fists on the tray table.

The gin and juice bounces in one motion
all over my lap and the smell of it becomes intense,
more like diesel than liquor.

My hands are shaking
and I stare at them for a long time.

When I look up
I'm standing outside the airport.
There's nobody else
and it's cold.

Eventually a cab pulls up.
The Pakistani driver opens the door.
He smiles
and I see that his mouth is full of gold teeth,
his scabs gone.
The drive isn't long into town
and when we approach Munro Park,
I tap him on the shoulder.

I walk to the centre of the rugby field.
There is no body, no blood.
Just a briefcase lying on the cold soil.

I open it
and see that it's full of colourful birds of song –
nightingales, swallows, babblers.

They are all dead.

2

The morning is waiting to be created.

Coffee on stove; toast, eggs, pickles.

A shot of *rakia* to take the edge off the hangover.

Shot, shudder, smack of the lips.

Aleks' grandfather Mitko sent a bottle last week straight from the village, made from cherries, strong enough to clean wounds with. Aleks smiles. *Dedo* Mitko has had a shot every morning of his life, before heading to the fields to plough and plant. 'Get the blood going before you face the day, Aleksandar – a shot of *rakia* is a good friend, but someone to be treated with respect!'

He thinks of his grandfather, so frail now, next to the window in a sweat-heavy room, his big, calcified hands the only testament to a life's labour. Ten years in a German factory, the rest in the fields the family had ploughed for centuries. He would be watching the tomcats stalking through the weeds of the garden and the cars passing intermittently on the way to Ohrid; his eyes shining with frustration. Poor old *dedo*, waiting all day for news from town, from Australia, from anywhere really, and exclaiming 'Mashallah!' if the news is good. Aleks would have to make up some good news and give the old man a call.

He puts J Dilla on the stereo at a low volume.

His hands are huge and hairless, the knuckles scabbed up; they move efficiently, with resolve. He scrubs the stove, then the pan. Streaks of egg and pickled green tomatoes. Then he packs a lunchbox – an apple, a packet of chips, a ham sandwich and an orange juice popper. He sets it on the counter and calls out in Macedonian:

'Hurry up, sweetheart. Gotta get ta work.'

'Yes, Dad.'

He moves swiftly, blue bead swinging, and soon the cupboards and marble kitchen top are shining. He proudly observes his kitchen (which he built with his own hands), lights a cigarette and opens the blinds. Aleks can see the whole Town from here, mostly low-lying houses in orange brick or white stucco, with flatblocks in between like dice tumbled randomly from an unseen hand. Everywhere is construction, trucks and scaffolding, and cranes like predatory birds and, winding throughout, the shining body of the river.

The sun whets itself on distant hills and comes in low and mean.

Aleks' own street curves down a hill in a new part of Town, covered in a scribble of burnt rubber. Several houses down, standing out against the monotony of suburbia, is a phone box with tags all over it, various shades of dripping red and black, Poscas and Molotow flowies. An endless cycle of scrawling and buffing, buffing and re-scrawling – the signatures of generations. He imagines a magic machine stretching out every layer in 2D planes like an accordion.

Down the bottom of the street, a boy is throwing a pair of sneakers over a phone line, sending a gaggle of sulphur-crested cockatoos squawking. A cluster of shoes already there, like grapes on a vine. Aleks smiles, turns and takes a gym bag from the top cupboard, well out of reach of little hands.

'Come on, Mila!' he yells.

'Coming!'

He reaches for a pair of old boots, caked in clay and spattered with paint, and thinks for a second of all the brand-new sneakers in Solomon's room. As he slips his boots on, he looks through the bedroom door at his wife Sonya, still asleep, her blonde hair halfway across her face. He tiptoes in, bends down to clear her face of hair, then kisses her forehead. She doesn't wake.

As he ties his laces in the doorway, his daughter appears at his shoulder with a mischievous grin. He wipes a smudge of Vegemite off her cheek then pinches it. She squeals when he tickles her and then bounds out the door ahead of him. 'Hurry up, Dad.'

'You should eat *ajvar*, not that Vegemite crap,' he says half-heartedly.

He throws the gym bag into the back of his white Hilux with the cans of paint and rollers. It's suffocatingly hot inside the vehicle and the belt buckle burns his hand when he touches it. '*Pitchka ti mater!*' he swears, then immediately looks around to make sure Mila hasn't heard him. He picks up a stack of CDs, stops to look at the Souls of Mischief one but instead throws on a Tose Proeski album that his cousin Nicko burned for him. These are the rules he has made – Macedonian at home and in the car. Australia, the outside, takes care of teaching her English. He stops at a petrol station to fill up and chats about the World Cup with the owner, an enormous, shaved head Samoan man with big teeth. Aleks has always loved how Islanders can convey so much with a simple arch of the eyebrows. He speaks to the man in a soft, ingratiating voice and claps him tenderly on the shoulder. The man once tried to converse with Solomon in Samoan. Solomon looked like a child and couldn't answer the simplest questions; how impotent and ashamed he had seemed. Aleks heads back to the car, chewing a Mars Bar.

'*Tat?*'

'*Da?*'

'Mum's birthday's coming up.'

'I know, baby.'

'Can we go on a holiday? Pleeease?'

He turns his head and sees that her eyes are on him, an unnerving, mirror-like blue. She reminds him of his sister Jana. Aleks passes a hand through his sandy hair, winds down the window and drums his fingers on the side of the door. She's right – the family needs a holiday. Soon. Somewhere tropical with long beaches and rosewater sunsets where Sonya can have some time to get better. Or maybe even back to Macedonia to see the family. He knows it's unrealistic, unless he can find a way to earn a lot of cash, quickly.

'Maybe we could go to Madagascar,' says Mila.

'What's in Madagascar?'

'Lemurs. Chameleons.' She says the words in English with a broad Aussie accent. Aleks smiles.

'You know, you look like a little lemur. Where's ya tail?'

'Daaaaad!'

'All right, all right, relax. I'll see what I can do. Maybe we can build a raft outta coconuts to get there.'

'Would that even work?'

'Well, you won't know until you try.' He winks.

'You're the best, Dad.'

'Hey, you know the rules. Macedonian only in the car.'

'*Da, da.*'

A police car drives by and Aleks turns his cheek, his whole body tightening. He's driving on a suspended licence. Shouldn't have had that shot in the morning; in fact, he might still be a bit pissed from the night before. He has to be more careful, for his family's sake.

'What's wrong, Dad?' Mila is cocking her head. Nothing escapes this one.

'Nothing sweetheart. What are you studying at school today?' He ruffles her hair.

As she speaks about assignments and the upcoming swimming competition, he passes the courthouse. He sees two people he knows smoking outside, looking uncomfortable in suits. They wave at him as he passes. He gives them the thumbs up.

When he pulls up at the primary school, Mila is already unbuckling her seatbelt. 'Don't forget your lunch.' She kisses him on the cheek and clambers out of the Hilux. He leans across the seat and yells, '*Te sakam, Mila!*' She looks back once with those neon-blue eyes and yells back, 'I love you too, Dad!' in English. Then she turns and becomes another eight-year-old streaming into the schoolyard. Aleks exhales and opens the glove box. He sifts among the papers and takes out a crumpled packet of durries. There is one left, which he lights. *Ahhh.* He reaches into his shirt and rolls the bead between his fingers, lets the strap fall over his thumb, middle and index. A thrill goes through him.

'Goodness me. Fucken lovely,' he says.

He starts up the engine and drives off. As he drives, he passes an abandoned building that was supposed to be demolished years ago. A yellow crane crouches next to it. He looks up and sees something he painted at the top of the building almost fifteen years ago. Tall, dripping, black letters: 'Greece is Macedonia,' and a yellow Vergina Sun next to it. Amazing that it's still there.

He and Solomon had scaled the heights of the building and twice they nearly fell to certain death. The building had been a general store in the early 1900s and was falling apart. It was two-storeys high and the wooden beams they climbed were rotten, the iron railings rusted. Neither would admit their terror, so they had egged each other on. They had to crawl on their bellies over the corrugated iron, staining their shirts yellow and red, to get a good position to spray-paint the slogan on the streetside wall, starlit.

Solomon had asked what the slogan meant. Aleks tried to explain it the way his father had explained it to him: that Macedonia had been at the centre of a tug-of-war since time immemorial, that heaps of people claimed it didn't even exist. However, he had found it difficult to explain and had become tongue-tied.

Solomon had shrugged and said, 'Sounds good to me,' then started plotting how to rack some tins of paint. They were twelve at the time. Aleks wishes he could explain it to his mate now, properly, but Solomon always seemed so uneasy discussing nationality.

Back then, Jimmy had been too scared to climb, so he stood below and kept watch for cops. Solomon had ridiculed him mercilessly, even though they needed a lookout. Jimmy turned away, and afterward they didn't see him for two whole days.

No one knew where he'd gone.

Aleks considers Jimmy and Solomon's relationship to be one predicated on a struggle for power and Jimmy had been born into a losing war. It was bad blood, Aleks was sure of it.

He passes a small block of flats that sits next to the river.

Only derros, alcos and new immigrants living there.

He keeps driving at a leisurely pace. Dead grass, eucalypts, low river, even the empty driveways: all seems bare and hungry from drought. Some gardens have been planted with the drought in mind, and bloom with tough plants like wisteria, sage and bush sarsaparilla, their lilacs and purples slurring in the heat haze. A Christmas beetle drops onto his bonnet.

Aleks is closer to the heart of Town now. On the main street he passes several redbrick pubs from the early 1900s, a small war memorial shaped like an obelisk, a dry fountain and a bronze statue of a bearded man carrying a book. There is a TAB, several kebab shops, charcoal chicken joints and pide houses, and on every block is the scaffolding of construction. He stops the car at a traffic light and an African girl in a hijab crosses the street. They catch eyes. Aleks nods at her but she looks down and keeps walking, books close to her chest.

Unlike many in his family, Aleks has always liked Muslims. He even has a grudging respect for Albanians. *They may all be criminals, but at least the proceeds of their crime go back to their country, back to the cause.* He thinks with shame of some of the Macos here, who are Macedonian by name only, so eager to become like the Aussies, the *kengurs* (based on the word 'kangaroo'). Like Julian, the local car dealer. Aleks can't stand people like him: Macos who won't speak their own language, who know no music or folklore, who never go back, who keep stacking money higher and higher as if it would make a staircase to God. *If every Maco in Australia went back to the homeland with even $20,000, it would save the failing economy*, he thinks.

Aleks pulls up at a nearly completed block of new apartments next to a barren soccer oval. He gets his gear out and climbs the stairs, nodding at the foreman on the way up. A day of hard work ahead, but he looks forward to it. His work ethic is what ensures his and his family's survival.

His partner is already there; a young skater in his late teens, who Aleks knows had some problems with heroin but is now on methadone. He works for half the price but twice as hard. Aleks lets him play his own music on a paint-splattered radio, because it helps him keep up with the latest shit. Today, it is mostly a jumble of Odd Future's lo-fi, off-kilter horrorcore and Yelawolf's mercurial drawl.

'Seventy-five per cent of painting a room is prep – always remember that,' says Aleks. The boy nods.

They lay plastic sheeting on the floor, check the wall for discrepancies with a light and sand away the few they see. They put down the base coat with a paintgun. Then they begin painting the trim of a bedroom. Aleks is careful but moves with ease and is soon finished. He stands back, admiring his work with pride. Flawless.

His phone lights up with a message. Number unknown.

Well well look at the big boy comin in2 the playground. how dare u come here and steal all my friends?

Aleks smiles. It could only be one of two people. He pauses, then types back with two thumbs.

I dont giv a fuk whoz playground it iz. Ne time I wanna drink from the bubbla, Ill do it and theres fuk all u can do bout it.

Send.

Then he starts to paint the dry walls with a roller, keeping a wet edge to avoid lap marks. Where these apartments now stand there was once a big block of land where an old Croatian couple lived and tended to their flourishing vegetable garden. All summer there would be a grapevine covering the whole fence, free for all who passed. The boys would gorge themselves and do chin-ups on the old plum tree that hung over the fence. All of that was gone now.

His phone lights up again, this time with the message, *we'll see bout that cunt.* He texts back immediately – *lets talk pursonaly. meet me tmorro at the old cemetery. i got a proposal for ya.* He clicks send then switches the phone off. He'll deal with all of that later – there's work to be done.

At lunchtime, he makes an excuse to his co-worker and drives a few blocks to meet Solomon. There are barely any people on the street, and those few cast no shadows. A red-brick pub stands on the corner and Solomon is lounging outside, in the middle of telling a story to two Tongan blokes. *Aren't Samoans and Tongans supposed to hate each other?* Solomon is wearing a singlet and honey-tinted sunnies and is gesticulating as precisely as an orator, his face serious. The two men are rapt, eyebrows knitted. Suddenly Solomon says something with a final jab of the index finger and the two men begin laughing hysterically. He leans back in his chair, smiling, rubbing papaya ointment into his lips and then his elbows.

Aleks and Solomon order chicken schnitties and mash with schooners of draft and sit inside to escape the sun. The pub had once been a notorious, sweat-reeking, liquor-soaked bloodhouse. There had even been several murders in the rooms above it. However, it had recently been renovated by a local entrepreneur and was now clean and airy, lavender scented and surprisingly, full of people. Solomon is suddenly sullen, but Aleks makes no comment, used to his shifting moods, from charismatic to brooding to street to booksmart. It is something women find mysterious and attractive, Jimmy finds endlessly annoying and contrived, and Aleks ignores. Solomon keeps looking around at the trendy decor, paintings on the wall and trim barstaff and eventually mutters, 'It's a fucken disgrace, man. I swear to God.'

'*Tsk*. It was a shithole, brother. It's a lot nicer now.'

'Should've left it how it was.'

Solomon, adamant that hip hop should change and progress, is equally adamant that the Town is changing too fast, losing its working-class identity, becoming yuppified. This is his town and repository of his life's story. Aleks looks at him and thinks: *everything in the world exists with its death alive in it.* Every fire dies, every story, every star, every town. Every nation? Childhoods are macadamed beneath asphalt and paint rolls, but just for other childhoods to exist. This, the nature of change, of modernity. Buildings go up, dreamings wander in search of graves or new owners; some remnant will stir occasionally, but these buildings will one day turn to dust and float through the bushland like ghosts. Eventually, the bush would die, too.

And besides, it's not like Solomon contributes anything – at twenty-seven lazing around with a half-arsed dishwashing job, still living at his mum's place, monkey-swinging from woman to woman, feeling sorry for himself about an injury he had almost ten years ago. *Nah, there is dignity in hard work.*

Solomon cheers up after a second beer and starts telling Aleks about a perfect spot for a mission, a fuel depot on the edge of town where a piece would be seen by everyone leaving for the City in early morning traffic. Aleks is mopping up some mash and gravy with a piece of bread, nodding. He knows the spot.

When he gets back to the apartment block, the kid is working at a furious pace, painting meticulously. Must've done a good apprenticeship. If you're taught to paint badly in the first place, you'll go thirty years painting like shit. Aleks is glad he didn't take the kid with him to lunch – Solomon has complete disdain for bogans.

It is now Freddie Gibbs' deep voice booming from the radio with fuck the woooorld attitude. Aleks paints with the bassline reverberating deep within him, completely calm. They are both in a zone. Before he knows it, they're finished for the day. He switches his phone back on and gets another text from the unknown number. *Done. Seeya then.*

He picks up Mila from school, takes her to ballet practice and waits outside in the Hilux, drawing in his blackbook. An hour passes, then fifteen minutes more. It has become dark. Getting tired of waiting, he gets out of the Hilux. He spies the bag in the back of the truck, among the tins of paint. The street is empty, but for an owl that swoops down onto a fence, its eyes two yellow phosphors. He is about to reach for the bag when he hears a voice.

It's another parent, a bloke Aleks calls Mr Chuckles because he can't remember his real name. The man is a lawyer and speaks with a patrician's briskness, giving off the impression of a civilised man marooned among savages, a benevolent dictator. Aleks smiles, remembering that the man is a renowned lawyer, an unscrupulous but aggressive tiger on the court circuit, and you never know when someone like that might come in handy.

He excuses himself and goes in search of his daughter. He opens the door into the mirrored light of the dance studio and sees her and ten other girls lined up, twirling around and around with varying degrees of skill. She sees him in the mirror, and smiles at him, open-faced, then twirls again, but trips and falls onto the ground. He laughs, eyes glittering. When she's finished, he takes her sweetly by the chin, kisses her on the cheek, then hoists her onto his shoulders and carries her out.

When he gets home, his wife is just waking up.

3

Pure bogan, this one. Trying to act all classy. Look atter, ay.

Against an enormous map of the world, the woman pouts, all blonde hair and bleached teeth. Jimmy examines her nose keenly. Pinched, upturned. Unconsciously, he touches his own hawkish nose, then runs a hand over his ponytail. Here, in the City, it's public servant land, where people get paid big bucks for doing fuck all, where a sign pointing to a national institution can be found next to a sign for plastic surgery. The vain and the bored. Jimmy should know. He's worked in a call centre in the public service ever since high school and he sees it every day. The more money earned, the more capacity to trade insecurities for even more illusions. The buildings reflect it, too – trendy new bars and coffee shops striving to mimic the styles of Melbourne but falling just short. They should chuck a nuke into the whole place.

'Nice scarf.' He smiles. 'Where's it from?'

She touches the blue silk protectively and doesn't smile back. 'I'm not sure. Um . . . Milan,' she decides.

'So how does the trip go again?' Jimmy puts on his work voice, clipped and professional.

She sighs. 'Okay, like I said *last week*, you'll fly into LAX. Then to

JFK. Then back to LAX. Then Apia, Samoa. Then back here.'

'Great.'

'You wanna put down a deposit this time?' The corner of her mouth twitches.

'Yep, yep, just ah, gotta make a call to my bank.'

She sighs again. This is a game they play at least once a week. Jimmy stares at the map of the world, focusing on the blue span of the Pacific, the neat lines delineating territories, and he can just make out the name: Samoa. Samoa – such an awesome ring to it. He remembers his stepfather's descriptions of the wind singing off the sea, alive with guitar music and salt and smoke, of the laughter of families bouncing in the flatbed of trucks, of the sun setting on the western tip of Savai'i, leaving a blood-red trail on the sea. 'God created those islands especially for the people of Samoa, James.'

One day, soon, Jimmy was gonna go there. If his lazycunt brother wasn't gonna get off his arse and do it, to pay homage to his own dad, then Jimmy would do it. Hit the sandy roads in search of a village called Fagamalo. Or maybe even seek out that real father of his and find some answers. Steady now. All he has to do is work and wait. In the meantime, it's fun to imagine he's about to escape this shithole once and for all, and to talk to the hot travel agent bitch. There's fuck-all other customers, and she's bored as, like everyone else, so she plays the game for shits and giggles. Jimmy wonders if his breath is stale from the morning shift at the call centre. He sees a wisp of hair dislodge from her tight blonde bun. Her name tag says Hailee.

'Hey . . . you into cars at all?' he asks.

'Yeah, I guess,' she says uncertainly, as if he's asking a trick question. 'Why?'

'Check this out.' He finds a picture on his phone and hands it to her. It is a 1967 Dodge Coronet, fire-engine red, white interior. His stepfather loved that car – it was one of the few material things Jimmy ever saw him covet. 'I'm gonna buy it soon.'

She looks at it warily. 'Sure . . . I mean, really?'

'Yep, just saving up.'

She tilts it back and forward, as if it were a hologram. 'Looks good.
I prefer sports cars, though. My ex-boyfriend had a Corvette.'

His stomach lurches, but, thinking of what Solomon would do, Jimmy
nods calmly and smiles. 'Ah, you'd change your mind if you saw it in person.'

She smiles back, for the first time. 'Maybe. Anything's possible,
I guess.'

He brightens, then says spontaneously. 'Hey . . . when d'you get off
work?'

'Why?'

'Just wondering.'

'Five.'

'Wanna grab a drink sometime?'

'With you?'

'Ah . . . Yeh.'

'No. I've got a boyfriend.' She smiles, relishing it.

'Oh righto . . . just asking.' His voice falls into its normal cadence,
rising at the end of the sentence. 'Um, I better get going, ay.'

'No worries. Say hi to Solomon for me.'

Solomon? What the fuck?

She looks at him, still smiling, but her eyes are impenetrable, looking
just past his shoulder. What the fuck is she thinking? Maybe he doesn't
want to know. He looks away, then back with hatred. He wants to grab
her face and make her look right at him, magically change her opinion of
him somehow, *make* her see him in a fresh light.

She looks puzzled then a little bit scared, and says, 'We'll arrange
those tickets for you soon, James.'

Jimmy tries to steady his breathing as he leaves. Walking to the bus
interchange, he counts numbers in his head, from ten to one, breathing
slowly. Then he repeats the Bruce Willis line from *Pulp Fiction* – 'They
keep underestimating you, Butch.'

They keep underestimating you, Jimmy.

Seven bucks twenty for a half-hour bus ride over the state border. Fucken
extortion. One buck, two bucks, three bucks, four. One buck, two bucks,
three bucks, more.

'There you go, mate,' he says. The bus driver grunts and takes the shrappers. This same bloke has given the boys shit since they were eight years old and looks exactly the same – aviator shades, spade-shaped beard. He tears off the ticket and slaps it in Jimmy's palm without a word. There can't be a group of people in society as cuntish as bus drivers. Parking inspectors maybe.

'Yeh, you're welcome, ya fucken thief,' Jimmy mumbles.

'What's that, mate?'

'Have a good day, buddy,' Jimmy says brightly.

The man growls and the engine growls louder. Jimmy sits down a few seats in front of two loud bogans, who are wasted at two p.m., slurping on longies. One of them says 'right?' at the end of every sentence and pronounces it 'rawt'. Jimmy thinks he used to work with one of them at the fried chicken shop.

The bus has air con, thank fuck, the cool air edged with cigarettes and body odour. It dries his temple sweat. On the back of the seat in front of him love memorandums and Aboriginal flags are scratched into the metal. In Wite-Out someone has scrawled a picture of a man aiming a gun at a woman with huge tits. Then he realises the barrel of the gun is a cock, veins and all, and the balls are grenades.

He starts to scratch it off with his thumb. As he does so, he looks out the window and sees Solomon's girlfriend Georgie handing out flyers, wearing a headwrap. Georgie is a bit of a pain in the arse, going on about women's rights and refugees all the time; but Jimmy doesn't mind her, unlike Aleks. Jimmy remembers her once saying, 'I never go out with white guys. It's so boring – Australia just doesn't have any *culture*.' She's from a well-to-do farming family from western New South Wales and it's obvious to everyone (Solomon included) that Georgie is just slumming it with Solomon, having her fling with a big Islander bloke before she settles with some white cunt with a dog and a law degree. Jimmy thinks of the word white and wonders . . .

Maybe if he got a hot girlfriend, it'd prove to everyone that he's not a shit cunt. But how to make it happen? Chicks like cars, don't they? The travel agent was just playing hard to get, surely –

a bit of persistence would pay off. What was it Solomon always said? 'Boyfriends are just details.' Jimmy knows he's none of the things his half-brother is: brawny or charismatic. But he knows he's resourceful. And determined as fuck.

The bogans are getting louder. Jimmy can smell alcohol vapours from his seat, even though his back is turned.

'Johnno sold his Holden, rawt. Got a pretty decent price too, *ae*. Now he has wunna them Chink cars, rawt.'

Despite himself, Jimmy turns around sharply to look at them. Feral cunts in uniform: wifebeaters, flat brim caps, neck-tatts, shaggy peroxide hair. Yeh, it's deffo him. Damo Cudgell. Cruel fucker used to run trains on drunk footy chicks with his boys, piss on them and ditch them unconscious in parking lots.

'Chink car?' Jimmy says.

'Yer mate. What about it?' Damo can't believe his luck.

Jimmy knows he shoulda kept his mouth shut but he continues regardless. 'Dunno. Not the type of word you should be slinging around, y'know? Not the type of word some people appreciate, y'know?'

Damo kisses his teeth and looks at his mate. 'Ha. Well I'll cross that bridge when I come to it, rawt? No offence if you are one though, *ae*. A Chink that is.' He's staring hard at Jimmy, obviously trying to figure out what he is. He brings up two empty longneck bottles and clinks them together. His mate raises his eyebrows. 'Chink, Chink, Chink,' they say in unison.

Jimmy turns back around. The bus driver is staring in his mirror. He's seen it all but says nothing. He looks real tired and for the first time Jimmy feels sorry for him, ferrying losers and lost souls

from one shithole to another

every

day

of

his

shit-kicking

life.

Jimmy puts on his headphones and turns the music up loud, Ice Cube's voice drowning out the bogans' nasal voices.

He tries to stay alert, recognising the trouble he has called on himself, but the music and the tiredness from his early shift suspend him in a hazy limbo. He watches the dry world spool by.

Paddock – pub – skatepark – construction site – park – funeral parlour – motel – flatblock – pub.

A lot of the new buildings going up are freshly painted, completely clean, ready to be bombed with paint. He begins to imagine a new piece. A fire-red Dodge, on a tropical beach. Palm trees, blue sky. But something is missing. That's it. A gorgeous blonde, like the travel agent, sitting on the bonnet. He's never been good at painting faces, unlike Aleks, who seems to always get the proportions right. He's about to take out his blackbook and do a sketch when the bogans' nasal voices pierce his headphones.

'Faggot, faggot, faggot,' they are saying.

Always on public transport.

He closes his eyes. He imagines locking the bogans in the bus, setting it on fire and watching them run up and down the aisle, screaming like banshees – hair, clothes, skin on fire. He turns up his headphones and keeps scratching away at the Wite-Out. He looks at his bird-boned wrists and hands. He wishes he were stronger.

He wishes he were Solomon or Aleks.

When he gets off the bus he still has a fifteen-minute walk home. As he walks, he shades his eyes, cursing himself for leaving his cap at work. The sky is a gradient of white to blue, with clouds like lonely skiffs adrift, high above the heat haze. He passes a basketball court where Solomon used to play with the older kids, its chain-link fence strangely curved at the bottom to accommodate generations of arses sitting against it. There was always a strange crosswind above the court that trapped birds, sometimes for minutes at a time, before sending them flapping and tumbling away. He crosses the court and sees a fire truck next to a small patch of smoking grass. Two firefighters are drinking from water bottles, their faces sweaty.

'Close call, ay boys?' calls Jimmy, looking at the charred ground.

'Bloody oath. Can't be too careful this time of the year. Bunch of idiots running around,' one replies.

'Too right. You reckon it was kids?'

'Probably.'

'Keep up the good work, boys.'

'Cheers, mate.'

Jimmy's house is a duplex made of light-coloured bricks. There is a single shrub in the front yard of dark red scoria. He lives alone. Once inside, he breathes in the scent of air freshener. There's a mounted Sin One record on the wall, from the early days, when Sin supposedly still lived with his heroin-addicted auntie. It is a standard hip hop cover, with Sin One crouched against a graffiti wall, hiding his nearly seven-foot frame. His famous green eyes ablaze. Why is it that mixed-blood Aboriginal people get the most hectic green eyes?

Jimmy looks around. Everything is perfectly in order, but he quickly wipes down the kitchen bench anyway. He has a long glass of water, which soothes the headache tolling in his temples.

The internet is one of his favourite sanctuaries – a rabbit warren of adventure. Once he has logged in to YouTube, he begins trolling well-known rappers and hip hop fans using anonymous names (he has five different fake email accounts). He does it methodically and kicks off three big arguments in a row on Facebook, the updates popping up every few seconds. His day is made when he gets an impassioned reaction from 360 himself.

The heat is a sedative. He puts on some porn and tries to have a wank, but can't get his dick hard, so he falls asleep fully clothed.

When he wakes up it's dark and he tries to wank again, but still no luck. What would he say if he ever met a real pornstar, like Kayden Kross or Jenna Jameson? Not much probably, but he reckons if they got to know him they'd like him. He's never been with a blonde girl; in fact, he's only ever been with two girls, even though he tells the lads different. One was Filo, the other was white, a redhead. Jimmy thinks of being lost in pussy, a pink-peach swirl of it, clits and tits and platinum hair.

Seriously, but. Who needs real women when you have porn, ay? Far less trouble, same result in the end.

He clicks the light on and reaches under the bed to lift out a heavy shoebox. It once held a pair of Air Max, but now it holds nothing but two-dollar coins, layer upon layer. He adds another ten coins. He's been saving twenty dollars a week for nearly four years, converting notes into two-dollars coins at a nearby laundry. The Korean lady at first gave him hell because he never washed his clothes there, but now accepts it with a shrug.

This box is how he is gonna buy the Dodge.

It represents so much energy expended, so many calls received from ungrateful motherfuckers. It is the future, the road that will lead him out of this yawn factory. Of course, the box is just a fraction of the money, the tip of the iceberg. He's not a dumb cunt. Most of it is in the bank, but Jimmy likes looking at the coins in the box, like a square of dragon hide. He's never told anyone about it, not even the boys. And he's close. He's gonna buy the car outright, call up the bloke in Sydney who sells them and wire the money straight through – no loans, no deposits. Just hard work. Unlike Solomon. Unlike his father.

Can't wait to see the looks on their faces. Give me a couple of months, and I'm out of this shithole for good. Trust me.

4

The man, Ulysses Amosa, scoops up his heavy newborn and approaches the boy who is not his blood, but most definitely his charge. The boy looks afraid and retreats slightly, but Ulysses beckons and places the raw baby in the boy's arms. The boy cradles him delicately, the baby dark against his light-brown skin. The baby cries and blinks and cycles its feet in the pine-scented air. Ulysses now bends his great head and whispers to the pair of them, addressing them equally, saying that they are brothers, that they are linked by a divine bond of responsibility, stronger even than blood, and that it must always be so.

The boy vows to carry in his heart this edict and for the first two years sits next to his half-brother protectively, smoothing curly wisps of hair, kissing him on the forehead and whispering into his ear, 'hello brother, hello little brother, my friend.' Yet to all observers, it takes just one look at their young eyes – the baby's steady and black, the boy's wavering like candleflames trying to right themselves – to recognise that the seeds have been sown for a different relationship altogether.

5

Familiar somehow

I roll up my sleeves so they can see my tatts.

The lecture theatre is full
when I walk in,
and I sense all eyes on me,
        even the guest lecturer's.

Still got it, boy, still got it.

I squeeze in next to Georgie.
She kisses me quickly
then faces the front.

Only two other ethnics in here:
        An Eritrean girl in a hijab and a pretty Polynesian chick.

Stuffy as a rape dungeon in here.

The lecturer, who is visiting from Brisbane, is talking about 'lateral violence' and 'the patriarchy'. The Polynesian girl raises her hand and explains that, in Samoa, there is a covenant of respect between brother and sister with special honour given to the sister. It is called *feagaiga*. She looks over at me as if she wants some back-up. The discussion is soon about something called 'intersectionality'.

How the fuck did I get myself into this whole greyhound shemozzle?

> Drug-fuelled fuckwittery, that's how.
> > Sheeeit, you gotta laugh.
> But what's mum gonna think when I
> bring a dog up into our tiny flat.

Cross that bridge when I see it, ay.

The lecturer is a willowy blonde in a well-cut navy suit.
> Firm jaw, very blue eyes –
> familiar somehow.

I started a degree at this uni, doing English and history. Mum was heart-broken when I dropped out, kept reminding me how disappointed Dad would've been.

> Do you take a greyhound for a walk everyday?
> Or does it have to be a *run*?
> Do you have to feed them fresh meat?
> Could cost a fucken fortune.

A guy with glasses and frizzy red hair raises his hand and asks the lecturer, in a vaguely aggressive tone, if she believes in 'misandry'. A groan goes around the room.
> 'What's misandry?' I whisper to Georgie.

'Hatred of men.'

The lecturer taps her pen on the table, smiling, as if she has spent her whole life preparing for questions like this, in deed and in word.

'Where do I start with this old chestnut? I get a lot of these so-called Men's Rights activists asking the same question online, I can tell you, mate.' When she says the last word it sounds anything but matey. 'As far as I'm concerned, sexism, just like racism, must have a power element involved to make it potent and/or relevant. And you cannot deny, statistically, that women are disproportionately affected by both economic and physical violence.'

I swear she looked in my direction when she said that. A to and fro begins between frizzy hair and the lecturer, its gladiatorial vibe almost reminding me of a rap battle.

Battle raps

Battles are heaps lame nowadays.

No beats,
No freestyles,
No flow –
        basically just rhyming stand-up comedy.

Jimmy loves em
but we never go anymore.

Old Jimmy –
        what's that cunt up to?

He's been pretty straight since
he got locked up as a teen,
but something diabolical is going on.

        I can feel it.

The frizzy-haired bastard won't die easily . . .

His voice timid:

'You mentioned intersectionality . . . but if I can, um, I was wondering where you think class fits into all of this. I mean, what about class privilege? Could, say, the privilege of an upper-class Muslim woman outweigh the status of a poor white Australian man?'

. . . but the lecturer is a tigress

'White male privilege supersedes all else. Misandry is like reverse racism. It's a fallacy – a concept that exists only in the minds of vapid, delusional people, not in the real world. The world, the weight of its history, the structures ingrained with sexism, would have to be turned on their heads in almost every way for me to believe that concept has any validity. It's bullshit.'

When she says that word,
her clipped speech drops for a second
and sounds Woggy, familiar.

Then it hits me. I do know this woman.
                It's Jana Janeski. Aleks' sister.

Holy shit.

I wonder if I should tell him she's in town.
What would he *do* if he knew she was here?

        I think of that white-hot summer,
        when he snatched the blue bead.

Georgie whispers, 'What's wrong, Solomon?'

'Nothing. Nothing.'

I look at the man
and his frizzy head is down,
embarrassed and dejected.

I wonder if he'll ever ask a question again.

The uni toilets

There are shittily drawn
cocks, balls and pussies on the wall.
        Aren't students supposed to be clever?

I take out a Molotow
and bomb up the bathroom mirror,
the felt squeaking on the glass
leaving black letters
        quote marks,
                a crown.

        LUMIN

Just to let em know.

A glass of water

'That bloke is an idiot. He always butts in with his contrarian questions.'
    'Yeah. Sexist prick.'
    'Typical.'
    A long wooden table at a new cafe on the edge of uni, packed
with Georgie's classmates. Nothing is under thirty bucks in this joint.
Things on the menu I've never heard of – spirulina, quinoa, goji berries,
Himalayan pink salt. I perch on the end and order a glass of water.

'So I think I'm going to go to Africa these holidays to do some aid work,' Georgie announces. It is all white faces, besides the Eritrean girl, who looks away and adjusts her headscarf.

'Wow, that is so brilliant,' says a redheaded girl with two moles on her chin. 'I worked in Bangladesh at an orphanage last year for six weeks. I got this blouse there, actually. The children were such sweethearts. It felt really amazing to give something back.'

The Eritrean girl again shifts uncomfortably and I am filled with a sudden rage. 'There aren't any people here in Australia you could help out?' I ask drily. The table turns to me. It's the first thing I've said all day.

'True,' Georgie says accommodatingly, also seemingly surprised I've piped up. 'I guess I could go to a remote Aboriginal community . . . '

'No,' I say, 'I mean here. In the City, in the Town. You know how many homeless people there are? Kids with no dads, bored outta their skulls. Three generations on ice. Start in your own backyard.'

'That's not the point, Solomon. Does it really matter where in the world you help out, as long as you do? There's just something about Africa that really draws me to it.'

'Look, I'm not talking about anyone here,' I say uncertainly, before deciding to plough in. 'All I'm saying is that I hate it when people head overseas on their big exotic adventure when there are people in need here. It's so they can wash their hands of it and come back to their boring, middle-class lives, sit around at uni and brag to their friends about how they helped some real, authentic people of colour.' I pinch my middle finger and thumb together to accentuate my point. 'People do that with hip hop workshops. Go to a community for three days, make good money, then never return.'

'So what is it that you do, then? To actively help the community?' says mole-chin with a heart-eating grin.

That gets me for a moment, but I ignore it. 'That's beside the point. It's the self-congratulation I hate. Like in that classroom. You crush some useless dickhead like that, or post a status on Facebook, then dust your hands off for the day. Tiny, pointless victories, while the world rolls on regardless.'

'No, it was about making him recognise his privilege. You have to call it when you see it,' retorts Georgie.

'How do you define privilege?' I ask, warming up. Been a long time since I discussed something like this.

'Well, it's access to a certain right or advantage by a particular group or person. For example, yours is being male,' says Georgie, wrinkling her nose.

'And yours is being white,' I shoot back. 'Privilege is power. Privilege is the opportunity to exert power over others, to be corrupt.'

'No, that's abuse of privilege.'

They are all staring at me, and I am feeling like I am holding court, warming to my subject. 'Abuse is inherent *within* privilege – they're one and the same. The feeling I get most of the time is that the fervour that fuels these so-called activists is the same that fuels a racist or a sexist. They're not actually aiming for equality. They're aiming for a direct exchange so they can be the one in the privileged position and lord it over someone else. Different side of the same coin.'

'That's a really cynical way of looking at the world.'

'Yeah? Well, it's dog-eat-dog out there,' I say, shrugging.

They all go silent for a moment, mulling something over. I'm not sure whether it's my arguments or the fact that a guy who looks like me can speak on their level. Then mole-chin says, 'Looks like a male ego has yet again hijacked the conversation.'

'Yeah, because there's no such thing as a woman with a big ego —' I stop, and look around. Staring faces. Mole-chin is smiling. I feel like I've fallen into some sort of a trap; but what kind, I don't know. Tiredness overwhelms me and I remember something I saw on a Facebook meme, 'Yep. Sorry. I guess I have to check *my* privilege. My bad.'

The conversation scurries on. I sip my water and stare away, still taken aback by seeing Jana Janeski. A boiling torment in my spine. I wish I could twist a valve in my shoulders and release it like steam, like I used to with basketball. Georgie, always conciliatory, scratches me on the shoulder and then rubs the back of my hand tenderly. When we first got together she couldn't get enough of putting her hand next to mine, admiring the contrast of brown and white, touching my tatts, telling her mates how spiritual I was. She couldn't stop asking questions about Samoa, questions I found hard to answer.

'There's a new exhibition of Pacific art on at the gallery, Solomon. Should be amazing,' she whispers. 'Wanna go on the weekend?'

'I dunno.'

'But I thought you'd be into it.'

'Why?' I say sharply. I'm about to add something else when I hear a familiar voice.

'Oi, Solomon, ya dumb cunt.'

I turn and see Jimmy grinning lopsidedly,

Some of the uni students look at him angrily,

but he doesn't seem to notice.

He strokes his chin like a faux-intellectual and nods to himself,

as if he's come up with a brilliant idea.

Silly bastard,

but thank fuck he's here.

'Come on, bro, let's go get Mercury Fire,' says Jimmy. 'Hey, Georgie.'

Georgie doesn't look at him. He has never been of interest to her.

She gazes at me steadily then sighs.

'Go on then.'

6

The day hot and strange and flattened, almost monochrome.

Aleks drives calmly, rolling the blue bead between forefinger and thumb. Spice 1's voice rat-ta-tats over funked-out keys and synths as the land unfolds before the Hilux. This part of suburbia has a wildness, as if the flats and houses on the edge of the bushland are in danger of being overtaken by it. He stops at a red light, and on the corner is a large electricity box with the ghost of a buffed chromie on it, its letters only vaguely decipherable.

Near the Greek Orthodox church, he sees a man in an orange hi-vis jacket standing in the middle of a field where there were once massive blackberry bushes, long since poisoned. The man has a measuring tape in his hands and the grass at his feet is almost white, bleached by drought. Aleks swings the wheel and turns into the old graveyard. He goes down a blue metal driveway lined by a calligraphy of ghost gums and observes a bird settle on a tombstone. As it lands, its wings take the shape of hands in supplication.

A ute is parked next to the far fence under an ironbark. He pulls up beside it. It's covered in Southern Cross stickers and bikie insignia. There are two men inside, both with long hair and thick, bristly beards. The driver climbs out. He's a bikie, wearing wraparound sunnies, and has a strange triangular dent in his forehead, almost squarely above the gap in his eyebrows. Tattoos cover his arms, hands and throat. He offers Aleks a cigarette. They smoke together for a while, looking at the gravestones, between which are patches of dying daisies and purple bush sarsaparilla, the stones slanting in opposite directions, stained maroon and green by rust and moss. A magpie hops sideways down the cemetery's far fence and beyond that is the river, drying up.

After a while, the man speaks.

'This is one of the oldest cemeteries in the state, you know. It's divided into four sections, see.' He gestures with a hairy hand towards the opposite fence, which is buckling and dark with treeshadow, then makes a chopping motion four times in the air, hand moving left to right. 'Presbyterian, Anglican, Methodist, Catholic. A few Jews over there. A few gravestones in Arabic there – Syrians who came during the goldrush, you know? All the Abos and Chinks were buried outside the fence cos they were heathens. No headstones for the unconsecrated. Somewhere beneath us, there's hundreds of em. Thousands maybe.' He taps the ground three times with his shoe, as if knocking on a door. 'A hundred years ago, most people in the Town couldn't even be buried here with a gravestone.' He smiles vaguely, then says, 'Well . . . maybe you or me.'

'Fuck that. I wouldn't wanna be buried here anyway.' Aleks catches himself and stamps out his cigarette. 'No offence . . . '

'None taken, mate.'

'How do you know all that shit, anyway?'

'Library card.'

'Good for you.' Aleks scratches his ear. 'So.'

'So.' The man plucks a gum leaf from a branch and methodically folds it in half. He has very dry lips, which he wets with his tongue before speaking. 'I've heard things, Janeski. Things that offend me. Things that make my life more complicated. I like my things to be simple.'

'Life is never simple, brother.'

'True. But a bloke can dream, can't he? You know, I wasn't even sure if I should come here today. I almost sent someone else.'

The men look across the headstones at a stand of poplar trees on the other side of the river. A boy in a wheelchair rolls off an unseen track and parks beneath them.

'But you're here now,' says Aleks.

'I am, indeed. But we're jumping the gun, Janeski. I feel like you had something to say to me.'

Aleks smiles magnanimously. 'Look here, brother. Let's not mess around, all right? I know you're not here to fuck spiders. You're a smart fella. You'd be able to tell that I'm what you call a people's person. I meet all sorts of characters in this funny game. So recently, I made the acquaintance of some fellas in Sydney. Fellas with a bit of dash. Fellas that it's better to be friends with than enemies, understand? More importantly, these fellas have a lot of product in their possession. Cheap. Good quality. Direct from Afghanistan.'

'How cheap?' the bikie asks. The man in the passenger seat of the ute is cocking his head, obviously trying to catch every word.

Aleks cracks his knuckles and says a number. The bikie nods. 'Competitive. But what if I don't want to meet your friends?'

'Well. Then things get . . . complicated again,' says Aleks. The boy in the wheelchair whirs a handline over his head and hurls it into the river. 'But there's no need for that, brother. Let's be businessmen about this. Not animals. Let's . . . how do you say? Compromise. The way nations do it.'

'Really? I thought they do it by force.'

Aleks laughs. 'True. But in this situation it's not mutually beneficial for anyone to use force. Play this thing right, we can be winners. You get direct access to the good shit. My friends make money. You make money. You'll be rich as bloody Ottomans, mate.'

'Then why shouldn't I go straight to them myself?' the bikie says.

'Because they're fond of me, these fellas. They value loyalty. And loyalty's a hard commodity to come by in this country. It's at a premium, don't you reckon?'

'All right. Then you? What's in it for you?'

Aleks looks across the river again. The boy is reeling something in.

Carp? Redfin? The water must be so low right now. *What fish would be in there?* he wonders.

'Me? I work for myself. Just a little extra cream will do me fine. A sip from the bubbler, like I said.'

'A bit of a rogue then, ay?'

'Fuck noath, brother.' Aleks grins and makes a mental note to use the word later. The bikie was right – Aleks treasures his position as an outsider among outsiders, a solo operator, doing as he pleases at a mid to low level in the criminal world. Over the years, he has acted as muscle, as a liaison, negotiated drug deals, intimidated and used fraud, all the while doing his day job. He doesn't consider himself a criminal, merely an opportunist. In the chaos of a war-torn country, he'd learned that you have to take what you can get, when you can get it. The same, it turns out, applies here. At times the urge is there to go all in, but he's been slow and steady, ready at any point to fade into the background. For his family, all for his family. 'A rogue. Yeh, I like that. Look, at this point, don't worry about me. I'm just sorting them out and the rest'll follow. We all win.' He claps his hands together then makes an open gesture, as if releasing pigeons from a rooftop.

The bikie has taken his sunnies off and squints at Aleks, studying him. He sees something, then slowly nods. They shake hands. Aleks waits for the ute to leave then he drives slowly up the long, bluestone driveway. As he swings onto the road, he nods at someone in the tree line.

7

Jimmy and Solomon stand with Mercury Fire in between them. Gladys is talking in a torrent. The boys try to shuffle back into the shade of a tree, as the sun is burning their skin. She carries on, unperturbed:

'He fell from the sky.

I was looking over me backyard,
making a sandwich.
The lad next door skied his cricket ball.
We both looked up
but both lost it against the sun.

I saw something moving waaay up high,
gliding,
        a V shape.
I couldn't believe the ball had gone that far.

I saw the ball drop in the corner of me eye,
but I kept looking at the V.

It turned and rose and turned.
Me head was right back.

Suddenly
it split into two and a black blob
fell
towards the ground.

I felt it hit the earth,
and maybe I heard it, too,
but I couldn't see where it landed.
I ran towards the fence and I knew it was something important.
                                        A change.

Even before all that,
        luck had played a huge part in me life.

I was always a street fighter,
a tough old bird.
You have to be, growing up in Streatham.
            South London.'

Jimmy whispers something about the rapper Roots Manuva to Solomon, who shushes him. The old lady continues.

'It's not all luck,
but that's what has played the biggest part.

That's what I think I thought.

I looked underneath the old plum tree
and saw something against the fence.
I didn't want to touch it,
then it made a sound.

It looked like a bloody grey tennis ball.
Then I realised,
a tiny face was looking back at me.
I thought it was a possum or a water rat at first.
But it wasn't.

It was a little puppy,
a bloody and broken little critter,
with fur the colour of mercury.

I scooped it up and squinted at the sky again.
I saw an eagle with wings
maybe as long as a man's arms.
Could've been a wedgetail.
The little grey ball whimpered in me hands.
It looked as if its leg was broken
and it had one eye staring at me,
                              bright as a button.

The other had been scratched,
maybe even torn out, by the eagle.

Who'da known that pathetic lil thing –
lil gift of the sky –
would be a champion one day.

I could hear the kids start their game again
on the other side of the fence.

I went inside and called a vet.'

She is crying now and the brothers, one with his hand on Mercury's
head, the other on its twitching withers, don't know where to look.

8

'Bro . . . I'm drunk as.'

'Me too, brother.'

'How the fuck we get here? This place is way too posh for us.'

'Aw, we're celebrating, bro.'

'Celebrating what?'

'Buying the hound.'

'Oh, that's right, ay.'

The bar is brand new, the latest hotspot in town, with a line almost around the corner. Young chicks totter like fresh-born foals. The boys are smoking just outside the door. Solomon is handed an ID by a nervous teenager who mistakes him for a bouncer. All the staff wear waistcoats and the wall shows raw brick in places. Concrete and a rust wall. The couches are rich brocade and the curtains have a bullion fringe. Despite all attempts, it is a parade of vulgarity. Neon lights shine through Alizé and Patrón bottles behind the bar. Metro roidheads and wannabe footy players wear shirts printed with the names of foreign cities they'll never visit and compare copycat tatts and gym muscles. Women with fake breasts and fake tans flick tousled hair over shoulders with manicured hands, waiting for someone to shake a bag of coke like a polaroid and lead them to the bathroom.

'Live by the bag, die by the bag', says Aleks.

A woman is yelling, 'Where's Caitlin? I've lost Caitlin,' while men stand against the wall, observing her, hands crossed over genitals, bobbing their heads to the beat. Everyone's eyes are elsewhere, on the door especially, to see if someone new comes in, each person ignoring exes, tracing hands around waists, heads thrown back with exaggerated laughter. A small, awkward dancefloor has formed, and the DJ switches from ambient tunes to old Ja Rule and TLC. Jimmy yells at him to play some Gang Starr. The DJ is a hip hop head from way back who does this lark on the side. He smiles tiredly and says, 'Yeh, for sure, bro, a bit later.'

Jimmy sprinkles some MDMA crystals into Solomon's palm, and watches as Solomon licks them off discreetly. Georgie looks away. Aleks is toying with his keys, chatting to a scientist who has just been laid off in the latest round of government cuts. A man, by himself at the edge of the bar, watches them all. Jimmy begins to tell a story, his voice loud and slurring.

'You know how Sin One became so good at rapping? He ran away from his auntie's place when she was on the heroin, bro; ran into the bush as far as he could. He was only six. He couldn't read or write. He couldn't even speak, did you know that? He was mute. He ran up into the hills, chasing a feral dog, and found a cave. He sat in the cave for five fucken days straight and when he was there, a swarm of bees came in. They went in his eyes, in his nose, in his ears, his throat, but they never stung him and he sat there, still as a Buddha. When he came out, he had a different voice; his mind had been rearranged somehow. He could fit words together like a mosaic. Then his Tongan neighbour gave him a Big Daddy Kane tape. The rest is history, bra.'

Aleks, Georgie and Solomon are staring over their drinks at him. Then Aleks says, 'Where the fuck do you come up with this shit, Jimmy?'

Jimmy starts laughing, then so do Aleks and Solomon. Solomon throws his head back and big gusts of laughter sweep through him and he's shaking his dreds side to side with tears in his eyes. A group of women at another table all stare at him slyly, lingering over their cocktails.

Jimmy notices that Solomon's the only dark-skinned person in the room, besides a Maori bouncer and a table of well-to-do looking Indians, who stare at the boys like they're an unpleasant joke or a foul smell hanging in the air. Why is it that ethnics always hate other ethnics? The boys stare staunchly back at the Indians, who soon stand up to leave. Georgie looks away again and orders a lime and soda.

'I heard your story. What a load of horseshit. How many lines have you had tonight, mate?'

The bloke on the edge of the bar says it. Jimmy squints and he comes into focus. The man is wearing grey, with husky blue eyes and light-blond hair whipped into a wave.

'Who the fuck are you?' asks Solomon.

The man smiles and doesn't seem offended in the least. 'Damien Crawford. Nice to meet you.'

Soon, a bit confused, the boys are shaking his hand. He tells them immediately he is a spokesperson for a government minister. He orders round after extravagant round for everyone, spending thousands. He begins to tell the boys that he studied law overseas, that before that he was dux of his high school, that at university he was heavily involved in student politics. Jimmy can't catch which party he belongs to. Who's in power anyway? Who the fuck knows?

Aleks smirks and says, 'What's uni? Is it like TAFE but with better cappuccinos?'

The man smiles again. Soon he and Solomon are in a debate about boat people and the attention is immediately on Solomon, and his big hands that accentuate his words in a strangely delicate way. Jimmy notices how his brother's voice changes, the private school modulation, how he can immediately slip into the back-and-forth of argument, using words Jimmy's never heard him say. It suddenly hits him – Solomon is bilingual.

'What we need is compassionate onshore processing,' says Solomon.

'And relocation of funds,' adds Georgie.

'Exactly. The current system doesn't work morally or economically. Costs the taxpayer billions every year that we could use way better —'
Solomon is about to continue when Aleks butts in.

'My parents, they came here with fuck-all, mate; they made something of themselves. They both had two jobs. We shared a tiny flat with another family. They came the right way and no one felt sorry for us. It's bullshit. People need to just get on with it. The government's doing the right thing – getting ready for when there's ten times more refugees.'

Georgie is shaking with anger. 'Ugh.'

Aleks curls his lip. 'Look. When NATO fucked us up the arse, we had one million Albanian refugees come across the border into Macedonia. You know how much that fucked the economy? Set us back decades.'

Solomon and Aleks have had this argument numerous times and for the most part agree to disagree, so Solomon speaks softly but firmly, using the Macedonian diminutive of Aleks' name. 'But *Atse*, we're not talking about millions of people. We're talking about a few thousand. Also, it's not *illegal* to seek asylum.'

'Yeah, but you let one in, you let em all in.'

'Bro, you of all people should know how war can make people desperate.'

Solomon is about to speak again when Crawford claps his hand on Aleks' shoulders. '*This* is a man who's talking some sense.' He turns to Solomon. 'What school did you go to?'

Solomon tells him.

'Rugby scholarship?' asks Crawford.

Solomon flinches, but replies truthfully. 'Basketball.'

'Right.'

'How you know I'm not a maths freak or something?'

Crawford shrugs and smiles again. 'Just a hunch. Tell you what though, you'd make a good footy player. We definitely need it at the moment. The Wallabies are atrocious. No heart.'

'Yeah, well, I'm not.'

Crawford sizes them up, looking at Jimmy's cap and Solomon's Elefant Traks shirt. 'I heard you talking about Sin One. You must have heard he's coming back to town. He might very well be the only Aussie rapper who really competes on the world stage. Party, political, personal – he does it all. Pity time's moved on without him, though.'

Crawford sounds passionate as he speaks – there's something entrancing and terrifying about him. How does he know about hip hop? About Sin One? His eyes seem to change colour, and then he becomes suddenly dismissive. 'Aussie rap – bit of a joke, don't you think? Can never compare to the real thing. Boys. Let me tell you another story.' Crawford begins to speak about boats and wars, deserts and islands. He says that truth is a metal you can bend with your will and with heat. He talks about an alley cat that tried to act like a tiger. The alley cat walked tall, it growled, it stalked through the city as if it was the jungle, but no matter how hard the alley cat tried, he could never shake the stink of the gutter. People always knew what he was and he was eventually castrated. 'This alley cat should have known his station,' Crawford concludes. He must have drunk a full bottle of liquor to himself but is still speaking in clipped, perfect phrases, as if he has rehearsed everything he is saying. Georgie excuses herself and leaves the bar.

Jimmy goes to the bathroom to take a shit. He scratches a tag into the toilet roll dispenser with a key but his mind is spinning. He sits with his head in his hands and spits out the saliva that is flooding his mouth. When he goes back to the bar, the place is almost empty. He goes into the smoking area and sees Solomon beating Crawford savagely and silently in the corner. The blood sparks off his face like garnets and he is grimacing or smiling. Aleks is nowhere to be seen. Jimmy joins Solomon and soon Crawford's face is unrecognisable. 'Wrong place at the wrong time buddy,' one of them says. 'They teach you 'bout that at university?' Holding him by his collar, Jimmy looks up and sees the bouncer standing in the doorway. He nods at them. They turn back to their task and continue to punch, now crouched over him, thrashing him against the bloodsprent cement. Crawford has not made a sound and is soon so disfigured that he couldn't even if he wanted to.

Solomon and Jimmy look up and the bouncer is no longer in the doorway.

9

Hand tatts

There are five men in the studio,
each one bigger than the next.
A woman walks in confidently
and says,
'Who's Wil?'
'Me.'
'Sweet. Over here.'

I scan the walls.
Thousands of tattoo designs –
pin-up girls, Southern Crosses, skulls.
The tattoo artist has dark hair.
She moves to the CD player
and puts on a David Dallas album.

The man called Wil reclines in the seat
and she points to his neck.

'Right here?'

'Yeah.'

'Too easy.'

She starts to tattoo

the postcode of the Town

onto his neck.

His face is emotionless.

She is mumbling along to the song –

        'From the Pacific Isle of Samoa

        via Middlemore, still as raw as the day a baby boy

        was delivered on.'

Delicate with the needle,

efficiently wiping away blood and ink

with a paper towel,

she is finished quickly.

'And now?'

'A joker. Right here.'

'On your hand?'

'Yeh.'

'Can you prove you've got a job that lets you have a hand tatt?'

'Ah . . . What?'

'I don't do face or hand tatts if you can't prove you're not gonna lose

your job if you get one.'

'Nah. I mean, I can pay.'

'I'm sure you can, babe. I just don't do it. Sebastien should have told you.'

'Orright.'

He sits back down with his mates. They talk among themselves.

'It says Johnno's next.'

'How much longer till me?'

'You Solomon?'

'Yeh.'

'Ah, shouldn't be long. Maybe twenty minutes. Sorry, babe, Seb called

in sick. Probably hungover. Fucked everything up.'

'No worries. I'll be back.'

A joint

I duck out the back and roll up a joint.
This weed is wet.
That dodgy fucker Grunt
  flysprays his weed
  to make it heavier, I heard.

Gotta be careful.

The main street is changing.
It even has a coffee shop. With a barista.
  Fucken sacrilege.

I think of some mad lines from a Horrorshow song:
  'Every day, the heritage fades/
  Gentrification, nothing's gonna get in the way.'

Change is a nest of white ants in the wall,
  acid to the face.
Sudden or slow,
  it terrifies me.

Today's heat like a fillet blade,
taking strips off me.
I blow smoke,
mouth tasting ashy but the weed working nicely.
Someone joins me. It's the tatt artist.
She has a smooth, pale throat.
'Finished already?'
'Yeh. Those fellas chucked a tantrum cos I wouldn't do hand tatts.'
'Ah.'
'Idiots. I'm not gonna take responsibility if they wanna fuck their lives up.'

'You gave that guy a neck tatt, though. What's the difference?'
'Dunno. Gotta draw the line somewhere, I guess.'
'You want some of this?'
'Don't smoke. Thanks, though. Come in, babe.'

Skin

I point at an elephant in an art book I brought with me.
It's stylised, with swirling designs on its hide.
An Albanian king had it on his chest,
supposedly.

>Suddenly Aleks' voice comes into my head.
>*Anytime you hear of someone getting clipped in Melbourne,*
>*it was probably an Albo that done it.*

'Nice piece. Why this one?' she says.
'My mum's favourite animal.'
'Aww, a mama's boy.'

>Truth is,
>I don't spend enough time with Mum,
>even though I still live with her,

but I say, 'Yep. Heaven lies at the feet of the mother.'
She looks up, her eyes a startling green. 'I like that.'
'Yeh. It's in the Qur'an. I think.'
'You Muslim?'
'Once upon a time.'
'Well, it's nice. Problem with most hip hop guys is that they all think
their mum's a queen but every other woman's a whore.'
'True.'
'And you?'
'I got a girlfriend.'
'And?' Her cat eyes shine.
'I treat her very well, thank you very much. You worked here long?'

'A while. Moved from Auckland a few years back. Hey, you've got nice skin. You must eat well.'

'Dunno.'

'You get all types. If you're lucky, it's lovely and buttery. You should thank your parents.' She wipes some ink and blood away.

'I'll try to remember.'

'You a coconut?'

'Samoan.'

'*Afakasi?*'

'I'm Samoan.'

'Woah. Calm down. Just asking. When was the last time you went?'

'Never been.'

'Well, I like those,' she gestures at my sleeve tatts.

'Cheers.'

'What do they represent?'

'Oh, you know. Power, money, respect,' I say nonchalantly, trying to throw her off the scent.

She looks up again. 'Tatts like that are a pretty modern thing. Based on *tapa* designs.'

'Ah, okay.' I didn't know that.

The *zzzzz* of the tattoo machine.

After a while she says, 'Sometimes you get skin that's coarse and dotted with pores as big as bullet holes. People who've been eating chips and gravy every day since they were ten. Two-minute noodles and toast. Drinking beer and smoking bongs twenty-four seven, getting psoriasis. But whatever the case, skin's the best canvas. Bleeds, fights, fucks. Skin tells a story like nothing else.'

'But not the whole story,' I say, thinking of Jimmy.

She doesn't reply. The outline is nearly complete.

'You got a boyfriend?' I ask.

'Used to. Now I date women. Mostly.'

'Sweet. We got something in common then.'

She laughs, showing very white teeth.
She's the least-inked tattoo artist
I've ever seen.
Her skin is perfectly bare
but for one teardrop
tatted under her right eye.
She has messy black hair piled on her head
and is wearing a loose white singlet
with a black bra visible from the side.

'What's your name?'
'Scarlett.'
'Scarlett what?'
'Planning to look me up?'
'Nah, just wondering.'
'Snow. Scarlett Snow.'
'Really?'
'Yeh, yeh, I know. Sounds like a porn name. Or a metal band.'
'Nah, I think it's cool. It's . . . evocative. You should thank your parents.'
She laughs again.

When I leave, I call Georgie
but she doesn't answer.

Broke as, now

At the paint shop looking at Beltons and Montanas.
　　Good paints.
Can't afford em, but.
I momentarily think of racking them
but there are people everywhere.

Racking paint

The rush of theft
turned into a part-time occupation,
        back in the day.

Stash the tins in an anorak.
Wheel a bin full of paint
out the back of a hardware store.
        Whatever.

Jimmy, Aleks and me kept our spots secret,
        guarded them *viciously*.
It was like a game to see who
could get the best paints.

Back then,
Bunnings was good for Dulux and Wattyl.
Autobahn for Krylon.
Magnet Mart for PlastiKote.
Shoe stores for Tuxan.
Horse saddle places for raven oil to make stainer.

Art stores always
cottoned on quickly
and stopped stocking cans.

Fuck those were good times.

There is one thing I could do

I walk to the basketball courts with Mercury Fire on a leash.
I chain him up and he stands stock-still,

staring far off,
a muscle in his shoulder twitching.

The afternoon's cooling down at last,
the sky as pink as a cat's mouth,
spires of smoke on the hills.
I do some lazy stretches and
my hamstrings scream.
I almost feel like crying at the pain.

Mercury starts barking
at a bunch of colourful parrots sitting in the bending fennel.
        I let him off the leash,
     and they twitter and fly away,
             points
                in a
           moving constellation.

Dad used to say Aussie birds reminded him
of fish in the reef near his village,
      Free, multicoloured, dreamlike.

This court's been here ages,
      blacktop crumbling around the edges.
Beneath the hoop is a hopscotch grid in yellow chalk.

Common's 'Be' playing from my phone.

I pound the ball on the ground a few times,
the ring alien at first,
but soon I'm sweating,
getting my range back.
I take my shirt off to feel the dying sun,
being careful of the cling wrap over my new tatt.

Bounce, bounce,
        fingertips, rhythm,
        limbs turn to fire,
Bounce, bounce,
         my body an instrument
            of knowing,
            of knowledge,
            of concentration,
Bounce, bounce,
the flick of the wrist,
the release,
        swish.

Just like before the injury.

A scar the size of a caterpillar
          hums on my Achilles.

Now I'm in the rhythm,
counting my shots:
         miss, miss, one,
         miss, two, miss,
         three, four, five,
         miss, six, seven,
         miss.

That word floats into my head.
        Afakasi – the Samoanisation of 'half-caste'.
    Not white, not brown.
    Outcasts, loners, entitled.

I keep shooting, angry and imprecise,
until the rhythm calms me down again.

My knees and ankles ache after minutes
and I take a long draught of water,
squinting at the sun,
      when a man calls out.

His name is Fred,
a small Filipino dude with a transatlantic accent
         and a furry lip.
He's excited to have made a new friend.
As he shoots wildly,
he explains that he just moved from Perth.
He's shirtless as well,
lean and muscled,
which makes me feel self-conscious.

'First to five?' he says.

I'm worried about the new tatt,
but I nod.

He starts quickly,
feinting to the right then throwing up an improbable shot,
which banks hard off the backboard and in.

1–0

He has no technique,
but makes up for it with quick feet and floaty,
         almost boneless movement.
He's difficult to read.
    He dribbles to his left,
    gets trapped,
    slips,

then suddenly jumps and scoops a shot up with his right.
                          Swish.
I land awkwardly
and there's a dull toll in the back of my head.

            2–0

Everything swollen and tight already.
I try to focus.
This time, this time I'll get him.
I stretch out my arms in a defensive stance,
showing off my wingspan
            and getting in his face.
Fred trips forward,
suddenly unsure,
apologises when he steps on my foot,
then runs in circles around the three-point line before I get an easy
strip.

I face him and it takes only a flicker
            for my mind to register every possibility,
                                    the lie of the court,
                                    his uncertain feet.
I jab step to the left.
He bites, so I drive hard to the right
            and bully the shorter man out of the way for an easy lay-up.

            1–2

            Check ball.

I wipe sweat away with my forearm,
then begin dribbling from the three-point line.
I drive right,

cross him up with my left hand,
the Shammgod move leaving him stranded.
I finger roll the ball in smoothly.

2–2

He looks at me in awe. 'Did you used to play? Properly, I mean?'
'Nah. Just messing around.'
'Damn. You should join a team, bro.'

I don't reply.

The next points don't come for several minutes.

I shake beads of sweat off my dreds,
lungs small as a baby's fist.
My Achilles white hot.
     Impotence and fury.
I try to rearrange my features into the mask I used to wear,
but I'm breathing so heavily it's difficult to.
Fred seems to notice the change in atmosphere
and has fear on his mug.
He hadn't anticipated being drawn into a battle of this kind.
The sound of the ball on the asphalt
               like a war drum.
I post him up,
use my size against him
and back him down,
slowly, slowly,
facing away from the basket,
slowly, slowly, wearing him down.
It's ugly but effective,
not the fancy moves I once prided myself on.
I pivot and my hook shot drops in.

One more to win.

I summon my fury and focus it into my body.

I drive for a fadeaway,
mishandle and bounce the ball off my shin.
It shoots over the dry grass
and rolls down a ditch next to the dilapidated wooden fence.
As I jog to retrieve it,
I'm suddenly filled with a deep sadness
    at this deteriorating body,
      my waning manhood,
and I feel tired.

I wish I were alone.

Fred shoots and misses.
I finish it off with a feathery jumper that he praises exuberantly.

'Mad shot, bro!'

As I drink deep from my water bottle
    and twist on my hips,
I notice crumbs of light sparkling on the edge of the court,
like the glow of treasure.
I stand for a moment,
half bent,
staring,
thinking about how it was luck that won it,
how I only shot the last one
because I was too damn tired to run
      or back him down.

From a house nearby
I hear that ubiquitous Lorde song, 'Royals'.
I realise the sparkle on the blacktop
    is the remnants of a beer bottle broken long ago.
High above is a red kite,
    twisting and turning.

I walk away from the court,
thinking of the sparkle and the kite.
I feel a bit ashamed at not saying goodbye to Fred,
but I keep walking,
    faster and faster.
I hear yelling,
    and ignore it until it gets to my shoulder.
It's Fred, breathless. 'Your dog! Your dog!'
'Ah shit, thanks mate.'

I try to smile.

Up close, Mercury Fire unnerves me.
He once inspired excitement and joy
but now he seems the portent of something dangerous,
something tragic and shameful.
        Of failure.
He yawns
and the silt of resentment boils up in me.
When I look into his eye,
it's my own eyes I see.

10

Jimmy and Solomon wander through the supermarket, bored, while Ulysses squeezes avocados and raps on coconuts. First, they have a chilli-eating contest, which Jimmy wins determinedly. Panting and fanning their mouths, they go into the cold room to see how long they can stay in there. Soon bored, they move to the toy aisle and find a packet of plastic cowboys and Indians. The whole packet only one dollar.

A voice from above, 'I reckon I could spare a buck.'

An immaculately dressed man is standing next to them, pencil thin with a smile on his face. Wearing fashionable sunglasses, he has light-brown skin and is of ambiguous ethnicity. He crouches.

'Hi, James,' he says.

'Who are you?' says Solomon.

'You must be Solomon. Big fella.' The man offers his hand and Solomon shakes it reluctantly, by the fingertips only. The man's hand is bone-dry. He lets go and conjures a two-dollar coin, as if from nowhere. He lets it trip down the knuckles of his right hand and drop into his left palm, then holds out the coin to Jimmy. As he does, a shadow appears over him and he is knocked to the ground by a crushing blow. Ulysses Amosa. The man stands up, bleeding from his nose onto his starched white shirt, afraid and blinking. He tries to

smile and reminds Ulysses that they were once best of friends. As soon as he stands to full height, another blow. This time Ulysses hisses, 'Get out. Get the fuck out of here now.' The man scrambles away. His sunglasses bounce on the tiles and a manager waddles over to berate Ulysses, who is shaking. The boys are astonished – they have never heard Ulysses Amosa swear.

11

Aleks has a day off work and is in his basement.

Steel, paint, chemicals, petrol. There is a big workbench jumbled with carpenter's tools and a tall shelf behind it. Aleks picks up a ball bearing, the size of a marble, turns it between forefinger and thumb, and observes it in the meagre light, silver, before placing it on the shelf. As children, he and the boys were constantly on the hunt for ball bearings, the king cheat of marble games. He smiles, climbs on a stool, reaches up high and pulls down the gym bag.

He opens it and takes out what is inside: a 22-calibre handgun, black snout gleaming. He lays it in his lap and disassembles it, then cleans it slowly. A .22 is light and perfect for wounding, good for hits because the bullet doesn't break the sound barrier and lodges in the brain. Guns are nothing new to him – in the Balkans, most homes would have one.

Tomorrow was going to be a dangerous day.

Once he has cleaned it, he places it back in the bag and hides it on the top shelf, then visits the pharmacy to get his father's heart medicine. When he collects Mila from school, she leaps into the passenger seat of the Hilux. She tells him about a science experiment she did in class where they put some Mentos into a Coke bottle and the chemical reaction caused the soft drink to shoot up into the sky like a fountain. Aleks doesn't think it sounds like a very educational experiment, but wonders whether he ought to get her an iPad to help her study. He pulls up at her ballet school and, before she jumps out, he smoothes her hair back and kisses her on the forehead, then arranges her collar, which has flicked up.

'I love you, sweetheart.'

'Have you thought any more about the holiday, *tat?*'

'Of course. We'll go soon, don't worry.'

'Promise.' Those eyes again. She adds in an almost professional voice, 'Could help mum get better.'

This time, he doesn't point out that she has dropped into English, but stares straight back into her eyes and gives her hand a squeeze. 'I promise, baby. Go on. Mrs. Hua will drop you home, all right?'

When he arrives at his parents' flat, his father, Petar, is watching the Macedonian news. There are flags waving and a man at a podium speaking hoarsely into a microphone. Petar is a dark, lugubrious man, wearing a white singlet at a table covered in paints. A half-finished icon of St Clement is on an easel by his side, eyes staring out gravely, gold background glowing. Petar is pinching at a faded tattoo above his elbow. It reads *Sloboda ily Smrt* – Freedom or Death. He stands up to shake his son's hand. His mother, Biljana, appears from the kitchen, smiling. Aleks hands her some flowers before clearing a space on the table and dividing his father's medicine into a pillbox.

Petar Janeski had grown up in Communist Yugoslavia with a photo of Marshall Tito on his wall, like every other family. His home life in the village had been one of crushing poverty, his father a poor farmer and secret Macedonian patriot who sold vegetables in the market. One day, as they tilled the fields, his father was telling Petar folk stories and reminding him that Macedonians were descended from Philip of Macedon, and a great line of warriors and kings. Cultural and church expression were repressed; spies were everywhere. A passerby, who happened to be listening in, reported him. The family was blacklisted by the Communist Party and, as life got harder, Petar's father became more and more harsh towards him. Petar didn't consider his father a bad man, but he grew up knowing the discipline of knuckles and fist. The blacklisting clung to his family name like a curse, meaning he could never get a proper job, just menial labour from time to time. He dreamed of a life that would offer him more.

One day, digging up a garden for his neighbours, Petar overheard the couple talking about emigration. The Party had eased travel restrictions in the 1960s and many people were heading to Australia, where it was said you could earn great wealth. There was already a community there, and the church had sent priests to educate the Macedonians abroad, so the transition to a new country would not be so difficult. As he dug, the field in front of him changed from dark soil to sunlit sand in his mind.

Weeks later, he met a young woman, Biljana, at a dance. She too had heard of the opportunities in Australia and after several years of marriage sent Petar off to *Matica*, the agency for emigration in Skopje, and then to the Australian Embassy in Belgrade. After countless interviews, letters and months of waiting, he, Biljana and their boy Aleks, were winging their way from the crumbling body of Europe.

Once Aleks has divided up the pills, his father leans back, satisfied. His hands are covered in paint. How fearsome those hands had once been. Petar lights a cigarette. 'You should quit those things,' says Aleks, reaching for a cigarette himself. 'Bad for your health.'

His father raises his eyebrows and says, 'I will when you do.' He speaks in Macedonian. Before relocating to the Town, they had lived in Wollongong. When they first moved there, Petar would have liked to learn English, but almost straight off the plane he had started working alongside other Macos in a steel factory in Port Kembla. He soon got a second job to help keep the family afloat, meaning he went years without learning a working use of English.

The Macedonian news then changes to some footage of Bitola in the summer. Petar turns to Aleks, grinning. 'Bitola girls – good for the circulation.'

'I heard that,' calls Biljana from the kitchen.

'I don't know how women put up with us,' says Aleks.

'So, you know Nicko has bought his parents a new house?' says Biljana, setting down two cups of coffee in front of the men.

'Really? Good for him,' says Aleks, bristling. He loves his cousin, but Nicko always seems to be two steps ahead. 'I'll do that for you, soon. Just have to handle my business, that's all,' he says, patting his mother's hand.

'Oh, yeah? How?'

'Got a big job coming up. Real big.'

* * *

Once home, Aleks dreams of the blue bead on his neck.

The blue bead is obsession and power –
    a frozen well,
    a bullet.

He dreams it is a blue galaxy,
    each gold fleck a planet.
On each planet, tableaux of moments in his life
    are frozen in place like a Nativity scene.

He floats among them.
    His father playing chess with Ulysses Amosa here.
    His sister Jana crouched over a girl with a bloody face there.

In his dream,
    he alights on the centre of one of the gold planets.

Running around him,
    endlessly,
        is a greyhound.

This blue bead,
    forged in a time so ancient,
    a workshop in Venice, by men

who were nothing but dusty whispers now,
had once been worth the soul of a man.

Isn't that what she'd said,
        all those years ago?
Before . . .
        Before the moment everything changed.

'Aleks. Aleks. Jimmy's here.' Sonya is shaking him softly in the darkness.

'Fuck. Forgot about that. Let him in.'

Jimmy's watching TV in the lounge room already and rises to embrace Aleks.

'You hungry, brother?' Aleks asks.

'Starving,' says Jimmy.

Sonya is already sprinkling salt and pepper on some chicken breasts on the marble kitchen top that overlooks the large lounge room. Aleks leaps up. 'You leave that, baby. Go and sit with Jimmy. *Fala*. I'll handle that.' Aleks rubs her neck, kisses her behind the ear, then guides her to the couch. Massaging her with one hand, he flicks through channels, fussing over finding the right program. He decides on *Chopper*, a movie he and Jimmy have watched numerous times and quote endlessly. Once back in the kitchen, he knows what he is doing. As the chicken breasts fry in a pan, he throws together a salty salad. 'Helps with a hangover, this one,' he says, slicing cucumbers. '*Rakia?*'

'Fuck yeh.'

'May you walk naked in the house of your enemies, brother.' They drain shots and Aleks smacks his lips, then exclaims, 'Good grief!'

Jimmy laughs. Aleks has a hotchpotch vernacular, pieced together out of rap music, woggy slang, movies and Aussie colloquialisms, but Jimmy's favourite is when he uses old-fashioned expressions, something you might hear a grandma saying – 'dearo me' or 'goodness gracious'. He says it whenever he's about to do something dangerous or bad for his health. Aleks pours another *rakia*.

'What'd you do today?' Jimmy says, eyeing him keenly. Aleks knows what Jimmy is up to. He loves to feel in touch with the criminal world without having to partake in any of it. Aleks once enjoyed telling him, but now throws him red herrings – close to but never the complete truth. Betrayal is in the kiss.

Today he doesn't feel like talking about crime. It'll bring down his delicately balanced mood. 'Ah, just painted a house on the other side of town, brother. Nothing too much. The couple were happy with it.' He keeps his eye on the television but can see that Jimmy is scratching his Adam's apple in disappointment. On the TV, it's the scene where Chopper is trying to convince his mates to kidnap the prison guards and lay siege to the jail. 'What a plan. Dumb cunt,' snorts Aleks. 'You'd get fucken forty more years.'

Jimmy looks at him again, trying to glean some insight from his mate's offhand comment. Aleks places plates in front of his wife and Jimmy. '*Pileshko*,' Sonya says shyly, gesturing at the chicken with her chin. '*Fala mnogu*, Aleks.'

Sonya is Anglo but she's been with Aleks for so long that she speaks Macedonian almost fluently. She took immediately to the structure and Aleks' obsession with all things traditional. He beams with pride and kisses her, then says to Jimmy, 'Not too shabby, ay? Come on. Eat up, both of you. You're all skin and bone.'

Sonya begins to tell Jimmy a story. He listens to her, almost childlike, experiencing each emotion as she tells it, eyes shining when hers do. Aleks knows she's always had a soft spot for Jimmy, that he reminds her of a hurt dog she once found on the side of a street, all kicking legs and wounded eyes. She regards Solomon as flashy and shark-like, and feels as if Jimmy is someone who could flourish if given the oxygen. Or explode?

12

The hound

As I untie the leash,
I put my nose to his head.
The fine fur is almost odourless,
     a scar from the muzzle on his face.

I trace a finger over it.

Cradling the long head in my hands,
I look into the lone alert eye.
It would be easy to crush his skull
with a cricket bat or a rock,
in one perfect stroke.

Fuck, what am I thinking?

I pull the leash away.

Mercury Fire pauses,
           streamlined and legged
           to a grass-warped shadow.
Then he dances away with the shadow,
cantering off and building to a sprint within bounds,
his spine as flexible as a bow,
body extended,
charged with blood,
           with ancient chases
and deer courses in forests long gone.

Like him,
I used to run and run,
from here to the stone gazebo
on the edge of the park
and back again, to keep lean.

He's bounding towards some joggers
on the far side of the oval,
           long legs still powerful.
Contracting, extending,
           contracting, extending.

Is he imagining the race?
The arena,
the ceremony of gamblers and luckseekers,
the strange smells coming to him from the stands,
the straining hounds on either side,
eager and competitive souls in their chests?

A pointless struggle,
actors in a strange tragedy
where the winner never wins,
           never gets its prey.

The true winner is removed,
a tall figure in the stands
with a ticket in his hands.

When I quit basketball,
I forfeited adulation
and the weekly engagement of muscle and will.

I used to walk home
            through this oval,
lie in the dew,
                drunk and reeking,
thinking of the times I pured a three
or threaded a pass perfectly.
Misses,
      awards,
          failure.

No basketball, no dad to play for –
       been rudderless ever since.

Maybe that's why I bought the hound.
Maybe it was a reason to be responsible for something again.

I see a figure in a red polka dot dress approaching
then I look back to Mercury Fire.

He changes direction and veers towards me –
something in his sight streak has appeared.
He's snapping after a butterfly,
       bright yellow and out of reach.

My affinity with him,

my fear of him,
        deeper than appreciation of speed.

We're nothing but spray cans,
used up and thrown away,
creating something that gets painted over within a day.

He comes back to me,
panting and smiling.

The figure in the red polka dot dress is close.

'Good boy,' I say,
patting Mercury Fire.

'Hi,' says Scarlett Snow.
'Hi.'

The gazebo

There's no one around
and the windows are partially obscured
by bare rose bushes.
I hike her onto the stone bench
and offer my throat,
which she clasps with two hands.
I peel the red up
and the white down.
And now the consuming danger,
the fierceness of summer
        riding on our shoulders,
my thumbs on her ankles,
the minutes trickling down our backs

and her black hair.
I stare at the long, trembling dusk
as I lick a bead of sweat from the side of her face.

'Wanna meet up tomorrow?'
'Don't get ahead of yourself, mister.'

She's become cool again,
almost professional,
but the danger is still hot on my body.

She kisses me quickly.

'Seeya soon, mama's boy.'

An argument with Georgie

She just called the Samoan guy at the petrol station 'bro'.

No way.

'Can you not say that, Georgie. It's fucken annoying.'
'What?'
'Bro.'
'Bro,' she mimics back.
'Seriously.'
'Why not? You say it all the time.'
'I'm a dude. It sounds ugly when a chick says it.'
'Solomon, that's ridiculous.'
'I'm just saying. Doesn't sound right. That's a guy's word.'
'I'll stop saying it if you do.' Her lips set.
'Fuck that.'
'You're a pig.'

'Oh, yeh?'

'And an egomaniac.'

'That all?'

We walk in silence.

Of course that's not all.

I clear my throat. 'Hey, Georgie. You realise that no matter how hard you try, you'll never be one of us.'

'One of the boys? Wouldn't wanna be.'

'Nah. You know what I mean.' I cough. 'Ethnic.'

'Why are you saying this, Solomon?' Her voice is shaking. My mind is perfectly clear.

'Just letting you know. No matter how many politics courses you take, how much yoga you do, how many fucken Buddhist scrolls you hang in your room – you will never be.' I snort coldly. 'I know how you girls think. And I'll let you in on another secret: no matter how many times you fuck me, you'll always be white. I'm not gonna fuck some colour into ya and I'm not gonna fuck that white guilt outta ya. You will never be anything but what you are.'

She's crying now.

That felt brilliant.

13

In Woolworths, Jimmy grabs a tin of coffee before heading to the wall of fridges lined with frozen dinners. Maybe lasagne tomorrow night. There is something about all the packets stacked up in supermarkets that he likes. In petrol stations, too. All the brightly coloured boxes, piled high and deep – the gaudiness, the abundance of it. You're in charge, browsing where you like, and it's all on display for your pleasure. Take what you want.

When he closes the fridge door, he turns and catches a glimpse of the girl from the travel agency, Hailee, walking up the aisle with a basket. He keeps his head down and watches out of the corner of his eye as she stands in front of the rows of pasta. When she moves on, Jimmy glides to the head of the next aisle and watches her as she chooses some rice. She's in running pants and her hair is pulled back, and Jimmy can see what look like simple diamond studs in her ears. He can just make out a tattoo on the back of her neck – a coathanger? He shadows her again as she moves on to the deli. As he hovers by the cold shelves of fresh meat, she seems to look right at him, but offers no flicker of recognition. He pretends to be looking at Christmas crackers.

Jimmy keeps pace with her through the checkouts and follows her out, passing between parked cars at a remove, hoping she didn't drive.

When she walks out of the carpark and across the road, he keeps close to a hedge. They pass Centrelink, then the Jade Palace Chinese restaurant with its oily smoke. The day is darkening all around and shadows drape on everything. Headlights swing through the streets and Jimmy inhales the smell of dry grass.

She lives in a quiet street in a house dressed with bougainvillea. A birdbath stands in the front yard. Jimmy is glad to see the place is dark inside – she lives alone. From where he skulks on the footpath across the street, he sees her disappear inside, and he waits as lights turn on, hoping to catch a glimpse of her through a window. He wonders what her body looks like.

Jimmy leans on a skip filled with the debris from a construction site opposite her house. He can see her moving about in the kitchen, moving between the stove and the sink. He wishes he could join her. He wouldn't touch her. Not if she didn't want him to.

He takes note of the house number and walks away.

* * *

The next morning, the heat is savage in the City.

Coffee shops and clothes stores, office workers gossiping about colleagues and love. Next to a diamond-shaped fountain, young bloods are carrying skateboards or holding hands. Some Sudanese cats are laughing loudly, bumping fists and practising handshakes. Some awful crunk plays from one guy's phone. They bum a cigarette from Jimmy and saunter off, rapping to each other in American accents. Jimmy wants to chase after them and tell them that what hip hop needs is more good DJs, not rappers. Hip hop is nothing without DJs. Then he pictures the look they would give him if he did.

Jimmy ducks into the air-conditioned arcade, taking a well-worn route through David Jones, where he stops at the perfume counter to spray on some Armani. He ignores the filthy look from a middle-aged shop assistant. Striding a little taller, he heads for the food court, imagining for a moment he might bump into Aleks and Solomon and they'd head off to the pool or on a mission to rack paint and bomb shit. But they're not fifteen anymore.

He takes the escalator downstairs and goes to a sushi window. The travel agent is on her lunch break, eating a salad, several tables away. She has not seen him. Her hair is drawn into a severe ponytail above her pale face. She is talking to a slick-looking guy who Jimmy knows owns a cafe around the corner. His sleeves are rolled up, exposing tanned arms. He is immaculately dressed, like a wog version of Solomon, but leaner, maybe crueller. She seems intent on their conversation but Jimmy can't tell if it's professional or if she's truly interested. The guy checks his phone then leaves.

Jimmy pays quickly and makes his move, sitting at the table across from her. Remember to ask her heaps of questions. Someone once told him that women like it if you ask a lot of questions. She is gazing into her empty salad bowl, face drawn. She looks up and notices him. Jimmy feigns surprise. 'Oh, hey! How are you?'

'I'm good,' she says. 'Busy.' She smiles uncertainly, but her eyes are glistening.

'Are you all right?'

She rests on her elbows and sighs. 'Ah. Just a lot going on. Someone in my family is really sick.'

'Who?'

'My grandma. She's got dementia.' She casts her eyes down again. He seems to have caught her off-guard.

'Aw, man. Sorry to hear that. My mum works at a nursing home. Always tough seeing someone close to you go through that. Are you all right?'

While she talks he meticulously puts an equal amount of wasabi on each piece of sushi, then two drops of soy sauce. Keep asking her questions, it seems to be working. Soon she is talking freely about her dream of owning a beauty parlour, maybe in Brisbane; how life in the City has become boring. Jimmy listens and eats. Once he has eaten, he starts absent-mindedly twirling a marker in his fingers.

'What's that for? Graffiti?' she asks.

He nods. She seems intrigued.

'I always wondered about that stuff. How do you come up with a name?'

'You mean tag. Depends, ay. Sometimes it's a nickname that sticks or it can be a cool image you wanna put out there. Sometimes it's just a combo of the letters you do best. Sydney guys used to have a "four to five letters is best" rule. Melbourne guys had weird, long tags.' He laughs and looks at a faint scar on the edge of her eyebrow, then at her full lips. Usually secretive about anything graff-related, Jimmy continues talking rapidly. 'People usually go through a few different tags as they get better. Sometimes they have a legal one and an illegal one. You practise in a blackbook first. Blackbooks are like a holy grail. Get outlines from your mates, practise your own, have your photo album in there. Gotta protect it with your life.'

She begins smiling wider the more passionate he gets. On impulse, he asks, 'You going clubbing tonight, Hailee?'

'Yeah . . . I think so.'

'Well, I'm going to a gig then I'll definitely head out. Maybe I could, um, give you a call?' he stutters.

She bites her lip and looks away, decides on something, then says, 'Give me your phone.' She types her number into his phone and passes it back. Must mean she's broken up with her man. Perfect. 'See you, Jimmy. I'll be out around eleven.'

'Nice.' He smiles. 'Seeya soon.'

* * *

Jimmy lights a durry and walks beneath the enamelled sky, thinking of near-misses and what-ifs and never-wases and blowing them out with the smoke. He heads into Sideways Records, with its thick crust of band posters in the dusty front window, like rings of a tree that sliced open would reveal the growth of the local scene. He's unsurprised to see Gonzo there, a local producer, keenly digging through old Japanese pop records in the discount box. Gonzo looks up wild-eyed, like a fossicker who's struck a golden seam, then holds a record to his chest. Jimmy nods in recognition.

Sideways Records has always had the biggest selection of Aussie hip hop in town. When the boys were teenagers, people mocked Aussie rap, but now it's packing out stadiums. He reckons the stuff that's popular is fucken awful, but the change in the scene is still unbelievable, and the two brothers that run Sideways – one friendly, one grumpy, like the good cop/bad cop of beats – have played their part.

Still, Jimmy likes the old school, and he spins some Tribe Called Quest on the turntables for a spell, but a line builds up at the booth and the bad cop gives him the flick. He buys the Funkoars album *The Quickening,* cos he wore the last one out, and a Marvin Gaye CD for his mum for a bargain at eight bucks. He wonders what Hailee might be into. Dance shit, most likely.

With the records under his arm, Jimmy sits in the park. He puts his CDs down and sniffs his musty armpits, checking that no one sees him. The heat is unavoidable. As he studies an album sleeve, he thinks about Hailee.

He imagines a sunblessed day, and the fire-red Dodge he's going to buy. Maybe he'll pick her up and drive down to Shellfish Bay, where the beaches are long and white and wild. They'll listen to music, good old soul tunes, him driving with one hand, her holding his other hand in her lap. They'll walk along the beach by a choppy surf, he'll help her avoid bluebottles and she'll go ahead and look back at him, hair billowing, her long legs defined under her windblown dress. In an old shop with the catch of the day written on a chalkboard outside, they'll share lunch on a bench overlooking the sea. Smoke and salt, blue and white.

At night there'll be cigarettes and murmuring, even though they have the house to themselves. The bed will tilt and moan and they'll hold each other and lean apart and fall asleep, then wake, and kiss and fall asleep again. And through the clouds outside he'll see the five stars of the Southern Cross, each as bright as the other, and the moonlight will cover her as she sleeps.

Jimmy's got it all mapped out. If he can just play this cool, not rush her.

14

A new court

This one is near the train tracks,
      abandoned,
        lines long faded.

Little chance of bumping into someone,
      thank fuck.

The backboard has been turned into an Aboriginal flag
      by some clever person with a marker.
      Chain net.
An ants nest covers the whole back half of the court,
then there's a swale filled with empty cans and bottles,
      a tall rusted fence
      and the train tracks behind,
        going all the way to Sydney.

The sun is at its peak,

the apex of a blown-glass sky.
I squint at the hoop
and carefully stretch my quads,
grunting from the pain.

A low wind at my feet,
a ghostly shawl of dust.

At first I let Mercury run free,
but he keeps trying to chase the ball,
so I tie him up again.

He looks wounded.

Bloody thing.
Mum says the neighbours
keep complaining about his barking.

Yet another thing she can get on my case about.

Dishpig

Centrelink are yappy cunts
so it made more sense to get a job.

Mum's disappointed
that I'm 'just' a dishpig,
        but I like it.
No responsibility,
mindless,
headphones on,
beats all day.

Aim the dishwashing gun –
spray the congealed gunk off the plates –
make em brand-new,
all facing one direction like satellites.

Mum says I'm wasting my talent,
that I owe it to her, to Dad,
to do something more.

Don't wanna think about that now

I pound the ball hard for a minute with each hand
till my shoulders ache
      and the blood's coursing.
Then it's And One, streetball shit –
      feints, spin moves, crossovers.
A step slow, though,
          always a step slow.
I'm drenched after minutes.
Nothing like a chain net,
and how the ball chanks out the bottom of it.

Something forgotten starting to rekindle now.

My shirt's soaked so I take it off.
    Ahhhh.
The sun across my shoulders,
    skin darkening,
    back slick.
Sweat runs over my tatts
and I feel kinda ashamed
I don't really know what they mean.

Sometimes they feel like a burden.

I hear Dad's voice:
'If I save up enough money,
I'll send the boys back to Samoa.
They need to learn that in your *'aiga* it must be about we, not me.
The boys have to learn, Grace.'

Sometimes I wish he had sent me back.

As I'm working on a hook shot
    I feel someone watching me.

It's a skinny young boy
seated against a tree.
I avoid his eager eyes
and turn back to the hoop.

I wish I didn't give Mum
so much hell when she stopped sending cash
to Dad's village after he died.
    She was trying her best, ay.

Several minutes later
the boy moves back into my sightline,
again smiling,
standing on one of those dumb Razor scooters.

I wipe sweat off my brow,
collect my shit,
    and head home
to get ready for a massive night out.

15

An underground bar with sweating walls.

Jean Grae, rapping in a bloodstained wedding dress, has whipped the crowd into delirium. Moving bodies, silhouettes, paper cut-outs tinged with malevolent red. A general madness in the air.

'Can't believe Aleks isn't drinking,' says Jimmy to Solomon when Aleks goes to get a water.

'Fark, relax, bro. He's buying you drinks, isn't he? He's only out cos you bought him the ticket. He's got a missus at home.'

'Yeh, so do you.'

Solomon turns to the stage, ignoring him. To the right Jimmy can see Tall Simon, the biggest hip hop fanatic in town, who is at every single local or international rap show. A photographer darts in and out of the crowd, snapping away, wearing an Ishu tee. She too is at every gig. Against the wall are two old school heads, one in a Def Wish Cast shirt and a Kangol, the other in a Zulu Nation shirt, talking to the support act Dialectrix. The two old school heads look like relics of another era, before the streets gave way to the middle class in Aussie hip hop. At the front is a mix of hippies and young fans, reaching up to touch the performers, and a staunch bouncer. Several minutes later, a young hip hop fan, white-eyed and white at the corner of his mouth, starts freestyling in Solomon's ear, spraying him with saliva. He's pilling off his head. Always at least one of these cunts at a show. Jimmy grins as he watches Solomon trying to accommodate the pillhead for a minute, before he pushes him away.

The moment of epiphany about hip hop had come at age twelve. A cassette tape passed from paw to paw, backpack to backpack, had ended up in Jimmy's pencil case. On each side of the tape a name written in Wite-Out. Public Enemy. Wu Tang Clan. Jimmy, Aleks and Solomon had gathered around an old cassette player. A crackle, and then suddenly a maelstrom of noise from the tinny speakers – street, eloquent and masculine – tough as Smokin' Joe Frazier. It was love at first listen.

Hip hop was a readymade culture for the fatherless, those born of fracture – family, culture. They all loved listening to raps, of course, but Aleks leaned more towards graffiti, Solomon b-boying, and Jimmy production and DJing. Jimmy, especially, adhered to the idea of hip hop culture religiously. If he could have prayed at an altar of hip hop, he would have.

There was a taut string that yanked back and forth between individual and community, with each person's style and flourish encouraged, the way someone rode a beat or moved their hands when they rapped, but adherence to the tribe was paramount. And no school could teach it. You learned for yourself, you learned from your brothers and sisters.

One rhyme turned into a sixteen-bar verse that turned into a whole song then maybe even an album that could be pressed and performed live in front of your peers. A simple top rock turned into a whole routine, to be paraded in front of other b-boys in the arena of battle. Tags led to throw ups, which led to full-colour burners, which archaeologists would one day pore over like the chrysography of illuminated religious texts on vellum.

Pharoahe Monch is on stage now, already drenched in sweat, his tee bunched up around the biceps, tatts visible; lead and mic and human creating an amplified creature all new, a philosopher's stone for an alchemy where every molecule in the room came to a pristine understanding, something sublime in spirit and body, the rupture, the flow, the rapture, something conjured for a brave, hopeless few.

When the world-ending horns of 'Simon Says' come on, there is pandemonium.

Afterwards, Jimmy pushes through and gets a CD signed at the merch desk and a photo with Pharoahe. Outside, he and Solomon rap, word for word, Pharoahe's verse from the Kweli song 'Guerilla Monsoon Rap'. Jimmy smiles triumphantly. He wants to stay in that moment forever, then he realises he's agreed to meet Hailee at a club called Luxe.

* * *

Deep in the guts of Luxe.

Tequila.

    Whiskey.

        Sambuca.

'Ergh. Tomorrow's gonna be trouble.' Jimmy takes a sip of vodka and checks his phone. No messages. She did say twelve, didn't she? He holds up his drink and the ice cubes glow blue from the mirror balls and bar lights. He imagines goldfish swimming around in his glass.

'Buy this lovely lady another drink, Jimmy. A Cowboy!' yells Solomon.

'Nah, nah, no more for me, thanks.' The bar chick rolls her eyes.

He's scanning for Hailee again. There's a mess of people dancing and making out on the balcony. He moves to it and looks over. Below is the dancefloor, a moving puzzle of bodies. The strobes come on and send a shudder through him. His mouth tastes sour so he takes another sip of vodka and lets his eyes wander to the corner of the dancefloor, closest to the DJ. There she is. Hailee is dancing in a group of people, arms above her head, blonde hair swinging from side to side in a wave, like a model in a shampoo commercial. Too good for this fucken place. Jimmy's about to wave when a hand yanks him around. It's Aleks.

'Where you been, ya poof?' He laughs and hands Jimmy two more drinks, while he sips a water.

'Oi. Heaps of nice ones here, brother. Take your pick. Aw, to be single again, ay?'

'Yeah, man. Already got my eye on one. Chick from the travel agency, ay. Check her out.'

They lean over the balcony. The spot where she was dancing is now empty and soon fills with other bodies.

'Aw shit. She was just there, man.'

'Yeh, right. Does she even exist?'

They clink glasses so hard that Jimmy's glass breaks. Aleks takes him by the shoulders and looks him in the eye. 'Brother, don't ever let them tell you that you're nothing. You're worth something, all right? I'm here for ya.'

They hug, then Aleks' shoulders slacken and he yells, 'Another drink for Jimmy!'

'Hold on. Needa piss.'

Jimmy heads to the bathroom, bloated. The line is long but moves quickly. He takes a long slash and sees vomit in the urinal already. On top of the trough are half-finished beers and mixed drinks – some of the glasses are filled with piss. There's a bloke stripped to the waist resting on his elbows over the basin, hair hanging in sour, black bourbon-and-coke vomit.

'You all right, mate?'

He waves Jimmy away with a limp hand.

Jimmy lurches down a hallway and into the stairwell. A door closes behind him. The music is momentarily muted and he is by himself. It's dank and humid and he feels very alone. There's a door at the bottom of the stairs, and flaring behind it are lights and strafing strobes. He spits against the wall and a bit gets on his shirt so he wipes at it and pushes the door open. The music hits him hard and he immediately puts a hand in the air. It's auto-tuned bullshit but he doesn't care and torpedoes into the crowd, dancing and bobbing his head. He bumps into a big black dude who spills Coke on his shoes. Sorry, mate. He says nothing but pushes Jimmy forward and he stumbles further into the furrow of bodies. A Tongan bloke his brother knows appears in front of him, leering, and pushes another drink into his hand and starts talking in his ear. He can't hear a word and the voice over the speakers is saying 'MOVE, MOTHERFUCKER, MOVE,' but instead he rests an elbow on the bar, looking again for Hailee. He turns back and sees the Tongan's waiting for an answer and he doesn't really know what to say so he yells, 'For sure', which seems to satisfy him. He grabs a half-finished drink from a table and drains it. There's dry ice now and people's faces appear out of the smoke, like triangular masks, inebriated phantoms. He dances by himself near the DJ booth and ends up in a circle of lads who put their arms around his shoulders, jump up and down to the music like they've won a championship game. He tries to catch a pretty blonde's eye. She turns away. He can't quite hit the beat with his hips and knees so he stands still and bobs his head. With one hand he types a text to Hailee: *where u?* Smoke is dissipating and he thinks he sees Solomon dancing with a brunette. He cannonballs through the crowd and hears a domino of expletives as he bounces off people. He snatches a glance of Hailee through waving arms and pushes through, but nah it's not even her so he steadies himself against the bar and grabs some ice from a glass and presses it to his forehead. Aleks appears by his side, hands him another drink and says, 'One for the road buddy, we gotta go soon.' Jimmy shoots down the liquor, gags, calms himself, and then texts again. *Where u? im at bar.* He feels queasy in the bathroom and glass crunches underfoot. He throws up in the sink and it's full now. There's a used condom in there. He feels a bit better, but. Aleks is waiting for him and he must be stumbling because Aleks catches Jimmy under the arm and begins to guide him through the crowd. He's about to go up the stairs when he sees Hailee, sitting with a group on a couch. It's a bit dark but when his eyes adjust he sees that she's with that smarmy cunt from the cafe. 'Nah, Aleks, that's her, bra. I gotta go talk to her.' 'You're too . . . Ah, okay. I'll be having a ciggie outside. Come up ASAP. We gotta go.' Jimmy buys another shot and a bourbon and everything is tilting. He sits on the couch opposite Hailee and smiles. Her friends go silent, looking at

him expectantly, ammo and gossip in their bleached teeth. 'Hey.' 'Hey.'
She looks confused and scratches the back of her head. 'This is Greg.'
'Hey, man.' Jimmy feels confused. 'Big night?' 'Not really. I'm driving.'
'Aw, sweet.' 'You?' 'Nah not driving . . . Oh, big night? Yer. Yer, I'm, um,
I'm here with mates.' 'Oh, cool. Where are they?' Greg sniggers. 'What?
So . . . big night then?' 'No . . . I'm driving.' Fuck. 'Yeh, of course. Sorry.'
Music too loud in here. The others turn back to their conversations. Big
screen playing the latest Lil' Wayne and Drake song. Diamond teeth,
palm trees and cars. When did Drake get so big? 'Hey, I've got big plans
you know!' Greg and Hailee look at each other and then back at Jimmy,
grinning. 'Yeh, I wanna —' His mouth not forming the vowels. Hailee's
hand on Greg's knee. 'Cool . . . Have a good one then, guys. Good to
meet you, bro.' Jimmy stands up and looks back at her and she's smiling
in a way he can't quite pin down and he's furious but glad to be walking
up the stairs away away away. He's outside in the alley sharing a cigarette
and someone tells a joke and then he's inhaling sweet weed smoke, the
tip of the joint glowing like a cat's eye in the dark and he stares back at
it and blows the smoke. He's back in the club. Bar chick looking at him
dubiously but pouring another one and a chaser. Hailee. He'll find her
again and do better this time. Pissing and then sick again. He falls against
the wall and somebody has him by the collar and is helping him up,
left foot, right foot, dragging him and he's saying thanks mate sorry but
his feet aren't working and he throws up again next to the bouncers and
stumbles forward, slipping in the sick, gets balance and then falls again
and wishes for nothing else but to sleep. The club line upside down. Then
baubles of lights above and a certain type of darkness and he can hear
himself breathing but it's from afar, maybe down a long hallway. 'This
guy is fucked! He your mate?' And someone is pulling him up again and
pushing him forward on his unwilling feet and he gains lucidity for a
second to see blonde hair go by and he says Hailee but he's not sure cos
it could be anyone. Where's Aleks? 'I'm not taking him in this state. No
way. He'll throw up in the cab. Ah, for fuck's sake.'

* * *

Sitting.

      Oh.

            So.

                 Still.

Still fucked up but everything's silent now.
He's at his mum's place somehow,
in Solomon's room.
Solomon's not there.
Jimmy listens to himself breathing
as he looks out the window.
The carpark is lit by lamplight.
It is never dark.
He sits watching, feeling as if he is on the rim of the world.

The carpark was once a paddock,
      dark and calm.
There were apple trees
and a broken wall the boys scrawled
their first tags on.

The night reels back and forth
in his mind,
on repeat.

Gonna try to stay up till dawn.

16

Her skin is frost –
    like we've never met,
    like this is the first time.

She bites my bottom lip gently
and soon there's warmth.
We are trying to get a hold with our eyes,
but each of us is slippery with shadow.
    The Manuka honey moisturiser
    she wears is overpowering.

I've ended up at Jimmy's house somehow,
but he's not here.

She moves her hands upwards
and bunches her hair with them,
then bites me,
    almost to collarbone.

She says 'Solomon'
and I say 'Scarlett',
at exactly the same time.

We turn to steam.

My breathing rights
and I turn away,
        like I always do,
                always have,
waiting for something
that this time,
        I don't hear.

The moon outside
        the size of a bullethole.

We have sex again
and this time our skin stays cold,
and after several minutes,
        she pushes me away.

She leaves soon after,
                silently,
but I can still feel her eyes on me,
as if she is watching me
                through a bullet hole moon.

* * *

I head fake an imaginary defender,
spin down the sideline
and launch the ball from deep.

I didn't judge the angle properly,
so the ball hits the side of the backboard
and comes straight back to me.

The whole backboard shudders.

Who is Scarlett?
What is this?

Mercury is chasing something
down near the train tracks.
More noise complaints Mum reckons.

     I think of the greyhound killer in Wollongong
     with the bolt gun.

The kid's there again,
back against the fence.
He's not smiling this time,
just watching,
     eyes full of longing.

I ignore him,
and practise a Dirk Nowitzki fadeaway,
one-footed,
kicking out with the other for better balance,
narrating my moves in my head.

     'There's ten seconds left on the clock.
     Amosa's got the ball,
     the crowd is on its feet.
     He's sizing up Jarryd Hooper,
     biding his time,
     fakes left, spins right,

he shoots . . . '

A train clacks past
and I make sure to put on
a little show for the passengers,
launching the ball from deep.

Splash.

'HE SCORES! AMOSA WINS THE GAME!'

I reach down and pinch my ankle.
The scar tissue is still thick.
I grimace,
remembering the gruesome surgery,
not being able to walk,
the constant pain.

A text from Georgie –
        I see you moved on pretty fucken quickly.
Delete.

Bounce, bounce.
                Flick.

Forty minutes later,
the boy is still there.

I sigh,
pass the ball to him
and he jumps up.

He starts shooting,
sometimes hitting the backboard,

sometimes airballing it.
His shot is flat and has no arc.
He's clumsy but springylean –
a bit of strength
for someone his age.
I take the ball and wordlessly show him
how to hold it,
the straight extension of the arm,
        the flick of wrist.
He nods and I pass the ball back.

He nails the next shot.

Finally I talk to him.

His name is Toby.

17

Aleks is early. He likes to be early.

He's in the carpark of Macca's, eating chicken nuggets, waving at little bush flies with his spare hand. He dips the nuggets in barbecue sauce and feeds them into the side of his mouth, chewing slowly. Then a cheeseburger and large fries. On the radio, a man with a nasal voice is talking about a new pop song. *Why do Aussie radio DJs always have the most bogan names?* he wonders. 'G'day, listeners! It's Midday Madness with Kelly and Simmo on 103.7.' Aleks changes station and finds himself nodding along to a shock jock. He sips his Coke down to the ice. In front of him is a hedge blooming with wrappers and crushed cups. Beyond that, shimmering in the heat, is outer suburbia, that great maze of hidden monsters and freaks.

Some petrolheads are hanging out on the bonnet of a Supra, incongruously eating soft-serve cones, their biceps weighty but ineffective machinery. They all wear black singlets, snap-pants and gold chains, a baseline bleeding from the boot. One throws French Fries to pigeons. Another throws rocks to frighten them away.

Aleks rolls the blue bead between forefinger and thumb.

Wil turns up and climbs into Aleks' passenger seat. He's a well-built Fijian lad with a red kiss tattooed on his neck, just above his ex-girlfriend's name. Dumb cunt. He's got a new tattoo on the other side, the postcode of the Town, crusty and flaking. He's a big boy, obsessed with MMA, but Aleks knows that he lacks balls. If it came down to it, this motherfucker would wilt like baby spinach in hot butter. Between mouthfuls of a burger, he talks about his newborn, also called Will, but the extra 'L' is crucial. Wil's real name is Wilfred – something he is deeply embarrassed about and tries to keep a secret. Aleks only knows cos he once saw his passport. He wonders if Wil can speak Fijian and why he didn't call his baby something completely different if he hates his own name so much. He concludes that people are mysteries.

'She's driving me crazy, bro, seriously. Wants this, wants that. New clothes, perfumes. You're farkin kidding me! Sending me bankrupt.' Wilfred spits out a pickle in disgust.

'Ah, you gotta give it to em sometimes, brother. Show em you care, you know? Love is one and the same as loyalty,' says Aleks. The unspoken corollary is that it must be proved, again and again, through gifts, vocal affirmation, extreme violence.

'Yeah, but I've got this new place now, ay? Landlord is a cocksucker, bro, I'm telling ya. Nice bloke, but a cocksucker. Puts the rent up all the time, bro. You're farkin kidding me.' He keeps talking and Aleks fades out. He's thinking about Sonya, at home, catatonic from Xanax. He wishes he could tell the boys, but has too much pride for that. Her problem had started long ago, when she had given birth to Mila. She suffered from severe post-natal depression, and hadn't been the same since. Maybe he should ask a woman what to do. But who? He doesn't know that many, besides the ones in his family, and he doesn't want them to know either. No, a long holiday would give her time to recover, get back to how she used to be.

Wil is now talking about a new video game. Aleks has never liked video games or computers. For nerds and fat cunts, he reckons. Better to be outdoors. And violence on a screen could never equate to the real thing. Wil is gesticulating expansively and is wearing a childish grin. Aleks decides that he might be soft, but he is good-hearted. Dumb and good-hearted – a terrible combo.

A white guy, Dave, pulls up next to them in a Holden driven by another man. Dave has the lean look of a starving mongrel, and when he smiles, it's sardonic and without kindness. Yellow teeth, oily skin, no sense of loyalty, no honour, no culture – Aleks can't stand him, thinks he is trash. Aleks can tell that Dave is thinking exactly the same about Aleks, that he is unworthy of Australia, a stain that can't be removed, a necessary evil. *At least the cunt fears me*, thinks Aleks.

Aleks and Wil climb into Dave's car. The driver is Dave's brother, a good-looking white boy, who says nothing. Wil talks the whole time, still munching a burger, spraying flecks of cheese and meat patty everywhere. Aleks cringes when Kelly and Simmo introduce a new song on the radio. In the song, a man sings about meeting the woman of his dreams, then losing her in unexplained circumstances. He sings of searching the earth for her but never finding her, only signs of her presence: in shopfronts, in clouds, in trees.

The men arrive at the house. It has a simple facade, paint peeling, fibreglass roof. There's a tyre swing, an oleander bush, some broken gnomes and an old hose in the front yard. The door is unlocked and they enter without knocking.

It's filthy inside. The floor is hard to see beneath the food wrappers and pizza boxes, bottles and chicken bones. A half-dismantled Harley Davidson sits in one corner, surrounded by parts. Two small children are sitting on the floor, stupefied. They barely look up when the door opens, and Aleks can smell them from the doorway. A man is lying on the couch and starts when he sees the men enter. He has long black hair and a sweaty singlet.

Aleks speaks in a low voice. 'Mark?'

The man nods. Aleks gestures to the kitchen table. On it is a CB radio tuned to the police channel, and a photo of a handsome, suited man in front of Big Ben. It looks out of place. 'Come here, brother. Sit down.'

The man stands up but doesn't walk straight to the table. He goes to the sink and takes a long drink of water from the tap. It goes all over his unshaven chin. He wipes his mouth and then sits down. Wil and Dave stand behind him. From the CB radio they hear a low and steady stream of male voices. Aleks switches it off and the only sound now is a weak fan and cicadas outside. He picks up the photo and realises the well-dressed man is Mark. 'You know who I am, brother?'

The man nods. Aleks continues. 'Look, I don't know what you done. But I got two jobs to do. Number one. The man who sent me wants his cash, understand?'

'. . .'

'Speak up, brother.'

Mark is unseasonably pale and the sweat shines on his Adam's apple. He clears his throat and when he speaks again sounds surprisingly posh. 'I told him last time. I don't have it right now.'

Aleks shakes his head. 'I'm not messing around this time, brother.'

Mark looks away, then mumbles, 'In the laundry. Linen closet.'

Dave leaves the room. Aleks leans close and there's sweat on his forehead too. He smiles, ignoring the stench of the man's breath. 'Number two. How do I say this? The man who sent me can't have scoundrels like you running around saying they played him for a fool, understand? So there's a couple ways of doing this. Either you can carry on, make a scene, and there'll be a lot of blood – it'll be messy. Or you comply, all right? We'll bandage you up nice and tight, cut off the blood flow. It won't hurt a bit. You can take it to emergency and they'll sew it right back on. No problems.'

The man looks at his children on the floor, as if they might provide an excuse or answer. They look like twins, perhaps four years old.

Mark looks back to Aleks, as if seeing him for the first time. 'You gonna do this in front of my kids? Mr Janeski, it's no good for them to see their father —'

'*Father*?' Aleks' voice suddenly loud. The children look up. 'Father? Frying yourself up on a glass barbecue all day. Look at yourself. Look at them. Haven't eaten in days by the looks of things. Half high off the fucken secondhand ice smoke. And you're handling fifty large. Fifty thousand bucks and your own kids are starving. You fucken *disgust me,* mate.'

However, Aleks nods to Wil, who ushers the children into another room. For a few moments, there is only the sound of the fan and cicadas, before Wil returns. Aleks feels like a cigarette but smiles benignly and speaks to Mark in a low voice. 'This is the way it starts again for you, brother. Give and take, give and take. That's what the world's about right there.' He suppresses a cough. 'I once knew a man who was a soldier. He had two kids, just like yours. And just like yours, these kids had never done sin, never even thought it. Their father went for a walk to the market one day and when he was gone, another soldier came to their door. But this soldier, he was from the army their father was fighting against. He was starving, wounded, begging for water. These children led him into the house, gave him bread, drink. They let him sleep. As he did, they tied up his hands. When the soldier woke up, they're sitting there, watching him. At first he was confused, like what the fuck's goin on? But soon, he's full of poison, brother. He spat at them, cursed their country with every name under the sun, cursed the diseased cunt they were born out of, called their mother a whore, a Jezebel . . . Those children, they'd killed him by the time the sun went down and their father returned. The point? There is no point, brother. It's just a story.' He smiles for a moment but then his face becomes grim. He wants to ask the man how the fuck he got in this situation, how he had squandered all of his opportunities, but instead he says, 'So, brother. You're gonna co-operate, aren't ya?'

Mark looks out the window. Then he slowly places his hand on the table, smiling as if he's merely playing along with a prank.

'Good boy,' says Aleks.

Wil pulls out a length of rope and tourniquets Mark's arm tightly from the wrist, winding it up and out so that the hand is almost white and bloodless. Wil hands Aleks a cleaver. The type they cut up smoked ducks with in Chinatown. Aleks holds it to the light and looks at both sides, then inexplicably, sniffs the metal. It's sharp enough to shave with. Dave comes back into the room, holding a bag. Wil holds Mark in the chair now, as he's started to struggle, realising that the situation is real, and Dave seizes the bound arm and holds it on the table. Mark's eyes are wild, looking from Aleks to his hand to the door of the room where his children are. The door like a blank piece of paper.

The man's mouth isn't working properly and his vowels sound misshapen. 'No. No, please! Aleks. Mr Janeski —'

'Just relax, all right brother? Spread those fingers. That's it. Don't worry, brother. I won't take it off at the knuckle. I'll do it right here so they can sew it back on. No problems at all. That's right, brother. Relaaax.'

* * *

The men part ways with handshakes, no words. Wil still has vomit on his chin.

Aleks goes for a long drive. He then makes his way to a suburban tavern and sits behind the wheel for another hour. He finds a hat at his feet and pulls it low. He climbs out and stares for a minute at the gym bag next to the tins of paint. He hadn't even had to use it – fear always the strongest weapon. The carpark is mostly empty, besides three cars and a motorbike that appear and vanish in irregular blinks of light from a streetlamp. Behind them a pale copse of eucalypts, the limbs upflung like ballet dancers.

As soon as he enters the tavern, the bouncer asks him take his hat off. Aleks stares. The man's mouth twitches with recognition and he shrugs his shoulders deferentially. His voice is way too high for a man of his size. 'Sorry, mate. They're just the rules.'

'Rules?' Aleks grimaces then takes his hat off. He pats the bouncer on the shoulder and for a second feels sick, really sick, as if he might faint. All this violence. For what? 'No worries, brother. You gotta earn a living. I understand.'

He buys a beer and exchanges a fifty-dollar note for coins. He heads straight for the pokies, sits down and his face is lit by the lurid buttons. There are fluro pyramids floating on the screen and for a moment he wishes he were somewhere else. But where? He keeps drinking and there's something therapeutic about the rise and fall of his money in the poker machine. He is tapping the pokies with one finger. He stares at the finger and slowly shakes his head. He takes a break to smoke outside and the stars are dizzying. The streets veer off in every direction, lined with the abstract shapes of buildings and bushes. He stares upwards for a long time, then says to himself aloud, '*Neznam.*'

I don't know.

He buys more cigarettes, withdraws more cash, drinks more schooners. It takes the edge off, but only slightly, like a headache tablet for a deep wound. There is an old man playing the pokies who looks like he has endured a lot of pain, or at least witnessed it. He seems at peace somehow but Aleks pities him nonetheless.

Aleks rolls the bead in his other palm, the gold flecks demonic to him now. Yes, surely it is hell that lives within the bead, broken pieces of a gold mirror reflecting his private hell. He wishes he could split it between his thumb and forefinger like a nut and crush what is within. But he can't. It's too beautiful, too unbearably beautiful.

Some lads, all wearing high-vis work jackets, come in and one of them recognises him. They're drunk already and talking loudly. 'Oi. It's Janeski,' says the youngest of them. Aleks hasn't seen this halfwit in a long time.

'Aleks! *Kako si?*'

'*Dobar, brat.*'

'*Kay si be?*'

'*Eve be.*' Aleks tries to smile. Once, when both were on holiday in Ohrid from Australia, Aleks scored some Albanian coke for him so that he and his dumb cunt mates weren't beaten senseless looking for it. The younger fella, it seems, wants to pay back the favour.

'*Zhimi maika brat*, I swear to God, bro, I swear on my mum's life, nah nah nah, I swear on *your* mum's life. We could invest in a whole kilo. Pure white.' The boys laugh.

Aleks, even in his drunken state, stares at the lad as if witnessing a thrown boxing match where the loser is unintentionally but fatally injured. 'I don't know what you're talking about, champ. I think you got the wrong bloke.'

'Oh . . . yeah.' The bravado instantly gone. 'Sorry, Janeski. Sorry.' For a moment there's nothing but the bleep of poker machines, then Aleks looks at him.

'Got any on ya?'

A sly smile in return. 'Course.'

Between trips to the bathroom and more beers, Aleks starts chatting to a man who is selling tickets to a meat raffle. The man, it turns out, is a chiropractor, whose wife beside him is Lebanese. Aleks tries to engage her in a conversation about Islam. He tells her about the Cross Mosque in Ohrid, how when it had been a church it was devastated by earthquakes again and again until the priest had a dream that, if Muslims and Christians could both worship there, it would never fall. 'The man attached a crescent to the cross and the building has not fallen since. Can you believe that?'

The Lebanese woman tells him she is an atheist but her family is Maronite Christian. Aleks, confused, begins to talk in labyrinths. He taps his fingers on the tray of meat and tells them how you can't get good meat in Australia, that it's full of chemicals and not organic. 'You can only find good meat in villages. The chicken tastes better in Macedonia. Tender, sweet. Bloody orgasmic. Not just meat, but the chillies, the bananas too.' He counts on his fingers. 'The air itself, brother, the water!' Eventually he slams a beer on the table and says it's important to believe in God.

The wife smiles awkwardly and the man asks, 'So how about a ticket in the meat raffle, mate?'

What happens after that is unclear, and unfolds in flashes.

His hand around a young man's throat.

A bloody face . . . in the mirror?

A plateful of cocaine in a microwave.

Lines on lines on lines.

A steering wheel.

Blackness.

When he comes to, he's floating in water, swallowing it, choking. He sees red and blue lights bobbing all around him and hears a man's voice yelling. He sees his Hilux, nose down, full of water. Then a wooden fence with a Hilux-sized hole in it. Then a policeman holding up the gym bag. Aleks realises he is in a suburban swimming pool, up to his chest in water, and floating all around him are sausages and schnitzels and steaks. He begins to laugh, madly and with gusto. He doesn't stop laughing, even when they come to take him away.

18

A low, pale dusk.

Jimmy is at the window this time, watching through a chink in the curtains. He has a brick in his hand. He swears he can smell Hailee's moisturiser and shampoo through the glass. Her body itself some kind of unfairness. He examines her throat, her mid-sized breasts, tight under a T-shirt. She looks like she's going to take the shirt off. He leans closer. She's just adjusting the waistband of her gym pants. A glimpse of peach-coloured skin.

When he sees her leave the room, he heaves the brick as hard as he can through the window, like a shot-putter. The window explodes; there is a single shriek and the cascade of glass, but he is already walking away, fast. Fucken bitch. He rounds a corner, crosses a road and walks through the park before looking back. No one has followed him.

He buys a frozen pizza and an energy drink at the supermarket, a headache spiderwebbing on the inside of his skull. He's already forgotten the brick and Hailee. The streets are as silent as a field after a gunshot. Or before one. There seems to be dust everywhere today, but he's not sure where it blew in from. It's in the trees, in the grass, in the gutters. Enough to drown the world.

Be good to have housemates, ay? He rented the duplex for himself because he thought it would be good to have privacy, but he gets lonely. As soon as he opens the door, a beast leaps at him from the dark. He falls on his arse and scoots backwards instinctively. He puts up a hand to push it away but the beast nuzzles up and starts licking his nose.

'What the fuck?'

Mercury Fire.

The dog licks his face and its alert eye strikes him as compassionate, wise. He wipes saliva off his face and and walks through the house, switching on lights. As each one goes on, it lights up a different feature of the house. The cream carpet, the rack of cassettes he is so proud of (arranged in alphabetical order), his crates of vinyl, the signed Immortal Technique poster and a framed Shem RDC sketch – everything as it should be. Then, in a carved wooden frame, there is the black-and-white photo of a young Ulysses Amosa astride a motorbike, the one he crashed on the sandy roads of Savai'i. Jimmy remembers how Ulysses used to carry him and Solomon around the block, one on each shoulder, until the pain in his bad knee became too much.

Mercury Fire follows at his heels the whole way, excited.

Jimmy hears music from the garage – A$AP Rocky, who he can't stand. The garage is spare but for raw concrete, a Malcolm X poster, a wardrobe and Solomon lying on a bench lifting the weights Jimmy never uses. His shirt is off, his arms still considerably muscled, his skin shining. Once lean and fatless, he now has a small but obvious gut. The expression on his face is one of fury. Jimmy watches with pleasure. This cunt.

Jimmy stares at the Malcolm X poster. It was a present from his biological father. It's Malcolm in his later years with that longer red beard, after he left the Nation of Islam. Jimmy knows that Solomon would say Malcolm X was his personal hero. What a joke. Malcolm X: a disciplined and pious man. Solomon Amosa: a hedonist, a libertine who had lost any sense of discipline to booze, women and MDMA years ago. Solomon told Jimmy that he reckons Malcolm was a great man because he changed and eventually realised the true Islam as one of acceptance and peace. But Jimmy always liked the early Malcolm more – angry, militant, fuck the white man. When people die young, you don't get to see them become boring old fucks, lose their principles and become sellouts. We'd probably roll our eyes at Malcolm if he was still alive, that 2Pac woulda been a politician or doing Viagara ads or some shit. Better to die young, ay.

Solomon is grunting and breathing hard as he pushes the weights up, sweat lathering his skull. The bassline and 808 drums bounce around the raw concrete. On the last rep he looks dizzy and as though he is scared he'll get trapped under the bar. Jimmy doesn't move to help him. With one last yell Solomon pushes the bar up onto the rack. He sits up and swears, gulping for air. Jimmy's headache is gone now.

'Hard workout, mate?'

Solomon turns around and sees Jimmy in the doorway. 'How fucken long you been there?'

'A while. Looked hard,' Jimmy smiles.

'Not too bad. Been a while. You give it a go.'

'Nah. Needa cook dinner.'

'Of course not, ya gronk.'

Jimmy smiles again as Solomon dries his face on his shirt.

'You heard that new Maundz?' Solomon says.

'Nah. Not yet. Any good?'

'Yeah, bro. Kills it. Mad wordplay.'

Solomon's smug now. Jimmy tries to keep up to date with everything. How did he miss it? 'There's a new Drapht clip out, but. I seen that,' he says.

'Oh, true? Didn't see it.' Even though Solomon doesn't like Drapht, he looks crestfallen. Got 'im.

'You hungry?' says Jimmy.

Something is up. Solomon is unusually fidgety, almost nervous. He pats Mercury absentmindedly, but the dog ignores him and begins sniffing around the garbage bin. Jimmy lets him out into the backyard, puts the pizza in the microwave, sets up his Ipod and Action Bronson comes out the speakers.

'Bro, I need to ask you a big favour,' says Solomon.

'Yeh?'

'I can't look after Mercury anymore. It's doing my farkin head in. Mum's on my case about it everyday. Reckon . . . reckon you could take care of him?'

Jimmy's resentment dissolves. He almost wants to hug his brother. He gets on his computer and googles 'how to look after a greyhound'. Jimmy looks back at Solomon grinning and sees a vague look of shame on his brother's face turn to relief.

'This is the best present I've ever got, bar none.' He punches Solomon on the arm. For a moment, whirling movements in his brain are halted, slowed down at least, and he looks through the window and can see Mercury Fire staring right back, head cocked to one side.

'We gonna take over the world, Mercury Fire,' he yells out the window.

You always know when Solomon is about to leave – he looks for a mirror.

'I broke up with Georgie today,' he says.

19

On the television,
live from Parliament House.

Damien Crawford.

He is immaculate
in a shark-grey suit
and smiling confidently.
He is talking about the plight of ordinary Australian families.
He says that we need to demand a better standard
of compassion and tolerance from ourselves,
that, as Australia becomes more and more part of the region,
we need a better level of understanding between each other.
Then he stares right at the camera,
right at me,
and says,
'That is one thing we can all agree on.'

Only a week has passed,
but there is not a single mark on his face.

PART TWO

A red glow pulsed like a barbarous heart.

It emanated from a bark hut that stood on the edge of the limestone plains. A hand that gripped a hammer was black with smoke, and sweat ran down a blackened face. Embers whirled up from white-hot shapes that were being clanged into the wherewithal to create a Town – rakes, spades, tongs, bayonets, rifle barrels.

The fire in the forge burned on.

1

The answer

Allen Iverson retired today,
so I'm in my old 76ers jersey.
         A bit tight around the belly, ay?

                  Ooosh, remember
the maze braids, the cross braids,
the tatts,   the cool,   the crossover?

         Kids these days,
         man, they don't even know who A.I. is.

I bounce the ball hard, excited,
remembering game one in the finals against the Lakers.
Even though I'm a lot bigger,
I always wanted to play like A.I. –
                  cool, but with heart.
         As I handle the rock,

I look at my hands.

Scarlett paints her nails coral red,
       'Helps with depth perception,'
           she reckons.

Forget that now.

All I care about is the court,
       the ball,
       the net.

Phantom defenders –
       talk to em,
       break em,
       spin around em,
       shake em.

Ball –
       lace it behind back,
       between legs,
       under knees,
       cat's cradle it,
       manipulate it,
       roll it off fingers,
       put English on it,
       step back with it
       and cash it out the side of the chain net.

Body –
       feel the blood,
       the vein and breath,
       the moving, floating parts,
       sweet stink of armpit

and sweaty forehead,
hear coach yelling,
'It's all in the legs, Solomon!
get em right and everything else will follow.'
Feel toes and heels and fingers,
feel it all atomise
and become one with an incandescent sky.

I lean against the hoop's supporting pole
with my forearm,
    breathing hard.
There's graff on it,
nicely mixed red stainer,
letters dripping down like blood.
'ROZA' I think it says.
Melbourne boys always mixed dope stainer,
    back in the day.

I hear a voice.
    Toby.
He's with a mate,
    an audacious, thick-set boy with snaggle teeth.
'Who's this?'
Toby looks at his feet. 'A friend.' He pronounces it *fwend*.
    He doesn't hear so good
    and has a speech impediment.
Was he born that way?
'What's your name, cuz?'
'Muhammad. I wanna learn that shot,' says the boy with a surprisingly
deep voice.

I squint at them.
It's not so hot today and there's a nice breeze.
Why not?

'Orright. Warm up first. Otherwise you'll bust yaselves.'

I get em to run around the court
    then stretch.
I stretch with them.
    Jesus.
My muscles feel like rubber bands left in the sun.

'All right. Layups. Both hands.'

They do that for a few minutes,
    then I get them to play one-on-one.
Muhammad's a natural –
    quick first step, mongoose-like reflexes.
    He lords it over Toby and I see Toby's face cloud up.

'Relax boys. It's just for fun. You boys need more bounce. You should get skipping ropes.'
    'Like girls?' Muhammad's face lemony sour.
    'For your feet! Give ya a good leap. Quickness. Boxers use em.'
    'Like Anthony Mundine?'
    'Yer, Mundine. Roy Jones Jr. Muhammad Ali.'
    'Muhammad. See!' says Muhammad to no one in particular.
    I start dancing around them like a young Cassius,
    shadowboxing their ears.
    Soon they're laughing and squealing,
    avoiding the mock hooks and jabs.
    Muhammad scuttles off to dinner,
    practising flicking his wrist the way I taught him.
    'Can you shoot it from half-court, Solomon?' asks Toby,
      Big wide eyes and a weird puckering of the lips.
      Poor kid just doesn't want to go home.

I slap him on the back –
      'Let's go, big fella. I'll walk ya home.'

His house isn't far away.
I stand in the driveway and
as he turns into the govvo flat,
he waves but isn't smiling anymore.
Not a single plant in the yard,
but there are vines growing out of
a washing machine on the patio.

At home,
      Mum's not there.
Working a late shift,
      as usual.
I ice my knees with a bag of frozen peas.
Then, as I shower,
I slowly turn the water from
      scalding hot to cold,
and it swirls pink at my feet
      from the sneaker cuts on my heels.

hot – cold – hot – cold

      Delicious torture.

Letting on

'I heard like ninety per cent of rappers in NZ are Samoan.'

'That's true,' she says.

'I always dug Kiwi rappers.

King Kaps and Che Fu are all-time greats, I reckon.
        Mareko too.
What ever happened to Scribe? He was dope.'
'He's around.'
'My bro Jimmy never liked him,
cos of the accent thing.'

She rolls her eyes,
        holding her cocktail with both hands.

A constellation of light freckles
over shoulders, cheeks and nose.
        The dark hair unscrolled over one collarbone.
She has small expanders in her earlobes,
a subtle nose ring and pristine fingernails.
She's wearing a white singlet
and a gold chain,
and as she twists to the side
I can see a tattoo on her ribs of a sailboat.

She watches me watching her.   We drink.

'So tell me a story, Scheherazade,' I say at last.
'Like what?'
'Where'd you grow up?'
'Well, until I was fifteen, South Aucks. Papatoetoe.'
'Like David Dallas?'
She laughs easily. 'Exactly. My parents owned a dairy. Not heaps of
money, but pretty middle class. But my folks always stressed – said that
the kids in South Aucks were a bad influence. So when they got enough
cash, they moved me away from all my friends, to Parnell, insisted I go
to a private school, which I hated. Wanted me to be a lawyer or doctor.
Typical Asian father, you know? But then, I started winning portraiture

prizes, and he didn't seem to mind that. Nothing like success to change an Asian dad's mind, I guess. I picked up the tattoo gun at uni – practised it on friends, you know, then for a bit of money on the side, before I got properly registered. I always loved Samoan and Maori tattoos. Even attended some tattooing conventions, and met masters like Su'a Sulu'ape Alaiva'a Petelo.'

'You said that like an expert. Sure you got no Islander blood?'

'Nah. Mum's grandparents came from China during the goldrush. Dad's straight from Singapore. You ever been to Auckland?'

'Nah.'

'It's the best.'

'So why'd you leave?'

'Just . . . things. Became too much.'

'Things do that. But why Oz?'

She eyes me warily and seems to decide on an answer.

'I followed a woman here, I guess. Photographer from Sydney I met at a gig. As soon as we got here, I knew it was a mistake. She was so jealous.'

'My ex was like that. Made me delete all my other exes on Facebook.'

'Exactly. Same here. But like an idiot, I tried to make it work. One day, I decided I'd had enough. Moved here to the Town.'

'Good move.'

'I guess so. Not exactly the Australia I'd dreamed of. Boring, mediocre suburbia, quarter-acre blocks, roundabouts. I wanted red sands and rainforests and highways.'

I roll my eyes. 'Roundabouts. Always the roundabouts. That's the least of our problems. Plus, it's bloody beautiful here, actually – the lake, the bushland.'

'Jeez. Relax. Was just saying.'

I'm always talking shit about the City and the Town but hearing criticism from an outsider stings. It's like when I hear people paying out Jimmy – only I'm allow to do that. I let it go, though. 'So, what were you were saying about your ex?'

She wrinkles her nose and continues. 'The next few months were hell.

She called everyday, alternating between sweet, morose and threatening, before just stopping altogether.'

'Did you love her?'

She grins but her eyes squint strangely. 'Love? Nah. Never been in love.'

'Me neither,' I say.

2

A rectangle of sky, seamless and cyanic.

A bird hangs against the lidless sun, turns, wheels and turns back before disappearing. Half an hour later, a reef of water-coloured clouds drifts across, then a distant plane, like a fugitive, carving the blue in half with its contrails.

Aleks looks down.

The remand yard is full of men in jailhouse greens, squared off behind chain links and razor wire with barbs as long as an arrow's fletching, sharp enough to chop a line of coke. Past that is the high wall, a century old, patrolled by armoured guards trained to shoot out a man's brainstem if necessary. All around is a murmur, the intermittent thud of ball and boot, the march of pacing feet. Most of the men are in river-like lines, walking briskly as if they have somewhere to be, trying to burn off energy before they head back into their cells.

It is his second day inside. Aleks is at a slight remove from the rest, people he knows from the outside, who are sweating and gritting their teeth against the sun and the exertion of boxing, sit-ups and push-ups, an effort as much about forgetting as penitence. One of them, a raw, bent-nosed petrol station robber, walks over and hunkers down. 'Hot as fark.'

'Bloody oath.' Aleks draws a vague swirl in the dust at his feet with the tip of his index finger. He doesn't look up.

'Chemtrails,' the man says, looking at the white lines dissolving in the sky. 'Government uses that shit to control us, ay. Like crop dusting'

'Yeah, probably,' says Aleks. The silence sits.

The man is desperate for conversation. 'Heard about the terrorists' yard? Crazy cunts. Training like the army in there. Muscly as clouds.'

'None of my business.'

'Yair, they're gonna make it our business, but. Wanna kill the infidel, they reckon. Gonna get us all one day.'

'If they don't, something else will, brother,' says Aleks.

'That's one way of looking at it.' The man laughs and looks over the yard. 'First-prize shithole. Number one. Least you get a good feed here, but.'

'Not holding my breath.'

'Nah, serious! They feed us well, bro. Lessens the chance of a riot. Heard what's going on out there in Shellfish Bay?'

'Nah. What's up?' Aleks is interested for the first time.

'A riot. Abos, Aussies, Lebs, Sudis, Islanders. No one getting along. Hard to tell what the fuck happened. You're not in here long, anyway, ay?'

Aleks wants to ask more about the riots but instead replies, 'Nah. Not too long.' Thank god for Mr Chuckles.

'Been in before, haven't ya?'

'How do you know that?' Aleks says, still not looking up.

'Dunno. Just sorta . . . ya, know?' The man spits aside nervously. 'Heaps of people been in before. That's all.'

Aleks turns his moonface to the man and grins, remembering a quote from a movie. 'You're right. I have been in before. But this time I'm innocent.'

The man guffaws and slaps him on the back, then stands and claps dust off his knees. 'Aren't we all, ay? Aren't we all. You're a good cunt, bro. You'll be right.'

Aleks had not been afraid when he arrived at the jail and stepped from the paddy wagon. A tiny cold burn of nervousness at first, a little dampness in the armpits as he was processed and strip-searched. He'd walked high shouldered through the dank, dismal hallway, alert, aware of the ambiguous shapes and voices bouncing off the paint, flitting among the bars of light that filtered in through the roof. An unnamable thrill had run in him as he walked through dark, light, dark, light. Then he'd thought, *This place is ugly.* It has been designed to be hideously ugly. He'd thought of the goodbye, the lie to his daughter that he was going to the Gold Coast for two months for work, her disturbing eyes.

An inmate with a Swastika tattoo strides past in the yard at a distance and nods. Aleks nods back grimly, then looks away. Crouching and standing and smoking discreetly, the inmates are all arranged in attitudes of conspiracy, desperation or malevolence in their listless faces. He studies them, wondering which of this shifting hive could resolve into the shape of an attacker. He cracks his knuckles then erases what he has drawn in the dust.

He claps the dirt off his knees and stands up. Two men are now having a push-up competition. The sun warms Aleks' face and he smiles to himself. In his first day in the remand yard, prisoners began calling out to him, words that moved and clung together in an unrecognisable mass, like bees, before solidifying into two words: 'Mr Janeski.' And the truth was, as much dirt as he'd done, he'd also done a lot of favours on the street.

He spies a tall, dark figure, alone on the other side of the yard – his cellmate, the Sudanese man. *Did he say his name was Gabe?* He had been very abrupt. *Fuck him.*

Aleks had met Gabe the night before, after being ushered into the cell by a massive, dough-faced guard. The cell was old stone, smelling of sweat and Ajax. He placed his stuff in the cupboard before realising there were eyes on him. A very tall black man was lying on his side on the bottom bunk, limbs gathered together loosely like driftwood. Yellowed eyes. Aleks realised he'd never met a Sudanese person before. He offered his hand. 'Aleks.'

The man took it gingerly and his voice seemed to rumble up from his belly. 'Gabriel. Gabe.' Then silence.

After a moment, Aleks said, 'It'll make it easier if we get along, brother.'

Silence and eyes.

'No worries,' said Aleks, turning back to his belongings. 'No worries, at all.'

Two months, just two months. It could be a hell of a lot worse.

* * *

Aleks had been to jail once before, in Macedonia.

That cascade of events had started on a brisk day in September, in the town square. The wind was fleet-footed, as if it knew that winter was at its heels. Aleks was discussing chestnut-picking with his friends when a man approached and showed him a Yugoslavian pistol with a silencer.

Aleks was only fifteen and had been back in Macedonia for six months, on his father's insistence, and already he was in trouble because of two incidents. One was a fight, where he had beaten a schoolmate badly for making fun of his Aussie-accented Macedonian. The second was graffiti. To get his mind off such things, Aleks walked through the cool gullies and hills – the silent tapestry of trees. There was nothing as beautiful to him as autumn in Ohrid as the leaves were changing colour. Chestnut trees had been planted on either side of a gully and the nuts rolled down to a certain area where they could be collected and then sold for a good price. As breath smoked out his mouth and he told his friends about the chestnuts, he thought of Jimmy and Solomon. He knew neither of them had ever seen snow.

The man's black eyes had an extinguished quality, and the lower half of his face was disguised by a thick beard. He showed them a gun at waist level. It was light, a Zastava M70, easily concealed. The boys admired it and Aleks got a thrill out of holding the silencer, which was as thick as a ballerina's wrist. Aleks handed it back and the man disappeared into the market. Minutes later they heard screaming, and he came back past them over the cobblestones, not looking at them, the front of his shirt bloody as if he'd just slaughtered a pig.

With NATO in town and a peaceful image to uphold, authorities rounded up all local troublemakers and criminals and put them in a big holding cell, especially those who'd been seen in the town square. In the three days inside, Aleks was unfed and thirsty. He was pissed on, made to admit he was a homosexual, forced to walk on hands and knees by the private interrogation company.

All he could remember now was the smell of dozens of bodies, killers and crims, the freezing cold wind that wrapped around his bones like a tongue. And the terror.

3

*RelationshipandCommunicationRelationshipandCommunicationRelation-
shipandCommunication.*

Jimmy mouths the words like a mantra as he puts in eye drops. He
hears a drumroll of feet and Mercury Fire bounds in from the other room,
turning in circles, jumping up and down. Jimmy holds his shoulders and
nuzzles his forehead into the dog's snout, letting the paws pad on his
belly. For a moment, man and dog are welded into something misshapen
but brand new. Jimmy then says the mantra backwards, grinning into his
dog's face.

'CommunicationandRelationshipCommunicationandRelationship
CommunicationandRelationship.'

He lets Mercury into the backyard. 'Lucky I've got one, ay,' he says
aloud, sitting on the stairs and tossing a ball to the far fence. There is
a fierce determination in the dog's limbs. His speed and agility have
Jimmy shaking his head in wonder. They repeat the activity for twenty
minutes before the hound seems to get bored and overheated. Panting,
it squats down on the unmown grass to take a shit. Jimmy wraps a plastic
bag around his hand, picks up the cigar of turd and sniffs it. The dog
watches him with his head cocked. Jimmy talks to him, telling him not

to poo on the floor of the house, as he pours water into an empty ice cream tub. The dog drinks, sloshing it onto the concrete.

He's taken two days off to get used to the hound. Can't believe fucken Solomon kept the poor bloody thing locked up in a flat with their mum, leaving it alone on hot days while he went out chasing women. Jimmy thinks of something he read on the internet. Must've been hard to even get the dog onto the third level. Greyhounds hate stairs.

For the rest of the afternoon Mercury sleeps, so Jimmy cleans the already spotless house, then falls into an internet spiral. He watches a Tom Thum beatboxing video, a B. Two DJing video, Joe New's rappertag, then finds some rare Prowla songs. Hearing the chopped samples reminds him of when he first got into Aussie hip hop and a wave of inspiration hits him. He begins to make a beat on the MPC, but he can't find the right drums. He wonders where Plutonic Lab or M-Phazes get theirs from. After a frustrating hour, he gives up.

He goes back to the computer and scrolls through pictures of his favourite pornstars. At the moment, his favourites are Kayden Kross, Nikki Benz, Christie Mack, Stoya, Rachel Starr and Lisa Ann (in that order). He once even got a response from Christie Mack on Twitter. He's rearranged the list every few weeks since he was fifteen. He stops on one picture and stares at it for a whole minute, imagining that his body has become particulate and is floating through the screen to where Kayden Kross is lying, enamelled fingernail pulling her glossy lower lip down, blonde hair in a perfect swirl. For some reason, today it doesn't turn him on. He bends about his jellied dick for half a minute then has an idea. He types 'how to pick up a stripper' into Google and finds a blog that gives instructions.

1) Find out her real name

2) Befriend the bouncers

3) Don't look at their tits or pussies when you get a lap dance: look them in the eyes.

He takes note.

He's about to have a nap when he gets a call from Aleks in jail, who asks him if he can take Mila out to play somewhere. He beams at the responsibility. Aleks had asked him, not Solomon.

'I'll take her out with Mercury Fire, bra, no worries.'

'Is it safe around kids?' Aleks sounds distant.

'Of course, bro. Greyhounds are awesome around kids. In fact —'
He's about to launch into a spiel of his newly acquired knowledge but
Aleks says, 'Gotta go,' and the line falls silent. Jimmy looks at his phone
and smiles.

That afternoon Mercury Fire shits on the carpet and Jimmy steps in
it, the turd squelching between his toes. Jimmy yells and hops on one
foot, admonishing the dog, dragging him by the collar and rubbing
his nose in his mess. Then he remembers the mantra and he adopts a
conciliatory tone as he repeats 'relationship and communication' again
and again, switching delivery and emphasis on syllables like a rapper
experimenting with flow. The dog looks betrayed and stares sadly, but
Jimmy keeps speaking to him in a soothing, calm tone and the dog is
frisky again in no time. Jimmy puts the radio on as he cleans the carpet.
A voice says that there have been race riots somewhere down the coast.
He recognises the name of the commentator from somewhere – Damien
Crawford. 'In these times of disorder, we need to name people for what
they are – thugs.' Jimmy's paying no attention, though, fascinated by
the way Mercury is chewing on a rubber bone. 'You've still got the spirit
of a puppy, ay, boy?' he says. The dog looks up and right at him, as if he
understood.

He then sets off on the bus from the Town to the City. He walks
confidently and with purpose, avoiding the travel agency. He goes to
a hardware shop and buys some lengths of PVC pipe, PVC cement,
a hacksaw, a hand-drill, and all manner of wood screws, hitch pins and
fittings. As he walks back to the bus interchange with his precarious
load, Jimmy sees a door open at the community centre where Solomon
used to attend b-boy battles. Tables are laden with delicious-looking
cakes and curries and he mistakes it for a market or a food fair. Jimmy
hasn't eaten anything the whole day. He leaves his load outside the
door but, once inside, he realises that it's a local Muslim community's
Friday prayers.

He starts for the door but a man gestures vigorously for him to sit down. He pours Jimmy cardamom tea and serves him a piled plate of saffron rice and curry. There are splinters of cinnamon throughout the yellow rice and it smells delicious. The man's name, it turns out, is Amjad. He looks familiar to Jimmy somehow. He says that he is a cabbie, and begins to talk about Australia.

'This place is biting . . . ah, eating me. Being away from my family. These Aussies, they talk so much, always talking. So lazy, but they get paid so much. This one bastard ask me – which boat you come on? I tell him I come on a plane. I am doctor back in Pakistan. I tell him you think I wanna be here? Driving you around? That bastard left his phone in the cab. He call me, says where is the phone? I tell him, you'll find it on the bottom of the lake, so get some scuba. I threw it in the lake. My cousin tells me he is a cabbie in New Zealand. People are kind, money is shit. Here, the people are arseholes, but the money is good. What a choice.'

Another man sits down and begins to talk to Jimmy about God, about attending next Friday's prayers. Jimmy makes an excuse, picks up his stuff and leaves.

He finds that buses have stopped running and has to pay sixty bucks for a cab from the City to the Town.

* * *

The next day he wakes up early remembering he has to pick up Mila at twelve. He cuts the PVC into various lengths and begins to make a baby gate so that Mercury Fire can't get into the living room and mess up the carpet or sofa while he is out. He puts some albums in his CD player – Kings Konekted, Jehst, Fluent Form, Fraksha. He raps along to the albums as he saws, trims, glues and fits the gate, using detailed instructions he found on the internet. A few hours and several albums later, he stands back, dusting his hands off. He coaxes Mercury Fire into the hallway to see it. Mercury observes it momentarily then leaps over it in one bound.

* * *

The weather has turned strange.

Still no rain, no clouds, but the sky has been changing colours all day, from wine dark to lemon light and back every hour.

Jimmy knocks on Aleks' door and Sonya answers. Usually she has a smile for him, but today she's out of it, her eyes almost closed and her mouth ajar. He tells her that Aleks wants him to take Mila out and she nods, but he could swear she's sleepwalking.

Having the hound makes hanging with an anklebiter easier. Mila does most of the talking, patting Mercury, her hands fitting between his pointed hipbones. She's a bloody sharp one, heaps like Jana. Jimmy wonders whatever happened to Jana's girlfriend from all those years ago, whose neck Aleks had snatched the bead from. Maybe she went back to Malaysia.

Jimmy pushes his floppy hair back and wipes his hand on his shorts. The park is strangely bare, but for a single tree that stands far off, its branches against the sky like cracks on a plate. A few youngsters in the cricket nets – what a shit sport, ay. Mila throws a tennis ball towards the tree and Mercury Fire goes bounding after it. He retrieves it and drops it at their feet, panting, pink tongue out.

'What do you do, Uncle Jimmy?'

'I work in an office.'

'My dad's never worked in an office. I don't think, anyway.'

Jimmy smiles. 'Nah, different strokes for different folks.'

Mila mouths the words a few times, as if making sure she will remember to use the expression later. Like father, like daughter. Aleks has a keen talent for mimicry and at times gives off the impression that he had a far greater education than he ever actually had. Much of his vocabulary he cannot spell. In a life of rupture – back and forth between living in Macedonia and Australia several times in his teens – this talent, combined with quick-wittedness, has served him well.

'Look at Mercury, Uncle Jimmy! He found something . . . Does your dad work in an office, too?'

'My dad? He was . . . He's a chef.'

She seems uninterested. 'When's my dad coming back?'

'Soon. He's working. Your dad is a hard worker – everything he does, Mila, he does it for you.'

She smiles broadly then looks thoughtful. 'Are you a hard worker, Uncle Jimmy?'

'Yes. Yes, I am,' he says with more force than necessary.

He looks up and can see a man sitting cross-legged in a flower garden across the road. His face is in shadow. The man is very well dressed, even wearing gloves, watching Jimmy throw the ball to Mila. A bus passes, and when Jimmy looks again, the man is no longer there.

4

There is ferocity in Solomon's game, as if he can outplay the Reaper for his father's life. He practises jump shot after jump shot until the hoop feels as big as a sinkhole. But during games, he never lets his fury take hold. He siphons it into his body until he becomes a blur of motion, a dervish spinning to the hoop, unfuckwithable. Yet his face remains placid, almost impassive. Teammates begin to call him 'The Iceman', referring to the great scorer George Gervin – supreme calm and a bone-dry shirt – but soon they rename him 'The Mask'. The mask unnerves opponents and teammates alike. There is arrogance in his game, the crossovers and dancing feet designed to humiliate, the smouldering intensity a slow knife intended to torture the opposition throughout the game. The truth is that he put the mask on much earlier.

When Ulysses Amosa recovered from his first stroke, his obsession with church and tradition became fervent. Solomon resented going to church and didn't understand the fa'aaloalo, respect for elders, that Ulysses constantly went on about – Solomon saw Aussie kids treating their parents as equals. Wounded, he began to speak less and less at home. Despite this, behind the mask, Solomon seethed with love for his dignified, sick father. His mother, Grace, would take Ulysses in his wheelchair to watch his prodigious son.

Though he couldn't articulate it, Ulysses loved to watch him dance on the blonde hardwood as if the ball was attached to a string. The man and the boy barely exchanged words, but Ulysses knew that Solomon was playing for him.

5

Hail bursts suddenly out of the cloudless sky.

Solomon, Scarlett and the kids seek shelter in a bus stop, watching hailstones as big as fists crack windscreens and dent letterboxes, bouncing metres high off the asphalt and racing over the street like runaways. A complete fury of white. Several minutes later, it is over and the sky is blue. The sun shines again, bright and furious. They spend ten minutes kicking hailstones into the grass, where they lie like blind eyes, melting.

Solomon gets the boys, who now number five, to tie their laces tight. 'Okay, listen, boys. Dribbling's bloody important, all right? Especially for you two – Toby you listening? You're quick but not that big. If you learn to dribble, people won't be able to take the ball off ya. You'll be able to get anywhere on the court, get to the basket. Understand?'

'Yeh.'

'You need to master the ball, control it. I wanna see you pound it hard on the ground, like this. Keep your head up, too.' All five boys are staring at Solomon, trying to imitate his every move, magnetised, as he directs them.

'That feels weird.'

'You'll get used to it. Don't worry about fucking up, all right? That's gonna happen. One minute now – hard.' Toby begins to bounce the ball on the blacktop, concentrating. Solomon has a new gadget, a cylindrical set of speakers with Bluetooth. He puts it on and a Ta-ku beat thuds out. 'Keep it up. It's all about rhythm, like music, like dancing.'

'Dancing?' gasps Charlie, a chubby blond kid.

'Don't knock dancing, mate. It'll help you learn balance.' Solomon toprocks niftily and strikes a pose. They all laugh breathlessly, still bouncing the ball.

'You gotta keep calm. Keep your composure. In this world, there're plenty of people trying to get you angry. Make you lose it. Never give in to em.'

Scarlett takes out an artist pad and starts to sketch with a biro. The shapes of trees, backboard, powerlines, fence, children of various colours and sizes in different attitudes of exuberant movement, all begin to appear. Here Toby driving to his right, there Muhammad in mid-air with the ball just leaving his fingertips, in the bottom corner Charlie catching his breath with hands on hips; at the top a bird caught in a crosswind. Solomon at the centre, directing everything. With assured, gentle scrapes of the biro, slowly depth and shade and life appear on the paper.

Scarlett looks up. Solomon is next to her, smiling thoughtfully.

'A pretty raggedy crew,' he says. 'But maybe enough for a team.'

Even though the day is darkening now, he has shades on, and she looks away briefly before standing up. He's wearing a Chicago Bulls singlet and his skin is almost luminous with sweat. She runs her hands over his shoulders and kisses him quickly.

Some lads turn up and start shooting on the other net. They're loud and cocky, all donning Bryant and James and Griffin jerseys, shades and caps backwards. Solomon seems to know one of them from a long time ago and his demeanour changes. He continues talking to the kids in a low voice but his eyes keep returning to the men, as if sizing them up. One of them, clearly the leader, calls out. He's tall and muscular with a shaved head and a goatee, and by the way he moves appears to have played at a high level. He has a scornful smile on his face. 'Oi, Amosa. Wanna play with someone your own age? We need an extra player.'

Solomon's expression is hard to read. 'Yeh. I'll have a game.' He turns to the boys. 'Okay, you got some free time, lads. Practise lay-ups and shooting, just like I showed you. With both hands. Might seem boring, but I promise it'll be worth it; all right?' He looks like he is about to tousle Toby's hair, then seems to think better of it.

The game is physical from the get-go.

The man with the shaved head is guarding Solomon closely, reaching in, shoving him, hand in his face, setting hard screens. Solomon's brow darkens as he plays and he flicks the man's hand away with his left as he dribbles with his right.

'Stop reaching, cunt. You'll get burned that way.' Solomon threads the ball through his legs easily.

'*Psssh*. The only thing getting burned is your cock, playboy.'

'Now, now. Envy's an ugly trait, mate. Pussies get no pussy.' Solomon is still sizing him up, facing right up to him, dribbling dizzyingly fast for a man of his size.

'Ugly motherfucker,' the guy says. 'Tana Umaga-looking motherfucker.'

'You mean Sonny Bill, ay?' Solomon does a spin move and hits the guy hard in the chest, sending him bouncing back into position. Solomon head fakes but the guy is all over him.

'Nah, cunt. You heard me. Fat cunt. Has-been.'

'Better than a never-was, mate. Bank.' Solomon flicks a fadeaway up but it hits the front of the rim. Ugly. He looks up to see that the kids have stopped their drills and are watching.

'Bitch, please. Let's see how that ankle works.' The man shimmies and shakes off Solomon, who grasps for his arm as he passes. 'Cash. And one,' the man says, neatly scooping in an up-and-under. He runs backwards past Solomon, wagging his finger Dikembe Mutombo style. The angrier Solomon gets the worse he plays, well aware that Scarlett and the kids are watching. He can't seem to help himself. Eventually, after a light foul, he drops the ball and pushes the man against the pole supporting the backboard, holding him by the throat. The man grins as his friends pull Solomon away. Solomon walks to the fence, spitting.

When he looks back, Scarlett is gone.

6

The men somehow manage to avoid each other, despite the confines.

Aleks has his back to the wall, reading a book called *The Secret*. He mouths each word as he reads, rolls them around his mouth like barley sugar, tasting them and thinking hard. He realises he already knows many of the words, but he can only read a page at a time before his head and eyes hurt. He hasn't read a book since early high school. Every now and again he catches Gabe watching him in the stainless-steel mirror as he washes his hands or stands up to get something out of the cupboard. The man has a regal bearing and Aleks is intrigued. Is it that he's never been so close to an African before? Is it the man's astonishing height or the numerous books he reads (in English). He thinks he can smell the man, and wonders if his black skin holds sweat in a different way. He's wondering whether he ought to talk to him when the lights go out.

An hour passes.

The man begins to makes a curious sound – not a snore, more a croak or a wheeze. It seems he's fallen asleep, but in the darkness Aleks can't be sure. His first instinct is violence, the rage that flows into the fists and explodes like dynamite on chin or cheekbone. He breathes slowly and imagines three points of light, a triangle, on the century-old ceiling arched, above him. He stares at it and it pulses. After minutes, his wife's sleeping face resolves in the centre of it. She is in deep slumber, and he momentarily envies her. She is then replaced by his mother, sweeping the kitchen in the flat, her eyes giving the impression of someone who fears nothing but God: not fists, not death, not fear itself.

The triangle expands with each of Gabe's wheezes and croaks. Aleks feels a strange, cool breeze. Now there are shimmering shapes lighting up on the ceiling. Candles and crucifixes and, strangely, peacocks. He sees a boy walking over cobblestones, chasing the peacocks, then looking out over the whole of Lake Ohrid, the water and light from this height like shot silk. The boy walks into the dank rooms of St Naum Monastery, carefully placing votive candles in a sandbox at the entrance. The boy is him, aged fifteen, when he first returned to Macedonia. He is looking around at the frescoes of an ancient room, saints and scenes from the Bible. The air is damp and cool, the skinny candles throwing irregular patterns on the brickwork. He can smell the water flowing somewhere beneath, or over, old stone.

Gabe coughs and the triangle disappears.

In the darkness, Aleks' mind again turns to violence, how he would like to make the guy shut the fuck up. Instead he focuses on the thought of the room and its wet, ancient smell, and how it reminds him of God. Peacocks and candles and God's mystifying deliberations. What was his place among it all? What part played by God or the Devil?

He wonders if his life would turn around if he moved back to his homeland. He often hears Macos saying they want to, but they rarely do. Australia has never taken him seriously, though he has tried to fit in. He remembers, at school, a teacher telling him how lucky he was to be here, how violent and animalistic the Balkans must have been. He had stayed quiet then, but he now knew that Australia was the scene of great crimes. Make a nick in the corner of the country, peel back the facade like possum skin, and the truth beneath would be hideous.

When he finally does sleep, he sees the monastery's inner sanctum again, but this time the fresco is made flesh. Women are lamenting and pulling at their hair, angels are weeping, and a single face is speaking. Aleks can't hear a word the face is saying, only a resonant singing, as if from deep within a mountain or a lake.

Flakes of gold paint are falling from the face of a saint, falling on him like sunlight.

* * *

'When did that shit get to Oz, anyway? Fucken tidal wave.'

'World War II, bro. The Japs used to be high on the shit. *Shabu*, they called it. Kept em rampaging. Every army done that shit, throughout the ages. Nazis had amphetamines, too.'

'Nah, nah, it was the gay bars. Early nineties, mate. The faggots used it first for parties, then it got into other clubs.'

A semicircle of ten men, all white, most of them smoking. Aleks is in the Aussie yard. There's the Islander yard, the Aboriginal yard, the Lebanese yard, the Asian yard, the Terrorist yard and the Boneyard for people who need protection: dogs, rapists and informants. The heat waves unspool in great ripples, and through it the inmates walk in lines with the jerky movements of marionettes. High winds today. Aleks feels as if he is in a dream within a dream, marooned somehow in a place as lonely and desperate as a space station.

'It's our version of crack. Three generations hooked on the fucken shit. Dirty as,' says Clint, an old crook Aleks knows from the outside.

'Don't knock it till you tried it.'

'Sucking a glass dick? Fuck no.'

'Remember when it first come out? Big bags of shard-like diamonds.'

Aleks has another story. 'They call ice *kamche* in the Town. Rock, little pebble. That meant Macos first brought it here.'

'Nah, nah, no way!'

Another voice cuts in, and everyone goes silent, even Aleks. 'If some cunt is dumb enough to buy it, then I'm gonna be smart enough to sell it. This is Australia, mate. Race or get erased.'

Torture Terry is a redhead with a square jaw and a loose bottom lip.

A Queenslander, he slowly drifted down the coast making a piecemeal existence from armed robbery. But since getting inside, Terry has become infamous for the rape of new inmates. 'I do it till they start liking it, mate – then I get a new one,' he had whispered to Aleks early on. He knows the justice system inside out – sly enough to slip out of a few years here and there, but way too far gone to ever go straight. Mostly his tatts are homemade, probably done at a young age with a protractor and Bic ink, but on his wrist he has a delicate tattoo of a swallow in flight, the only beautiful thing about him. When asked about it, he is rumoured to point at the swallow and say, 'This is what I make em do.'

Aleks looks at his knees, scratches his throat then looks back at Terry. For all intents and purposes, this animal is considered his equal: same uniform, same yard, same company. Aleks feels ashamed. To people outside they were both to be demonised; or, even worse, pitied. Aleks wonders why Terry isn't in the Boneyard or why nobody has put a hit on him. Then again, death is almost too good for this animal.

Terry is now holding court. 'It's the fucken Asians, mate. They're the ones bringing it in. Ruining our country with drugs and whores. They take our jobs, too, mate. And they don't even speak English.'

Some of the men nod. Aleks speaks jovially. 'Oh, yeh. Suppose you got a degree in medicine, ay? They took that day job you had working in an office too, did they?'

The men laugh nervously.

'But this is my country, mate,' says Terry, smiling with lightless eyes.

'Oh, yeh. You a Mabo, are ya?' Aleks is still smiling, too, but the tension is palpable.

'Fuck that! Look, I grew here, they flew here.' For a tiny moment, every man is perfectly still, like statues or pieces on a chessboard, waiting for some divine revelation, when suddenly Clint nudges Aleks, breaking the tension.

'Hey, I got something to talk to you about, mate. Business opportunity.' He offers Aleks a ciggie and jerks his head.

Aleks takes the ciggie and turns with Clint. They walk away and fall in step with the river of pacing men who are all discussing crime: how they got caught, how they might succeed next time.

'Bloody Terry,' says Clint. 'Don't worry about him. Always carrying on like a half-sucked cock.' Aleks laughs. He's surprised to see Clint inside. The odd jobs they had done together were simple, a bit of cash on the side.

The sky is inescapable and there's smoke on the wind, most likely from a bushfire somewhere. Aleks remembers a story Ulysses Amosa had told him when he was a child.

In the story, a beautiful woman is about to be burned at the stake for murdering a baby. Just as the flames are about to close around her, she sends a message to her brother far, far away, who sends spirits in the form of bats to flap out the flames with their wings. When the astonished villagers see her alive, standing untouched among the cinders, she says to them, 'We meet on the crossroads of life.' Aleks finds himself saying these words to Clint, who looks at him strangely. They smoke and pace.

'So. How you going for cash, mate?' asks Clint.

'All right. Businessman like me always has a Plan B.' Aleks grins but he's lying. He had paid his lawyer ten thousand dollars straight off the bat and might have to pay another ten grand soon. He left Sonya a few grand in their bank account but it won't last long. What if he gets more time? Plans need to be made. His family would help her, of course, but they didn't have all that much either. Then there was the mortgage to worry about. If his trial went badly and he had to go back inside, the whole bloody thing would fall to pieces.

He feels a pang, wishing that Sonya could get up out of bed and work. She's a smart one with a medical science degree. He once knew a man hooked on Xanax who thought the government had turned his eyeball into a video camera. The man stared at the sun for three hours to try to burn out the retina.

'Well, never hurts to have a bit more cash,' says Clint. 'And this is a good one, like the old days.'

They laugh. They're both thinking of the same scam, something they'd done a few times. They would sit on a hill thirty kilometres from the City and watch the bushland. If they saw a car go down a certain road, then switch its lights of halfway, they knew it was where a weed plantation was being watered. They'd wait an hour for the car to leave, and then hit it. Easy money, especially if you make the weed a bit heavier. One occasion, as they had gathered the weed, Aleks had seen an old kangaroo bone on the ground, a perfectly clean femur with a big ball on the end. It glowed white in the moonlight. Aleks had picked it up and surreptitiously slipped it through his fly and told Clint to look over. He then tipped the enormous, moonlit appendage up through the zipper and Clint's look had been one of sheer horror.

'Anyway, just think about it. Not much risk. Just money. Get ya back on ya feet once you get out,' says Clint.

'Yeh, or put me back in here.'

7

She,
a twist of pale smoke
      between the criss-crossing lasers
         and cursive of bodies.

She,
all hips and legs and curves,
      floating, bending, popping
         into an alphabet
      of perfect b-girl control.

Me,
      chewing my chain,
      fixing my cap,
      looking around,
but soon, fuck it,
      I'm reacting
to her controlled explosions of movement.

Heaps of kids
     haven't seen a b-boy before.
What kind of shit is that?
There used to be more solidarity between the elements,
     b-boys performing between acts.

'I miss b-girling.'
'Yeah. The atmosphere. The smell,' says Solomon.
'Deep Heat?'
'Yeah. Someone working their arse off on a move and then nailing it at
a battle.'

We're at a Thundamentals concert.

She wanted to go,
     even though it was sold out.
She went along the line and eventually wrangled two tickets,
     one for free.

She matches me drink for drink at the bar.

'Pool? I'll kick your arse. I'm a real tomboy.'

Afterwards,
I tell her that I let her win.

She wants to talk about the race riots,
but that'll bring the mood down.
Word is that
     a young boy is in a coma.
Still unclear what happened –
seemed like a free-for-all.

Scarlett guides me through the door
with one hand on the small of my back.
          It feels weird.

'Oi. Loverboy.'

Jimmy is in a new polo.
Rather than looking hurt,
                    as usual,
he seems chilled as.

          'Pity more good acts don't come through here, ay?'

Scarlett seems to cautiously like Jimmy.

He shouts to be heard over the music.
          'Deadset bro, I swear when I look him in the eye —'
          'Ha.'
          'Yeah, yeah. When I look him in the eye,
          it's like he understands my thoughts,
          and I can understand him too.
          I send him messages, mental pictures in my mind.
          Saw a doco, right, where this chick could do it with big cats.
          They can understand heaps, bro, even complex ideas.
          Animals are way smarter than we give em credit for.
          They just have different, um, different frames of reference, bro.
          Like this thing I was watching, right —'
I haven't seen him so excited since the last Wu Tang album dropped.
They rib me about not looking after Mercury properly
and I laugh and buy a round.

A young black guy called Remi is warming up the stage
with a DJ and a drummer
and while it's sampled beats,

they sound fresh,
unlike anything else at the moment.
Rarely see a black dude in Aussie hip hop.
                    It's troubling, ay.
Scarlett notices, too.
It's her first time to an Aussie hip hop gig
and she is looking around between sips.
'So many white people here. Not like this in Auckland.'
'Yeah. Aussie hip hop is pretty bloody white. There's more women than
there used to be, but,' I say, a bit defensively.
'Not on stage.'

She once told me
that NZ has problems with racism, too,
but they can always point at Australia
and say, 'At least we're not as bad as them.'

When the dude finishes his set,
there is just the drunken chatter of the crowd.

Scarlett tells Jimmy a dirty joke
        and he cracks up.
She has a bold, open-mouthed laugh
that shows her white teeth.
        I'm observing her too closely to laugh
and she notices and whispers,
        'Scared of a little rude joke, Solomona?'
        'Nah, I think it's you I should be scared of.'

These Thundamental dudes put on a hectic live show,
bobbing and weaving
        over a mess of leads.
Haven't seen them perform in ages.
Tuka has a skater/hippie swag,

bouncing one-footed
off speakers into the air.
Morgs is mean on the cuts.
Jeswon floats at the back of the stage,
coming forward for his verses,
attacking the beat with vicious sixteens.
Something in the water up in the Blue Mountains, ay?
The soundman is fucking the levels
but it doesn't matter.

> The vibe's there.

They do their big love song, 'Smiles Don't Lie'
and as the crowd sings along,
> Scarlett and I kiss.

'Are we cheesy or what?' she says.
'Yep,' I reply.

Jimmy waits for Scarlett to go to the toilet
then leans over.
'Oi. Guess who I bumped into?'
'Who?'
'My old man.'
I suddenly feel sober. 'Bullshit.'
'Serious.'
'The fuck he want?'
'All right, I didn't talk to him. I saw him outside work, sitting in the
back of a ute.'
'The back of a ute?'
'I think he wants to talk.'
'The fuck for?'
'Dunno. I reckon he wants to make amends.'
I know that look. Somehow wounded, somehow excited by the danger.

'It doesn't make any sense. No one's seen the bloke in years,' I say.
'I know.'
'*Pssh*. If it is, we should beat the cunt senseless,' I say.
'Yeah. That's what I reckon.'
'Let's do it. I'll come with ya.'
'Nah, nah. I just wanna see what he says. I got it under control.'

I wrinkle my nose. 'Just be careful, James.'

I can't concentrate on the rest of the show.

* * *

Scarlett's place doesn't have air-con.

Against the doorframe,
she takes my dick out of my jeans.
She squeezes it between thumb and forefinger
and a droplet appears.
She teases it with the tip of her tongue.
I try to hold her head but she keeps unfastening
my fingers from her hair,
undressing me with one hand.
Her back is covered with purple tatts,
stars and swordfish and coral reefs.

On her legs are scars,
razor marks at perfect intervals,
twelve per leg,
moon coloured.

She climbs on top of me
and guides me in.
She's not very wet.

We begin to move slowly
and she parts her legs to accept me deeper.
This room is so hot.
I touch her nipples,
long and dark and pierced.
With her right hand she holds my throat
and with the other she slowly begins
to slap me on the right cheek,
once every few seconds.
We're moving faster now and she's wetter.
She tightens her grip on my throat.
The slaps become harder
and more painful,
but with the same regularity –
        each slap turns my head further to the left.
Something anchored deep in me rising.
My face is scalding.
Her teardrop tattoo becomes liquid,
runs down her face in a single trail,
falls onto my chest
and evaporates with a sizzle.
I'm losing my breath.
Now the pain on my cheeks
blade-sharp and my skin unbearably hot.
I'm holding her breasts tight.
When I come it is painful and explosive
and I lose breath completely.

Her eyes have been closed the whole time.

We're lying in bed,
not touching.
        It's too hot.
And something's wrong.

'Why did you buy the greyhound in the first place, Solomon?'

'Dunno.' What's she driving at? 'To be honest, I wanted to show the boys that I could be responsible for something, look after something. Fucked it up.'

'Ah, yeh. The boys.' She's staring straight up. I suddenly crave a cigarette and think about getting up when she speaks again. 'Do you have any female friends?'

'Course.'

'Ones you haven't slept with?'

' . . . '

'Your group of mates is a cock forest, Solomon. Admit it.'

'It's not that bad. They've been my mates forever, what do you want me to do?'

We lie in silence.

Unlike with Georgie, I don't want to argue.

Then she says, 'Don't you hate people who are all style over substance?' She's been dropping shit like that all night since the concert.

I try to smile. 'Ouch.'

'I'm serious. If you don't contribute anything, anything at all, what's the point?'

I realise she's for real. 'Why do you keep seeing me, then?'

'Because you're a good fuck.'

'Jesus.' Whatever she's doing, it's working. I've never been more angry or turned on.

'What about companionship? Don't you think you need that?'

She laughs. 'I don't need anything. Least of all from you.'

I want to make her take the words back.

She's loving it,

        suddenly self-destructive.

'Used to getting your way, aren't you Solomon?'

I stand up, shaking.

'See you again soon? I'll call you,' she says.

'I'll think about it.' I want to hit her.

'I'll see you next week. Don't take yourself so seriously, Solomona.'
    She's still smiling.

I leave,
thinking about Georgie,
lovely and safe and dependable.
            Dependent.

8

On the TV:

'Mr Crawford, we understand that you are in support of recent calls to change the Racial Discrimination Act. Don't you think, given the race riots in Shellfish Bay, that this is a rather inflammatory proposal?'

'On the contrary, I think this is exactly the time to take another look at it. The mood of the electorate is one of understandable frustration. The Australian identity is being contested as we speak and I believe that one essential part of the Australian identity is being forthright and honest, something that political correctness has been white-anting for quite some time. Amending the Act is not, as some contend, a green light for prejudice; rather, it is a green light to express ourselves more fully as Australians.'

'Mr Crawford, is there any truth to the claim that it was police brutality that started the riots?'

'Absolutely none. It is merely the actions of a few thugs and should be condemned as such.'

'And do you have any more information on the young man injured in the riots?'

'He remains in a critical condition. I grieve with his family and I am praying for his swift recovery.'

9

Jimmy slowly gets into bed and knows the hound will follow.

'Good boy.'

He tucks the pillow beneath his head and his eyes are aching from the twelve-hour shift. His inner thighs are chafed raw from the shabby material of his cheap suit – inexplicably, as he sits at a desk all day. He is so tired it feels as if the bed is radiating outwards around him, stretching like a desert. He feels something running towards him. Soon the hound bounds onto the blankets with him, lightly arranges itself – snuffle, pad, pad, snuffle – then twists into a ball with the motion of water spiralling down a drain. Jimmy rubs the dog behind its ears and Mercury Fire makes a sound of satisfaction, deeply reverberating in his throat, almost a purr. Then he yawns, and in the near darkness his teeth appear like some fine rock formation. His breath, the smell of dead meat, somehow pleases Jimmy. A warm-blooded, loyal, gentle being so close. Closer and more affectionate than Jimmy had ever been with a woman. The night is strangely cool. Jimmy draws the blankets around himself, moves so that their bodies can share some warmth, then falls asleep.

His bed stretches outwards
  and becomes an enormous limestone plain.
He stands and begins to run.
Mercury Fire keeps pace with him,
running towards a body of water
  in the distance.
With each step Jimmy can feel himself getting stronger
and he wonders if he is taking on
  the animal's spirit.
The dog is saying,
  'Run on, my friend, run on, run on, my master.'

When he reaches the water's edge,
  he doesn't slow,
but leaps perfectly into it
and becomes at one with the lithe body of a river.
He swims and can hear the dog's voice,
encouraging him forward,
but he can no longer sense him at his side.

Jimmy swims deep down,
into a grotto
where there are thousands of voices
  and golden lights.

He swims through a doorway
and finds himself standing at the back of a crowd,
  completely dry.
Run DMC is performing
and through the drift of dry ice
he sees Jam Master Jay's gold ring
as he scratches on vinyl
  as black as his leather jacket.
Jimmy pushes through the crowd to the front

and he is holding a pair of Adidas in the air,
    waving them from side to side.

Jimmy is hauled onstage
and joined by Rakim, Ghostface Killah,
who pours him a tall glass of Hennessy,
and a young Jay-Z,
    who hands him a mic.
Jimmy faces the crowd;
    lights and mirror balls are floating like seraphs.
He starts rapping,
    freestyling flawlessly, intricately,
        catching whatever beat DJ Premier
        (who is now behind the decks)
           is spinning.
When he finishes,
someone takes the microphone from him.
It is Sin One,
standing almost seven-foot tall,
rapping a famous verse from 'Orphan Slang'.
The crowd is on its feet
and Jimmy is leaping up and down,
    his hair in his eyes.

He goes offstage
and is ushered down a hallway to a door
    covered in dripping blue paint.
He opens the door
and it takes a moment
    for his eyes to adjust
to a concentrated darkness.
When he closes the door behind him,
there is sudden silence.
He sees the figure of a naked woman at the window,

overlooking a big, broken city.
He cannot see her face.
Without turning,
she beckons to him with a sweet voice
and her body is gilded in moonlight.
He goes to her and she undresses him
and gently kisses his ears and neck and eyebrows.
It is Kayden Kross
and she is wearing no makeup.
She whispers secrets to him,
revealing her authentic, tender self
        that nobody else has seen.
He kisses her eyelids
then she climbs on top of him,
but as she does,
her face changes
and starts scrolling through the faces of other women –
Hailee, Scarlett Snow, other pornstars.
Her pale belly is twitchy when he touches it.
Her ribs look like a pharaoh's headdress.
As she begins to move,
he looks down at his body
        and sees that it is Solomon's.
Blonde hair falls in a wave around him,
                        drowning him,
and her lips become as big as the night
and swallow him whole
        like a pill.

In the morning,
he is incredibly hungry.

No graff and music blogs to wake him up today:
the hunger alone

has made him alert and sharpened.

At McDonald's,
the cashier is talking about church.
        Her eyes widen when he makes his order.

'All for you?'

Two schoolkids
watch him eat three hash browns
and two servings of hotcakes.

'Hey, kids. Ever seen a greyhound?'
'Yeh.'
'Like em.'
'Nah.'
'You know they can reach up to seventy k's an hour? Crazy, huh?'

One shrugs,
One smiles.

As he leaves,
the cashier is talking about cleavage.

He feels light,
and stops to lick dew
from a blade of grass.

At work,
he is called into his boss's office.
'Look mate,
we've been monitoring your calls
and sad to say, you're not doing a good enough job.'
'You firing me?' says Jimmy, hopefully.

'No, no.'
'Didn't think so. Impossible to get fired from public service, ain't it?'
'I think you've got the wrong attitude, mate.'

Grey walls.

A spray can would change that.

With several callers,
he holds the phone away from his ear
and has to pinch himself so he doesn't scream.

Count. Breathe.

On his lunchbreak,
he sees a fabric shop.
        Colourful beads, cloth.

He buys a piece of felt
and keeps it in his pocket
as he answers calls,
        stroking it from time to time
to remind himself of Mercury Fire's ears.

As he walks from work
to the bus interchange,
he sees a protest in the centre of the City.
There are signs with Damien Crawford's
        smiling face crossed out.
A handsome Aboriginal man in a suit
        is speaking into a megaphone.

Jimmy walks past.

As he leaves the City on his bus,
he sees a man sitting on top of a street sign,
dressed immaculately with a scarf
around the lower part of his face,
    watching him.

10

'Secca?' asks Solomon.

'Yeah, there is one, but he's a lazy cunt. Only patrols once every two hours, if that. I saw him wanking in the office the other night,' says Jimmy.

'I'd do the same if I was him. Boring as,' says Solomon. 'Camera?'

'Haven't seen one.'

'Word.' Solomon nods. 'If we time this right, it'll be easy as.'

Jimmy is leaning on the wheel of their mother's car and Solomon's sunk deep in the seat, playing with a lighter, smoke filling the car. Jimmy looks up, scoping the spot, moonlight outside turning everything bone-coloured. Trem album on real low, sampled snares cracking.

Solomon thinks to himself for a second that he's getting a bit over hip hop. Most of what he hears in Australian hip hop is either glowstick-wielding, fast-food pop or purist garbage stuck in the nineties. Jimmy reckons there's heaps of good stuff out, but Solomon doesn't have the energy to dig for it anymore. On a night like this, though, doing this, it's perfect.

Jimmy is rapping along and points to the right. Solomon nods. The grass is thick and nearly as high as the barbed wire. Sick. It's the fuel depot on the edge of town, a big cylindrical building next to bushland

and a set of traffic lights on the highway. They see the spot they want
from here – freshly primed concrete, real high up roadside exposure, at
the top of some stairs that wind around the building. Holy grail. Every
cunt going to work in the morning is gonna see their masterpiece. But
that's not even why they're doing it. Jimmy lights up another ciggie and
they sit listening to Trem's voice winding up with the smoke.

'Borrowed time's got expiry dates/
Vindicated with a choice of either wrought iron or fiery gates.'

Jimmy rolls down the window and flicks the butt out. Heat, insects,
the smell of gum trees. The CD changes and the paranoid anthem
'They're Watching' by Ciecmate and Newsense comes on. Jimmy rolls
the window up and they drive off.

The next night they're there again, this time on foot.

'Ready?'

'Ready.'

They take out T-shirts, pull them over their faces and tie the sleeves at
the back of their heads, eyes peeping out their neck holes – instant bally.
Gloves on, bag over shoulder. Executioners. Jimmy stays low, so low that
the top of the grass is well above him. The secca just patrolled. Should
give them a good hour, maybe even two.

Boltcutters out.

Jimmy cuts a big hole in the wire and passes the boltcutters back
to Solomon in the tall grass. Jimmy waits quietly and a minute later
Solomon appears at the fence on the other side of the compound and
cuts a big circle out of it so they have another escape route. A nod, then
simultaneously they creep through the tears in space and time.

Their feet crunch on the gravel. Keeping low, creeping towards the
stairs, the smell of petrol and steel. A light is flickering in the secca's
office. They climb, trying to stay quiet on the iron stairs. It's higher than
they thought and by the time they get to the top they're sweating. They
stop, look at what's below: the whole town, the roads, the bush.

Then they unzip the bag, take a can out and mark up first with the
dregs of a Matador. Big, block letters:

FREE JAKEL

Jimmy hands Solomon a can – Soviet Red. Concrete like this is porous, soaks up paint. Ironlak is hard to buff, leaves a scar, like Killrust back in the day. Jimmy takes out his can – Pineapple Park Yellow.

'You do the top fill,' he whispers.

'Yep.' Solomon begins.

Ghost fatcaps on both cans. Used to be so hard to get fatcaps, so you'd stock up on nozzles from out of town. Fatcaps were worth their weight in gold, and Rusto's were the shit. A writer from Melbourne once told the boys they used to call Rusto's 'whistlers' down there cos of the sound they make. They begin to fill the letters in.

Yellow to red fade.

The ghost cap goes *hohhhhhhhhhhhhh*, projecting a wide circle of paint.

'Careful it doesn't drip,' Jimmy whispers.

Solomon nods and leans back to get maximum coverage, emptying the can quickly.

The brothers had argued over colours and design for ages. Jimmy sketched a few ideas in his blackbook, which has one of the best photo albums of anyone they know. Solomon was bouncing a tennis ball off the wall with his left hand, smoking a joint with the other. Jimmy sketched the letters first, then the characters – he wanted the piece to be red and yellow, Maco colours, for Aleks. Solomon, always vaguely uneasy about Aleks' patriotism, agreed only if they put black in it, 'like an Aboriginal flag,' even though he knows Aleks isn't all that fond of Kooris.

Red. Black. Yellow.

Strong colours but difficult to make work in a piece. Back in the nineties they wouldn't have even tried. A red to yellow fade is really extreme and good reds and yellows were hard to get. Yellow, especially, was watery. Pastels were always better with the paints available. Now that they have access to good, cheaper Ironlak paint they might as well try it. Nothing like a challenge, even though they know that Aleks, the best writer of them all, would warn against the colour scheme. Jimmy then argued that they should rack the paint, like the old days, but Solomon dismissed the idea straight away. 'And run the risk of doing community service or some shit? Fuck that. Too old for that.'

'A real writer racks his paint,' said Jimmy in an imperious tone.

'Yeah, yeah. And they only paint trains, I know. Who are ya, Jisoe or something? You can afford it now anyway, Jimmy.'

Now, they start the characters.

A skeleton smoking a ciggie.

Bushfire flames and a Vergina Sun.

Then the piece de resistance –

a muzzled greyhound with a patch over one eye leaning against the 'L'.

Perfect night for a mission. The Town turns ghost come Sunday night. No cars, the air warm and clear, stars above like grapeshot. Winter time is a bitch to paint in, so they leave that to the Lads and the young writers now. How did they do it all those years, heading out every night for weeks on end in minus-five cold, fingers freezing stiff as the propellant comes out, paint all drippy cos of the temperature. Solomon wonders what it would be like to grow up in Sydney – good weather and a proper trainline.

The outline now –

Montana Black. New York fatcap.

Sssssssssss.

This is the real shit. The pretty boys can keep their preening for the stage. No MC has ever died holding the mic. Writers are a different breed though – gotta be a bit crazy, a bit wild. People die on train lines everyday around the world, dying for their art. Dying for something that'll be painted over in a day.

Cutbacks.

Sss. Sss. Sss.

A car pulls up at the intersection. They crouch low in the shadows, hugging close to the stairs. Solomon coughs into his hand. The car sits there for what seems like hours, a house drumline pulsing from it. It's a done up Vectra, some terrible chameleon paintjob. The light turns green and it drives off. They look down. No sign of a secca.

Background now –

dark purple.

Fumes.

There's no way they could count how many times they've done this. Bus seats to drains to tennis courts to underpasses. The planning, the risk, the art, the pride. Jimmy wishes Aleks was here. He thinks back to when they did a door-to-door full-colour burner. It ran all the way to Sydney Central before it got buffed.

Now the highlights –

Aspen White.

Like Trem says, icing on the fucken cake.

Solomon is thinking what a liability Jimmy can be. One time, early on, he capped a dope piece by WERSE from Brissie, who's a king. Jimmy went over the top of it with this shit chromie but was all proud of himself. Toy.

A bird cries. They both look up sharply,

then it's silent again.

Now the keyline –

light purple makes it pop right out.

The piece is finished.

They stand there, appreciating,

grinning,

breathing.

Bold – crisp – emblazoned.

Best they've done in ages.

Solomon looks at his watch. It's been just over an hour.

'Beautiful,' whispers Jimmy. He pulls out his phone and takes a photo. The flash is blinding.

'Dumb cunt!' Solomon hisses.

'What did you want me to do? Fuck,' Jimmy whispers back with equal vehemence.

'Ay, you can see the mountains from here,' whispers Solomon, looking over his shoulder.

There they are, paperfolded mountains, far off. Soundless chains of lightning burning like filaments in between them.

'Fuck. That's dope.'

They stand up straight, stretching, looking over the lights and the blackness to the far mountains. Suddenly a voice rings out.

'OI!'

The secca is looking up at them, white face like a coin on the floor. Only one way out. 'Go!' They barrel down the stairs. Jimmy is zipping up the bag with one hand, making sure the bally's still on with the other. The secca is yelling something repeatedly but they can't tell what it is, with the ringing of the stairs and the sound of their breath. They get to the bottom. 'Oi, stop!' The secca's got something heavy in his hand but he doesn't seem to know what to do with it, a snake more scared of them than they are of him, so he just stands there. Solomon's still got a can in his hand, which he aims, blasting yellow paint right in the man's eyes. The secca yells, falling and holding his face.

Another man they hadn't seen appears from the right with a torch, running and shouting at them. Light swings through the dark and he yells, 'I called the fucken cops, you fucken idiots.' He tackles Solomon to the gravel and gets some good punches in before Jimmy gets there. Jimmy has got a can in his hand and he busts him in the side of the head with it. Red. The man pitches over and shivers on the ground, like he's having a fit. Solomon rolls away and they can see the dude's teeth in the moonlight and it's almost like he's smiling. They freeze for a second then the first secca comes at them again, with blood and dirt and yellow paint all over his uniform. Solomon twists his ankle as he tries to run and lets out a yelp of pain but Jimmy pulls him up and they're running.

Jimmy half dives, half falls through the hole in the fence, the one Solomon cut, tears his shirt, then is hurtling through the grass up a slope. He can feel blood trickling down his back, or it could be sweat. Solomon is behind him, puffing, swearing.

Neither of the seccas has followed them out of the yard, but the danger hasn't passed. They run across a big road and then hide for a moment behind a bush. They take the ballys off and they become T-shirts again. They stuff them in the bag, then the gloves, and chuck the whole lot deep into the bush. They peek out and see a cop car pull up at the intersection.

They run across the remainder of the road, leap a fence, bolting, ducking and rolling. A car screeches around and it's coming towards them. Jimmy is sprinting now, breath rattling like a ball bearing in a can. Can't keep this up much longer – he's getting dizzy, stomach curdling, metallic bile rising in his throat.

Then the sound of the car heads in the opposite direction.

'Thank fuck.'

They fall underneath a Hills Hoist in some rundown backyard, breathing hard. Sheets billow around them like the skirts of spectral dancers. 'Fuck. That was hectic.' says Solomon. His face is shining.

Jimmy is still breathing too heavily to answer and he begins coughing nuggets of black.

Nevertheless, it feels good.

Like brotherhood.

11

The smell of himself, a grin of moonlight, and the sound of an inmate who has been designated to sweep the floors outside the cells. The sweeper is the way prisoners trade goods, buy cigarettes and pass on messages, something the guards know but let go. Aleks can hear inmates on the lower floor yelling, 'Sweeper! Sweeper!', a murmuring in one of the other cells and the sound of someone sharpening a toothbrush.

He takes out a little wooden prison spoon. He snaps it into two pieces and begins to plane them down with a razor that has been melted into the handle of a toothbrush, making sure to get the proportions right. Below him, Gabe sings softly to himself. Aleks feels the violent urge building, but instead grips the handle hard and focuses on planing the pieces smooth. It takes a week to get them as he wants, smooth and flawless, both with overlap notches so they fit perfectly together.

Now he needs superglue, which is harder to come by than he imagined. It becomes a full-scale, clandestine operation, and eventually he gets a glob of glue in cling film from the sweeper, as a favour from a Turkish mate. The glue would've come from the minimum security workshop. Finally he puts the pieces together and lets the final product sit there. He wishes he could show it to his cousin Nicko, who is very religious.

He concentrates and in ten minutes is able to transport himself back to Ohrid. Every year a priest stands on the pier and throws a cross over his shoulder. Hundreds of men in the freezing water swim for it, splashing up little coronas of white foam and gasping for air. Aleks smiles and looks at his new cross, thinking that, if he drills a hole in it and uses red and black string from a towel to make a cord, it would make a fine necklace.

In the yard, he is treated with deference and shows no signs of weakness. Every now and again he spies the flash of red hair and thinks about teaching Torture Terry a lesson. But he must control himself. Concrete, bars, concrete, bars, alliances and enemies, each man within ruminating his own ruin, falls, failings and loves, his place in the animal hierarchy. Though most of them would've done the air jiggle a century ago, there is even a type of brotherhood among some. *The road to hell is paved with good intentions*, Aleks thinks.

The attack he expects never comes, but he sees every variation of violence. Unlike in Macedonia, here the prisoners are the ones to worry about, not the guards. He sees a man stomped to death, hears men raped in their cells. He sees jam packets heated into napalm in kettles and flung on the faces of paedophiles. Even the recreational boxing, where mitts are made from socks stuffed with stolen sponges, is just another outlet for tension and a way to show strength.

When he returns to the dark, silent cell, the presence beneath him almost seems big enough to devour him. There are times deep in the clockless hours when the man cries out and Aleks worries for him. Then he feels disgusted. So alien, so black.

In the morning, Aleks is about to go into the visitor's area. He pulls his shirt, pants and underpants off, spreads his legs and stands against the wall as naked as a newborn. The security guard checks his armpits, hair, ears and mouth, then gets him to spread his legs, pull his dick up, squat and cough.

'Nothing up there, mate? I found a mobile phone last week.'

'Bullshit,' says Aleks.

'No bullshit. Saw the antenna sticking out.'

'Old school. Motorola?'

'Yeh. Bloke got it up there in a condom. Punched him in the side and half the bloody thing came out.'

'Farkin hell. You gotta a find a better way to earn a living, brother,' Aleks says over his shoulder, grinning.

'Seriously, I've never worked around so many arseholes,' the man replies, giving him his prison whites.

Aleks is still chuckling when he enters the visitation room. Instead of his wife and parents, whom he expected, he sees his cousin Nicko. He burns with a sense of loyalty for his cousin, who has done a lot for the community and trodden the straight path. They smile at each other. Nicko, who has dark bags under his eyes, passes his hands over his eyes, nose, lips then down the back of his neck.

'What's wrong, Nicko?'

'Work. Don't worry about it.' He scratches at a birthmark on his arm.

'Nah, nah. What about it?'

Nicko sighs and stares at the ceiling. 'These people I work with, cuz . . . public service pricks. They look down on me so much, I swear. They're the cream of the dregs, *Atse*.'

'I bet. That's how the *kengurs* do it —' Aleks is about to go on a rant, but Nicko cuts him off.

'Ah, don't worry about it. How you going in here?'

Aleks, worried Nicko is going to go back to the community and gossip, says nonchalantly, 'The food's good. How are my ladies?'

Nicko seems to relax and his eyes brighten. 'Good. Mila came around for a birthday party at mine the other day —'

'Oh, of course! Happy birthday to little Suzana.'

'Thanks, cuz. Little princesses – they grow up so quickly, ay? Giving us a run for our money already.'

'I know.'

'And Sonya. You see her?' Aleks looks at him squarely.

Nicko scratches his birthmark again. 'Yep. She dropped Mila off. Just looked a bit tired, that's all. She couldn't come today cos she had a job interview. I thought she got the message through to you. Sorry you have to see my ugly mug instead.'

Aleks grins. 'No way. Your ugly mug makes me feel better about mine.' Then, thinking of Sonya, he says, 'Harder to get a job than it used to be, ay?'

'Yeah. Government's cutting jobs in the public service, too. *Atse.* If you need any help, just let me know, all right?'

'Of course. Of course,' Aleks mutters. 'You seen Jimmy around?'

'Yeh. Running around with that dog of his, talking to it like it was a human.'

'Sounds about right.' They laugh easily.

'Rare as rocking-horse shit, your mate. That's dog's lucky to have Jimmy. I heard most ex-racers get drained for their blood so vets can use it in transfusions. Poor doggies.'

'Yeah,' says Aleks. 'What about Solomon?'

'Dunno. Seems to have gone missing in action.'

12

Basketball playlist

Gang Starr – 'Full Clip'
Nas – 'Nas is Like'
Kanye West feat. Lupe Fiasco – 'Touch the Sky'
Cam'ron – 'Hey Ma'
Jurassic 5 – 'What's Golden?'
J. Cole – 'Workout'
Verbaleyes and Mute – 'Lingua Franca'
Jay-Z – 'Roc Boys'
The Tongue – 'The Show'
Talib Kweli – 'Get By'
Home Brew Crew – 'Basketball Court'
Method Man and Redman – 'The Rockwilder'
The Roots – 'Get Busy'
Outkast – 'So Fresh, So Clean'
Mos Def – 'Mathematics'
L-Fresh the Lion – 'One'

Muhammad's dad

A convivial Indian-Fijian shop owner
     with snowy hair.
He seems to like what he sees on the court,
     until his eyes alight on Toby.
'That one. A bad influence, I think. His parents.' He twirls a finger
around his temple then mimes drinking.
'Yeah, I heard. Just needs a push in the right direction, Mr Khan.
Basketball's good for him.'
He nods,
sizing me up,
     then crushes two fifty-dollar notes
          into my hand.
'Get the kids some stuff they need.'

Shopping night

At the sport's store,
     an attendant keeps following me and Jimmy around,
     looking at us heaps suss.
'You all right?' I call out.
     She looks embarrassed and leaves.

     I measure a few sizes of a Steph Curry jersey against myself
          then decide on one.
'That's way too fucken small for you,' says Jimmy.
'It's not for me, numbnuts. It's for a kid.'
     Sounds strange saying it.
'Huh? What kid?'
'A kid I'm teaching to play ball.'

Jimmy looks taken aback,

then grins.
'You didn't tell me about this. Watch out, bra. You might get put on
one of them lists.'
'Shut up.'
'Expensive present. Buy me one.'

I ignore him and go in search of sports cones.
        I also get cheap basketballs
                and water bottles.

Jimmy stares.

        'All right, it's actually a few kids.'

I pay for the jersey with my own money,
the other stuff with Mr Khan's.

I sniff the jersey on the way out
and almost wish I bought it for myself.
Fresh gear always makes you play better.

It's like Reebok Pumps –
        pure placebo.

Drinks

An outdoor bar with a Mexican theme.

Some boys I used to play ball with
are talking about Aussies in the NBA.
They're all clean cut,
        working in the public service now.
'Mate, we've got a fucken awesome national team. Bogut, Dellavedova,

Baynes. Patty Mills is crushing it, too.'
'Yair, heard of this new guy Dante Exum? He declared for the NBA
draft and everything. Jarryd Hooper's going well at college, too.'

I feel a pang at the mention of Jarryd's name.
Then I notice Jimmy,
    very still, by himself,
on the margin of conversation.

I know what's on his mind –
    'These people don't even know I'm here.
    I have nothing in common with
    these rich, successful, white cunts.'

Then he'll think about his dad.

Every small failure in Jimmy's life
is magnified by his paranoid brain;
a massive ugly picture
    of failure and loss.

    To Jimmy,
    it's always been him against the world.

Beige

At first,
Jimmy told the kids in high school
he was half-Samoan.

But one day at the interchange,
    I told them the truth –
    that he didn't know what he was.

After that,
everybody began to call him 'Beige'.

Beige Beige Beige

Jimmy was jealous of the fair-skinned Koori kids,
so proud of their culture.

Seems fucked up now,
but I loved to torture him –
ignore him at the bus interchange,
see how far I could push it,
how the smallest jibe would affect him
     like a lash to the back.

Hiding my own shame
at not being Samoan enough.

And Jimmy would take it
          and take it
          and take it,
until he found hip hop . . .
and that other stuff.

I wish I could rewind it all.

Sonya

He's still got a good heart, though.
He's worried that Sonya might not be going so well,
with her health,
     with her cash.

'Reckon we should help somehow?'
'Yeah, maybe. Not sure how. It's a bit awkward, don't ya reckon? Aleks
would hate that.'
'Yer.'

As Jimmy keeps talking,
my mind drifts to the court
and my team:

Amosa's All-Stars!

Toby's first present

Toby can't seem to believe it.

He holds the jersey to his nose
and closes his eyes as he breathes in the scent,
just like I did.
Then he tears his T-shirt off
    and puts the jersey on.
He shines on the court,
still a little clumsy,
but with gunpowder in his step now.
His jump shot like a heatseeker —
    everything I taught him working at once.
Muhammad stops acting cocky for a moment
    and seems pleased to see his mate so happy.

Some Sudanese kids have turned up,
one who's nearly six-foot-three tall
    at fifteen years old.
Diamond in the rough,
mad potential to be a good centre.

Word-of-mouth, ay?

I set up the cones
and I'm running drills with em
and finish with a proper five-on-five game.

I make sure to play music the whole time.
Most of kids are into Kerser,
but I play older shit
        they mightn't have ever heard.

Each one, teach one, ay?

The point of it all

Every point
a toe, heel or ball touches,
is a point on a map.

        And the map
        points to *something*.

When the kids leave

I put on my favourite album,
'A Long Hot Summer' by Masta Ace.
Something melancholy but resilient
about the rhymes and the chopped samples.
I dribble to the beats,
and for a moment it feels
as if my muscles and bone have sheared off

and I am one with the wind,   the music.

I think about Aleks again
        and feel guilty.

He'll feel betrayed
that I haven't visited him.

Sometimes I think his presence
is rupture to the music,
that negativity only breeds more of the same.

Shared history, though –
you can't just let it off
        a leash like a dog.

The ethereal synths of 'Beautiful'
come on.

I tilt my head,
sniff the air –
the dusty, sherbet sky enters my nostrils,
my mouth, ears, skin.

A sign of rain?

I square up to the hoop,
jump straight up,
        and flick the ball in a blazing arc
        from the sideline.
Swish.

13

High winds and willy willies.

Summer marches through the trees, a giant headhunter, taking off skulls. Jimmy has drawn the blinds against it. He's chopping weed in a bowl, watching Mercury as he sleeps. The room is dark but for an intermittent red light blink-blink blink-blinking from a computer screen. He lays the sticky scissors down, carefully rolls a joint on his knees and holds it up as one might an ancient conical shell found on a beach.

His eyes grow red as the orchids of smoke sink upwards and pancake on the ceiling.

He imagines optical fibre connecting him and the dog. It is taut, glowing, perfectly straight like a laser. He now tries to send shapes down the fibre with his mind – bones, balls, love hearts, race tracks, rabbits. As the smoke turns and uncoils, he stares, and images pulse down the invisible filament, growing bigger and bigger until they envelope the dog's sleeping head and soak into it.

After half an hour, the dog opens its eye and raises its head. They stare at each other.

Hello, little dog. Hello, my friend, Jimmy says in his mind.

The dog raises its head further, nose up, sniffing the air. It doesn't open its mouth, but the reply comes. 'Hello, Jimmy. Hello, Jimmy, my master.'

Jimmy goes for a walk to get food and Mercury trots at his side, the points of its hipbones visible behind the skinny waist. An old bloke yells from across the street, 'Give him the chilli finger, mate! He'll run faster.' Jimmy whispers to the dog, 'Ignore him, Mercury.'

The air is dense and smokey. At the foot of a telephone pole, Jimmy sees a dead yellow-crested cockatoo. He hunkers down and stares at it for a full minute – its outstretched wings, its open beak, claws, eyes swirling with ants, feathers a subtle grade of yellow and white. Its fellow birds, arranged evenly on the powerlines, look down in silent vigil like worshippers on a pew.

The dead bird is huge, as long as his forearm, and has already begun to stink. He resists the urge to pick it up and weigh it in his arms. He tries to send it messages and shapes with his mind, but the filament is frayed halfway and the shapes dissipate in the air. He peers down the street and can see the red sun setting across the wild ridge that borders the edge of town.

That night he sketches the cockatoo in his torn blackbook. Its wings are spread, about to land on the powerlines. Behind it he imagines a fierce blue sky. MTN 94 Azure maybe? Aspen white and Pineapple Park yellow? He sits back and admires his work. He'll get Aleks to paint it when he gets out.

He goes back the next day to see the dead cockatoo. There are now ten of them. All of them are strangely flattened, two-dimensional. Jimmy assumes it's a combination of ants and the heat that has eaten them from the inside and collapsed them. He sits for a long time, looking at them. *Hello, birds*, he thinks. *Hello, little birds, my friends.*

No reply.

Trudging back to towards home, he passes the fire station, where trucks are polished to a high red, and the orange and silver firefighting gear is bunched on the wall. He walks inside and begins to touch it, running both hands over a helmet like a phrenologist. He then takes out a marker and tags up the side of the truck. He has only done several letters when he hears a man's voice and Jimmy goes running.

The next day, the dead cockatoos are all gone.

14

'Mr Crawford, I'm a volunteer fireman.'

'Good for you, mate.'

'Mr Crawford, err, our job has got harder over the last few years. I personally believe climate change has something to do with it. Surely this current spate of bushfires is as much the fault of climate change as firebugs. I mean, the fires started in early spring, six weeks out from summer. What do you say to that?'

'I thank you for your question and applaud your good work. But let's be real about climate change. This hysteria about its authenticity has been largely manufactured. This is an economic question, not an environmental one. Fires have been a part of the Australian landscape from time immemorial.'

15

Solomon is trying on clothes and jewellery in Scarlett's room. He already has several sets of clothes there, neatly folded in the corner. There's a look of stress in his eyes as he meticulously tries on different combos. Scarlett goes to say something but instead lets the cool air from a cheap fan run over her. She checks Facebook and stares at the endless parade of social media: friends back home offering opinions about Teina Pora, something about a missing plane and Jimmy, as usual, posting graff pics and photos of the dog. She puts on the Hermitude album 'Hyperparadise' and, as the chunky beats bump, she starts to sketch. Solomon eventually decides on a black-and-white checkered shirt, dark jeans and a pair of cool grey, black and infrared Jordans.

When they get to the City, they walk hand in hand past the merry-go-round, past the restaurants with ironic menus and pink lemonade in jam jars, past the bus interchange and straight to the noodle house. Scarlett's surprised when Solomon ushers her towards a table where a woman is already sitting. She's half lit, middle-aged, her profile leonine. She turns and her dark-brown eyes rest on Scarlett's teardrop tattoo. Then she smiles broadly, shaking Scarlett's hand and patting it with the other.

'You must be Scarlett. I'm Grace – Solomon's mum. So lovely to finally meet you. Solomona hasn't stopped going on about you,' she says.

Solomon looks down and smooths the front of his shirt.

'And here I was thinking he took all this time to get ready for me. I knew it – such a mama's boy,' says Scarlett.

Solomon's nervous, as if sharing a secret. He had mentioned in passing that he'd never introduced Georgie to his mother. The waiter comes over and he and Grace are soon engaged in banter about whether laksa is still Australia's Asian noodle soup of choice, or pho. 'That is not the question,' he says with a wink, 'the question is whether laksa is still Australia's *national dish* or not.'

Solomon squeezes Scarlett's hand under the table.

'So how's Aleks?' says Grace.

'Who's that?' says Scarlett.

Grace looks horrified. 'Aleks is Solomon's best mate. Shame on you Solomona.' She turns back to Scarlett and shares the gossip in a stage whisper. 'Aleks is in jail. He's having a rough trot. This one hasn't even visited him yet.'

Solomon coughs into his fist. 'I need a ciggie. Order me the duck laksa, okay?'

He leaves and they can see him pacing on the street, blowing smoke out hurriedly. Grace shakes her head. 'Samoan men. Useless with their emotions. It was difficult for me to understand as a *palagi,* until I realised there are some things that we're not meant to understand. What do you see in that boy, anyway?'

'Dunno.' Scarlett looks at him bunching his dreds up and says, 'Actually, he looks just like my ex boyfriend. First thing I noticed about him.' She puts a hand to her mouth, seemingly horrified, but Grace nods.

'I know what you mean. After Ulysses passed, I kept dating men who looked just like him. No one was the same, though. Are you still in touch with your ex?'

Scarlett shakes her head and looks away. 'So. Aleks.'

'Aleks is a good boy, a real sweetheart, in a way. A bit of a contradiction, really. Used to cop it hard as a kid. But every morning, he'd be up the stairs to our place, poking his moonface around the door. He'd help me with washing, with shopping. He used to say, "It's better to conduct business on an empty stomach – it makes a businessman work harder."' They laugh. 'I'd give him a two-dollar coin, and say he'd make a fine businessman once day. Now look. Him, those sons of mine . . . ' She looks despondent, then brightens. 'Maybe you can help Solomona a bit.'

Scarlett shakes her head. 'I'm not his saviour, Grace. I'm not his —' She cuts herself short, again realising she may have put her foot in it. This time, Grace looks slightly offended and sips her laksa in silence. Solomon returns.

'Hope you haven't been talking about me.'

* * *

Before they know it, it's nighttime. Grace politely declines drinks and leaves. Fairy lights are strung through the centre of town like neon kelp. Scarlett and Solomon end up at a steamy salsa club, surrounded by Latin Americans doing complicated, sensuous dance moves. Neither of them knows the music, but they start to dance. At first she leans away from the synthetic edge of his cologne; as they move, she can smell his sweat beneath it, and sees his mask falling away, just briefly, his eyes open and dark; then he seems to catch himself and the reserve builds up, then the charm.

She invites him back anyway.

* * *

'This isn't a porno, Solomon.'

'But last time —'

'That's what I wanted then. But not now. Slow down,' she whispers into his shoulder.

Music plays softly, Dwele and J Dilla's 'Dime Piece'. They kiss each other's scars as they make love, seeking them out in the dark, by touch.

There's usually a stillness in his eyes, an unwavering knowingness, but tonight he's trembling all over, almost shuddering, and his eyes are needy and warm-blooded, terrified and terrifying.

They lie breathing and the biro sketches flap on the wall. He looks to the side and sees that she has packets of medication beneath a desk lamp. He is going to ask her about them, when she says, 'So what do you think you'll do with this basketball thing?'

'Dunno yet.'

'You've never applied yourself to anything, have you?' she says tentatively.

He's thoughtful. 'Nah. Not for a long time.'

'You can't carry on with all that macho bullshit if you're gonna be teaching kids, Solomon.'

'I know. I know.' He sucks in a breath. 'It's just frustrating. The injury —'

'That's in the past.'

He rolls over and faces her. 'Yeh . . . I guess it's not just the injury. It was this huge kind of . . . feeling of betrayal. It's stupid. I felt like Dad betrayed me, by dying, then Mum stopped sending the money back to Dad's village after he died. And then shame at feeling all that. At my body. But this team. It's a chance to be proud again, maybe.'

'It is.' She laces her little finger in his. 'Maybe you can get funding for it? Shouldn't be so hard. A local business could sponsor the jerseys.'

'Now you're thinking.' He reaches over and holds up a DVD. 'I could never get into this. Kinda boring.'

'You don't like *The Wire*? Shit, boy. You coulda been the one.'

They smile.

16

The next day in the remand yard, Aleks falls in step with Clint, who is pacing back and forth, smoking. There are high winds, so strong that the men almost lean into the wind diagonally. The fellas behind them are talking about selling the Bupe medicine they have scored from the prison doctor and managed to regurgitate. A skinny bloke is moving swiftly among the pacing feet, picking ciggie butts off the ground to scrounge himself some tobacco.

'Ah, you're back, mate,' says Clint.

'So. What's the job?'

'You strapped for cash?'

Aleks keeps his face straight. 'Nah, just wondering, brother.'

They continue struggling against the wind as Clint speaks. 'Janeski, you're straight-edged, you're a businessman. I know you wouldn't fuck it up. If you want work, I got a cousin up in Sydney with the rock.'

Aleks nods and they quicken their pace. 'I'll keep it in mind. Thanks.'

The smell of a barbecue floats to them from one of the other yards, who must've spent their buy-up on it. He can't tell which. Aleks looks through the fence and can see that they've been cycled next to the Viet yard. There is an almost military formation around a certain man, who is immaculately put together, hair parted and shining, looking both bookish and stylish. He has his hand to his chin and his nails are trimmed. Aleks wonders if he has known war. He's quite young, so maybe he came in a boat as a baby. Aleks and Clint stride past.

'So what else is new, mate?' says Clint.

'Dunno. Been thinking I might go back to Macedonia.'

'That's what they all say.'

'I'm serious.'

'Well, you'll need money for tickets.'

17

Toby hasn't worn the jersey the last few days.

I finally ask him about it.

'I lost it,' he says.

'Lost it?' Some of the kids look around at the sound of my raised voice.

'Yeh.' Then he repeats it, like a mantra. 'Lost it. Lost it.'

I look away, spit, then turn to him and grab him by the shoulders. 'You've got to take more care with other people's . . . with *your* shit.' It takes all my effort not to slap him.

'Fuck you, cunt,' he says and runs away.

I can't help myself and my voice explodes out of me. 'Fuck you, too, ya ungrateful little shit.' He's already around the corner. I'm almost shaking and even shooting hoops can't get my mind off him. The other kids watch me as I shoot for a while then slope away. As I'm walking home, Muhammad jumps out from behind a bush, and I throw my fists up straight away. Seeing who it is, I awkwardly rub my hands together then let them hang by my side.

'Mr Amosa.'

'Solomon.'

'Solomon. Don't be too angry at Toby.'
'Why not?'
'It's not his fault. His mum gave the jersey to his stepdad.'
'What? Why? It's way too small for a grown man.'
Muhammad shrugs and he looks down.
He knows more,
    but I don't press him.
I think of Jimmy's dad, The Prince,
    and stories Mum told me about him.
The torment in those sort of homes
    goes way past what's rational.

Toby's back the next week, though,
    wearing unwashed and ripped clothes.

    'Jersey? What jersey?'

18

Aleks is waiting in line for the phone. A man in front of him is yelling instructions to put bets on the Canterbury Bulldogs. It usually calms down after twelve p.m., once people's phone lists have run out. The man swears, hangs up and walks away. Aleks picks it up and Sonya answers after several rings.

'How you going, baby?'

'Good, good. I miss you, Aleks.' Her voice sounds clearer.

'I miss you so much, too, baby.' He's smiling and he can tell she is, too. 'And Mila?'

'All right. At school. Getting excited for you to come home.'

'You still on the job hunt?'

'Yeah. Still no luck.'

'I'll be home soon, baby. I promise I'll sort everything out. Call that bloody lawyer of mine, all right? He hasn't even visited yet.'

'I will.'

He has a thought and then says, 'Categories?'

She laughs out loud. 'Sure.'

The last real holiday they had as a family was in Shellfish Bay, when Mila was only three. When she was asleep, he and Sonya would unfold an old card table on the tiled balcony and play drinking games with the two harmless stoners who lived next door. One of the games they'd play was Categories. Name a category (European cities, Olympic sports, etc.) and list things until there are no more. They'd play for ages, smoking ciggies and listening to hip hop and old rock. Once the neighbours left, he and Sonya would lie on the tiles, side by side, watching moonlight leaping from tile to tile like a fish and, more often than not, make love right there.

'Car brands,' she says, and the smile in her voice almost makes him weep.

'Toyota.'

   'Audi.'

      'BMW.'

         'Ferrari.'

When they finish the game, they're both laughing, but a line for the phone has built up. 'I'll be back soon, sweetheart. Don't stress.'

'I know. I won't.'

'I love you, baby.'

* * *

In bed, he holds his cross and tries to think of God. But other things take in the darkness above him: knives, fangs, men with the faces of wolves. He can almost hear the snicker and pop of their teeth. He imagines himself running with them, running together through a big, broken city.

Maybe these are his gods. Solomon didn't believe in God. Aleks felt he had to.

What will he do if he moves back to Macedonia? Start the vineyard his father always talked about? Maybe run a tour company. All these things, he figured, he could gain an understanding and mastery of. The Balkans were chaos, but there seemed to be some inner reason to it, perhaps, the energy that propelled it even less opaque than in Australia. Mila would kick up a fuss, but she'd come around. He's getting ahead of himself, though – first he has to concentrate on getting out.

Gabe wheezes and puffs and moans, and Aleks is sure the man is going to jump him. *Animal*, he thinks. *Fucken black bastard.* The man's disquieting eyes, his narrow presence, surely it was the portent of something murderous. Who knew what he was truly in for or what he'd done in his own country. Something savage, no doubt. Aleks had seen what war did to people, how it could be used to excuse the most hideous acts.

Even as he sleeps, he swears he can hear it, the breath like hellish bellows. He wakes several times during the night and begins to clench his fists, open and closed, open and closed, thinking he will first hit the man with a short arm, an elbow to the nose bridge, hard enough to break it, then he'll sit on him and beat him until the screws come. Maybe use the razor a bit. No, that wouldn't do. It'd mean more time. It might mean solitary. But the question remains – what if the man gets him first?

He falls asleep and has a dream. In it he shivers. The darkness around him is absolute and unquestioned. He hears a door opening but still there is no light, just murmuring voices. He's being guided through a corridor by a hand made out of smoke. He steps down and can tell by the uneven rocking beneath his feet and the sound of the water that he is in a boat. The boat moves swiftly, but he hears no oars or motor. He thinks to himself that there is a beauty, even a lustre, to darkness this entire.

A light appears on the front of the boat and it is soothing, diffuse, like the spoors of a dandelion. It is being cupped and protected carefully by a bearded man who seems very ancient, and Aleks thinks he might be a soldier or a priest. Surroundings are starting to appear in the meagre light and he can see small dwellings on the shore, and grapevines, and willows, and he can tell he is on a river; but which one, he can't be sure. Is it the Drim River, which flows through Struga and is black and full of eels? Or the river in the Town where he and Solomon used to fish? Whichever it is, it's flowing rapidly, and Aleks clutches onto the side of the boat. He is being propelled towards an enormous whirlpool, bigger than the eye of God or the throat of the devil.

He hears a sound and emerges from the dream upwards, as if from a pool, and is off the bed and on his feet. There's a streak of movement and Aleks is ready. He sees Gabe upright and twisting with a great energy, dancing even, eyes bulging. Aleks then sees a strip of bedsheet around the man's neck, self-tied and looped into an air vent, and how the man gurgles and fights against himself with a will to die that overtakes the will to live. Aleks leaps up and holds the man by the struggling legs, grunting. He feels very scared and tries to yell but the man hisses, 'No, no, no', and for some reason Aleks becomes silent. He grabs his razor from beneath his pillow and cuts the man down, who falls, gasping and crying. He pulls Gabe up and makes him drink water.

Aleks thinks to himself that somewhere, at that exact moment, someone had succeeded. But not here, not this time.

19

Toby's mum

Grubby chin and port-sour breath.
'What do you want with these kids, ay?'
'I'm teaching them to play ball.'
'Why?'
'Just giving something back. I used to be a proper ball player.'
'Couldn't make it, ay?'
'I had a bad injury.'
Toby is hovering behind her,
        embarrassed and unsure.

The other kids continue to shoot.

Her pig eyes,
black and watery,
        are searching my face,
but she doesn't seem present somehow.
'So now you teach kids?'

'Yep.'
'And give them presents?'
'I gave Toby a jersey. It was a one-off thing —'
She leans in close. 'You saying I don't know how to look after my son?'
'Not at all. I —'
'Then why not buy them all presents?'
    She grabs Toby by the arm
    and I step to her.
    She smiles a yellow, wobbly smile
    and is then screaming.
'I don't need anyone else to look after my boy.
    Especially not some fucken coconut,
    some FOB cunt.'

    As she hobbles away,
    dragging Toby,
    she yells, 'YOU FUCKEN PAEDOPHILE.
                FUCKEN KIDDY FIDDLER.'

When the kids leave,
I sit on the court,
and cup my face in my hands.

    It feels like it's gonna spill over the sides.

The next day

I get all the kids' addresses.
Over four hours,
on foot,
I visit each house
(well, mostly flats)
and tell every parent what I'm doing,

that it's on public property,
that it's not illegal
          and that they're more than welcome to come along.

Most of them are single mums,
who seem confused at first,
wondering what's in it for me,
but are generally pretty stoked.

One of them
offers to help out as an assistant.
Used to play for Queensland,
          she reckons.

When I get home,
Mum's cooking something delicious,
but I head straight to bed
and collapse onto it.

The next morning

'I call it the Ulysses,' says Jimmy. 'An adventurer. Feel like an
adventure?'
'Chur bro!' I say in a Kiwi accent.
'Red like fire, red like the devil,' says Jimmy.

Red polished to a high gleam.
Headlights perfect in design and shape.

I squat,
          run a finger over the bonnet with wonder,
          as if the paint might still be wet.

My bro Jimmy.
     Unbelievable.
Dad loved this car.

Tears in my eyes,
     spliff in hand.
I'm trying to quit smoking
but this is a special occasion —
     tomorrow I'll quit.
I hold it like a dart,
     puff, puff, pass to Jimmy
     who holds it between curled forefinger and middle
     as if he's checking his nails for dirt,
     then blows the delicious smoke
     towards its brother clouds above.

Soon we're driving,
     Mercury Fire in the back,
     no destination in mind,
just towards the ocean somewhere.

We pass antique towns,
     places that were once rough-and-tumble outposts –
     bushranger, massacre land.

The Dodge doesn't have a proper system,
     so I play tunes on my phone.
New Aussie shit –
     Astronomy Class,
     a Big Village compilation,
     Joyride's baritone over washed out synths,
     Seth Sentry's multi-syllabled wordplay.
It's not Jimmy's style but he smiles and lets it go,
seeing how I'm yelling the words.

We head towards Shellfish Bay.

It's a coastal town that swells
    during holiday season
    and washes out in low season.
The southern beaches,
    just out of town,
are the most pristine you've ever seen,
as if they've been forgotten by time and humanity.

'How's Scarlett?' Jimmy asks tentatively. We don't often discuss my
women.
'Good. I think.'
'Getting serious?' asks Jimmy.
'Nah, man. True playa for life.' I laugh.
'Don't fuck it up, bro.'
Instead of getting annoyed,
    I nod.

We pass through rain,
    a fine mist,
bizarre rocky outcrops and green fields,
    climb slowly up a small mountain
    and are soon in cool rainforest.
We stop to smoke at a place
where a white cross is wreathed with flowers.

A little girl and her dad died here in a car crash.

As we wind down the mountain,
we can smell the ocean for the first time,
the saltwater tang.

Jimmy says, 'The beach. That's the true Australia.'
'Fuck noath.'

As we approach Shellfish Bay,
we're practically bouncing in our seats.
Jimmy is driving with one hand
and he looks at the sky.
It's restless,
          charged with electricity and moisture.
Mercury barks out the window.
We pass stores
that advertise bait and the catch of the day,
scallops and grenadier and gemfish
          and we grin at each other.
We cross the long bridge into town.
There are heaps of people on the streets,
          mostly kids –
shaved skulls, boardies and wife-beaters or shirtless,
lean and sun-dark, pockmarked and tatted,
          smoking or doing kickflips,
some with sun-bleached curls,
          some grinning and skinny as skeletons,
heads ballooning and enlarged –
          their faces turn to us
as we drive past and some of them yell
and we realise that we've passed no cars on our way here,
nor were we overtaken.

We are the only car going into town.

We see the first burned-out shop
when we get to the main street.
A middle-aged man
is leaning against the blackened doorframe,

crying or coughing.
There are burnt sneakers swinging from lampposts
    like dead rabbits.
Inside the obscene shattered maws of shopfronts,
graffiti drips with no rhyme or reason:
    FUCK THE PIGS
    FUCK OFF WE'RE FULL
    ALWAYS WAS, ALWAYS WILL BE
    LISA IS A SLUT.

Cops, cops everywhere,
    blue and red lights flashing on corners.

The riots.
    We'd forgotten about that.

We get fish and chips regardless.
    The shopkeeper is sombre.
'Animals,' he says,
    but who's he talking about?

Kids wandering along in groups of five or ten,
with eyes flashing from beneath hoods.
There are still fishermen along the water,
lines feeding into the black tides.
I stop a kid.
'What's all this about?'
The lad eyes me, then says, 'Cops bashed a young Koori fulla. There's
video of it and everything.'
'You seen it?'
'Nah, but me cousin reckons he has. Boy died this morning.'

We drive further down the coast in silence.
Take a sandy track off the main road

and at last – the beach we're looking for.
It's long and windswept,
subtly curved for what seems like kilometres
    until it reaches a promontory far off.

The fish and chips are still warm and we eat,
    watching the choppy waves.
Mercury Fire hurtles down the sand,
    a grey hyphen on a white page.
We walk down the beach
and soon come across a cluster of sheds
just over the sand dunes,
fishing shacks, at least eighty years old,
made from odd bits of rusted metal.
Latrines out the back
and the smell of trapped seaweed and bait.
    No one is around.

'Look like they're from another world,' I say.

The stink somehow comforting.
No way this type of place will last.

'James. Jimmy,' I say, looking at him seriously.
'Yeah?'
'Trust me, bro, if he reaches out to you, don't meet up with that cunt.
Nothing good will come of it, bro.'
Jimmy looks pained, cornered, trapped. He won't meet my eyes and
doesn't speak. I persist.
'Seriously. He's lied about everything else. What'll be different now?'
Jimmy clears his throat and finally looks at me. 'Now, I'm a man.'

    We just sit, looking out over the choppy surf.

20

Jimmy drops Solomon at Scarlett's house and drives to his mother's flat. Grace has just finished a long shift at the nursing home and is methodically watering the few plants she has on the landing. She's staring across the road at a stately, heritage-listed house when Jimmy climbs the stairs. She wraps him up in a hug.

When Ulysses Amosa had his second stroke, he lost the faculty of speech. He eventually regained it, but moved slowly and often spoke Samoan. He spent much of his time sitting on the landing. Sometimes he would play chess with Petar Janeski. The two men would speak in gentle and respectful tones to each other, punctuated by roaring laughter. They'd sit for hours talking about their plans to return to their homelands. They seemed to have a crystalline understanding of their parallel situations, of a certain type of manhood, of the centrality of the church. They'd repeated their plans like a mantra, to the point where Grace and the children would roll their eyes. Other times, Ulysses would pray, as if preparing for death. Grace fussed around him, saying he was silly for even thinking of it. Remembering his own father's congregation, Ulysses sang hymns and his voice was a ribbon that insinuated itself throughout the flats. He didn't know that people listened; that it moved the residents of the flats to see such an enormous figure, rocking slowly back and forth, singing.

When Jimmy enters the flat, he sees the hole in Grace's flyscreen where a neighbour cut a circle out of it to make a veggie strainer. Her cat, Biggie, arches and sniffs Jimmy before rolling on his back and rubbing his head against Jimmy's ankle. Biggie then leaps up onto the ledge and starts dabbing lazily at a blowfly.

'Miau,' says Biggie the cat.

'Mraow,' says Jimmy.

Grace puts an LP on her cherished record player and soon they hear Stevie Wonder singing 'Golden Lady'. She closes her eyes in pleasure. Jimmy stares out the window, also savouring it. All the dust and haze of dusk is boiling upwards and now the sound of people returning from work, turning on televisions and microwaves and irons and the clatter of skateboards and the whir of bike wheels and the forms of cats creeping and leaping and sphinxed on fencelines. Grace talks non-stop.

'All the air-conditioners broke at work today. Blackout. In the middle of a bloody heatwave. Four days above forty degrees. You felt how hot it was – like hell. We tried our best, James, but it was just too much. Two patients died. One of a heart attack. I had just fed lunch to one of them – Suzy. You know what the last thing she said to me was? She said, "I learned a new word today." Isn't that magical?'

'What word?'

'I didn't ask.'

As she keeps talking, Jimmy takes his shirt off, and begins working on her broken TV. He's always been good with electronics; in fact, he's the only one of the boys who could ever make a half-decent beat on an MPC or a computer. He even sold a couple of them to local MCs, beats with sped-up classical samples and crispy drums. Grace watches him from the kitchen while she sprinkles red capsicum, lemongrass and onions all over the snapper. His skinny frame – all elbows and ribs, inherited from her – is caged around the television like a spider. He turns his glittering, slanted eyes to his mother.

'I think I saw my father the other day,' he says.

She looks up from the oven. 'Where?'

'Outside work.'

'Don't be silly. No one's seen him in years.'

'Yeah. I'm not even sure it was him.'

'Well, tell him to get *fucked* if he says anything.' Grace swears rarely, but the emphasis is sharp. 'Can't be him.'

They're silent then Jimmy says, 'What did you see in him, Mum?'

Grace drips some soy sauce onto the fish and then puts it in the oven. She busies herself making a gin and tonic and Jimmy thinks she won't answer, staring deep into the glass as if there's a shipwreck in there. Then she tongues a tooth at the back of her mouth and says distractedly, 'I lost a filling today. Bloody nuisance. If only —' She breaks off. When she speaks again, she almost sounds wistful. 'Was young and dumb, I guess. Just had this danger about him . . . Stupid. I knew that I'd never be bored when I was with him, you know?'

'How could you be with someone when you knew nothing good could come of it?' Jimmy's voice is harsh.

She smiles. 'You came of it James. You came of it.'

They hold each other's gaze. Then he smiles and turns the television on, the picture perfect.

'There you go, Mum.'

'Good boy.'

'No worries.'

He looks out the window and she continues to talk and set the table. She can't see but he is biting into his thumb so hard he draws blood. The sun goes down like a swimmer lowering herself into a lake and one by one the stars come out.

21

REPORTER: Now a heartwarming story. A young, local man trying to make a difference in his community, through basketball and hip hop. Solomon Amosa was a star basketball player who led his high school to two championships, and even represented Australia at under-sixteen level. A promising career was cut short by injury, but now Amosa is using his skills in a different way: to coach a basketball program for local children. Solomon, what gave you the idea to start Amosa's All-Stars?

SOLOMON AMOSA: Well . . . um . . . it just happened, really. Started teaching a couple kids how to shoot, how to dribble, then more and more started to turning up. Pretty organic, really – just word-of-mouth. Keeps them out of trouble, and me too.

REPORTER: So can you show us around a bit?

SOLOMON AMOSA: Well, this is the basic set up. Pretty simple, as you can see. They do all their drills on this court, running, shooting, dribbling. Three-on-three games, five-on-five sometimes. It's public property; so anyone who wants to volunteer, come on down.

REPORTER: And this tent over here?

SOLOMON AMOSA: A local party-hire shop donated this marquee; not every kid's into basketball, you know. Here, you can hang out, have a yarn, learn to draw or paint.

SCARLETT SNOW: You can rub the charcoal in with your thumb, see? Getting shadows right is the most important thing.

REPORTER: So what do the kids think?

TOBY McCARTHY: It's real fun and gives us something to do and that. Otherwise, we might get heaps bored and that.

MUHAMMAD KHAN: It's got everything we need – hip hop, basketball, mates.

SOLOMON AMOSA: I'm a uni dropout, you know, but I know about basketball and hip hop. I thought this could be the way I give back.

REPORTER: And you do it for free?

SOLOMON AMOSA: Yeah. I'm just here to help out, build a bit of a community. Community is important and I think it's something we've lost a bit. My father always said you should think about *we,* not just *I.*

REPORTER: And I've noticed the music never stops playing.

SOLOMON AMOSA: Never. The beat goes on.

REPORTER: Well, there you are. The beat goes on. Back to you in the studio.

22

Jimmy watches Scarlett from the side. If she notices, she doesn't say anything.

His eyes move down her hair to her shoulders, the shadow of stubble beneath her armpit, down to her ankles and painted toenails. He runs his thumbnail along his jaw. Mercury Fire bounds up to him and Jimmy scratches him behind the ears, speaking to him quietly, keeping his eyes trained on his brother's girlfriend.

Practice is underway and the kids are playing five-on-five, half court. Solomon is barking orders, strutting up and down the sideline. 'Box out, Muhammad! That's it!'

Whenever criticised, some of the ethnic kids have started saying, almost subconsciously, 'Oh, racist!' Solomon calls a halt to practice.

'Oi. Where did you learn to say that?'

'Say what?' says Muhammad.

'Using racist like that.'

'Dunno.'

'You know you'll get away with more shit if you call a teacher racist, ay?'

'I guess.' Muhammad is looking at his feet. Solomon raises his voice and faces them all.

'I don't wanna hear that shit, all right? I won't fall for it. I don't know what your teachers are like, but if I criticise you here, it's about *basketball*, it's to do with your attitude. Believe me, there's plenty of racism out there, but you start crying wolf all the time, when the real shit goes down, who the fuck's gonna listen? So don't bring none of that shit here – no mind games, no feeling sorry for yaself. Just play ball. You hear me?'

They all nod and the game continues. Jimmy is stunned and observes Solomon closely. Solomon, in turn, is watching the children with a sad expression, as if they have been failed somehow.

A group of young men turn up in a black SUV with tinted windows, all in various jerseys. They clamber out of the vehicle like stick insects. The appearance of one in particular is causing a commotion – a tall, lean Aboriginal fella. Jimmy looks to Solomon and sees his jaw muscles pulsing and that he's standing to full height. Jarryd Hooper must be back from America. There's something different about him, something even more assured and slick than the boy Solomon faced all those years ago. He shouts to Solomon immediately. 'We need another player. You up, bro?'

Solomon doesn't hesitate. 'Yeah, man. Let's do it. Kids – keep running those drills.'

As Solomon walks across the court, Jimmy realises it is not Jarryd but his younger brother Jack.

Jarryd had been Solomon's nemesis on the basketball court many years ago. He was explosive and cocky, just like Solomon. They said he could dunk over two shopping trolleys and was headed for a professional career. Solomon wanted his blood. A huge crowd had gathered to watch to two wunderkinds face off in the division one finals. Right from the start, Jarryd was having the better game, his six-foot-nine wingspan and vertical leap almost impossible to guard. Solomon gritted his teeth and defended him even closer and was soon forcing Jarryd to make a few errors. In one play, Jarryd went for a lazy fadeaway and Solomon stripped the ball from him and took it up the sideline as Jarryd chased him. Solomon wasn't to know it was the last time they would ever face each other.

'Fundamentals, Solomon, focus on the fundamentals!' his coach yelled from the sideline. Solomon ignored him and went into streetball mode, imagining the blonde hardwood was blacktop. He waited for Jarryd to catch up and get into position in front of him. Then he began to dance. He faked right. Jarryd didn't bite. He hesitated to the left and Jarryd went for it completely, swiping for the ball. Solomon's mask dropped, and in a harsh whisper he said, 'Be a man. Go on, cunt. Get me. Be a man.' He then crossed it back swiftly, with authority, and felt a surge within himself when Jarryd stumbled, his ankles twisting and unsure. Solomon drove to the hoop, went in for the dunk and, just as he pushed off his left foot, heard a sound as loud as a gunshot and felt the tendon corkscrew up the back of his leg. His world burst into flames.

Now, almost ten years on, with Jarryd playing overseas, his younger brother Jack and Solomon bump fists. If he is wary of Solomon, he doesn't show it. Jimmy is watching close, completely forgetting Scarlett's presence. The kids ignore Solomon's order to keep practising and gather around the side of the court, some sitting, some leaning on each other's shoulders. Solomon is acutely aware of the audience. This is a test. A song is playing from the speakers – 'Trillmatic' by the A$AP Mob and Method Man, which is new but sounds like an early nineties song. It then drops into a Nas medley. The deadly, driving baseline of 'N.Y. State of Mind'.

From the start, it's clear that Jack is even more of a prodigy than his brother. He has the sleek moves of a big cat. Solomon doesn't try anything fancy. A few drives, a couple of shots from the elbow, one particular no-look pass that gets *oohs* and *ahhs* from the sidelines. He looks slow and is beaten easily off the dribble. With the game on the line, someone flicks an alley-oop over his head and he jumps but doesn't come close to touching it. Jack appears on the other end, hovering against the sunset, his hand cupping the ball then crushing it through the hoop. Solomon is shining with sweat.

He gets talked into a second game and this time he's on Jack's team. A few people complain but, after seeing that Solomon's no longer a threat, no one argues too much. His teeth are bared, but not with aggression, just with simple, dumb pain and resilience. He's warming now, though, enjoying playing distributor, second fiddle to Jack's flash. The younger man's razor movements are controlled and precise. The two seem to understand each other and are working together perfectly, separate parts in a mobile. Jimmy feels as if he is a witness to true beauty, an awakening, and Jack seems to feel it, too, having to say nothing, just communicating with his eyes. Solomon executes a pinpoint shovel pass between two defenders and Jack finishes the alley-oop smoothly.

Toby looks proud and Muhammad looks disappointed.

'Oi! Get back to doing those drills!'

Jack claps him on the back. 'Shit, cuzzo. You still got those moves.'

'Nah, man. Has-been. Useless.' Solomon sounds defeated.

'Doesn't look like it.' Jack nods at the kids. Solomon slowly nods back. Jack approaches the kids.

'You listen to this bloke. He was the meanest baller I ever saw. Used to torture my bro, no bullshit. He'll teach you a lot.'

Toby asks, 'Why didn't you go pro, Solomon? Like Jarryd?'

The atmosphere becomes awkward. 'Dunno. Injury . . . nah, guess I didn't have it in me.'

Jimmy can see the look in Solomon's eyes is one of realisation – didn't love the game as much as I felt sorry for myself, kid.

* * *

Lightning outside but no rain or thunder, the sky perfectly clear.

Jimmy is lying on his bed, feeling flimsy, a photograph developing in a bath of chemicals. He's about to fall asleep when his phone rings. Private number.

'James.' It's a man's voice, distant.

'Who is this?'

There's no reply, just something like the sound of wind moaning over a gravesite or a limestone plane. Then there's complete silence, as if the line has gone dead. Jimmy's about to hang up, but then the man on the other end clears his throat.

'Who is this?' says Jimmy again.

'James, I'm worried about you. About your future. You have a great honour, but also a great hatred. You think the worst of the world. I know you long to be taken seriously – we all do. But wilfully bearing the burden of hate is no way to live.'

Jimmy recognises the voice. It's his father's. But it has a peculiar quality to it, as if filtered through water. It's deeper and more formal than he remembers it. He does not reply and waits for the voice to continue. There's a click and it does.

'If they get recognised, mistakes are an important part of life; they enable us to change. Change in all its forms is unavoidable – peaceful change, violent change, inevitable change, change that cannot be expected at all. I was once standing on a plain facing a mountain. It was full of headless statues. The sky was black, no stars, no clouds, no moon, but I could see everything somehow. Everything was different shades of black. Then I saw a black river moving over the mountain towards me. It was moving very slowly and could only have been a few inches high. In hindsight, I think that river was the river of history. It was perfect and without ripple; it was like glass, and turned the whole plain into a mirror. But there was nothing to reflect in the sky. I heard a moaning and realised the statues were not headless at all. They were living humans; they were every person I had ever met. And we were all trying to move, but the river was up to our ankles, and it was tar.'

The line goes silent again. It sounds like the previous message had been recorded and then played down the phone line. Jimmy laughs. 'Look man. I have work tomorrow. This shit isn't funny, ay. Whoever this is —'

'You know who it is.' For the first time, it doesn't sound like a pre-recorded message.

Jimmy runs his index finger over his lips, eyes downcast. 'Well, yeah, if it is, I don't wanna talk to ya.'

'I would have thought you'd want to talk to me more than anyone else.' Jimmy is silent.

'Tell me, James, do you know how to cook?'

Jimmy's caught off guard. 'Um . . . Nah, normally I just eat takeaway or microwave meals.'

'Next time we talk, I'll teach you how to cook a curry.'

Jimmy snorts. 'Yeh, right —'

The line goes dead.

23

A shear of sunlight comes through the window, caroms off a mirror and falls onto Solomon's skin. Scarlett puts her hand on his shoulder and feels a shock of heat and sweat. He doesn't move. Outside, a kid wheels by on a bike, crushing the scattered casuarina seeds and plums on the pavement. The day is already white hot. A man across the street is buffing a full-colour graff piece. A labyrinth of interwoven pastel letters. Each roll of paint erases them. A woman is hosing down the driveway of her new house, despite the water restrictions. Scarlett switches on her laptop and puts on the acoustic version of 'You Know Who You Are' by Oddisee. She turns it down low.

Pinned biro sketches and photographs, built up over a few years. She peels a sketch back and it reveals two old Polaroid photographs, which she unpins. They're both of a young Maori man with dreadlocks. In the first, he is standing shirtless out the front of the Early Bird bakery in Ponsonby, holding a potato-topped pie and grinning. His eyes are feminine and long-lashed. It's the height of a temperamental Auckland summer, and around him pollen is drifting like gold dust. In the second, she's holding him by the waist on the black sands of Piha Beach. Behind them is Lion Rock and two brave souls slicing through the surf. It has rained and the black sand is mottled as a jaguar's back. She carefully puts the photos into a drawer, then shakes Solomon.

'Hm?'

'Solomon.'

'Yeh?'

'Wake up. Let's go on an adventure.'

'A what?'

'Come on.'

He showers and dresses, smiling at her spontaneity. Scarlett packs a thermos of coffee and two sandwiches. On the highway they pass an industrial suburb where local crews have run rampant on the freshly primed concrete. Solomon names the Ironlak colours as they pass them – Smurf, Guacamole, Pose Sushi, Sofles Violence. Daily Meds are playing on the stereo. The industrial wasteland soon gives way to scrub and then there are hills, spotted with granite tors, immense boulders and outcrops that bubbled up like a molten gift from the earth. They turn off the highway down a set of smooth valleys, where black cows escape the heat under gum trees and a single white colonial cottage stands far off. Their phones lose reception.

They park at the end of a short gravel road off the main stretch, next to a sign that warns not to light fires. Scarlett slings her bag over her shoulder and stares at the trees, tapping on a front tooth with a red fingernail. Far off is the snarl of a dirt bike, but somewhere nearer they can hear a steady roar. They go down a trail through the bush and on either side are granite boulders, nobbled eucalypts and black she-oaks that wimple in the breeze. They emerge into a clearing and beside them is a waterfall, fifty metres high, each droplet visible and singular as a crystal on a chandelier, connected into a chain of water that lands on rock below before flowing off to pool in calmer hollows.

Directly opposite them are sheer cliffs, segmented into squares and rectangles by rents in the rock, streaked with bird shit and waterstain. Almost impossibly, out of the rock, shrubs and flowers grow, interspersed by dead eucalypts, their branches blackened and sharp, pointing upwards like minarets. These were burnt during the bushfires ten years ago, and all in between is new growth. Another ten years uninterrupted, they would be crowded from sight. Despite the numberless tones and transformations of colour, there is a unity to the landscape. And above everything, a fierce, blue sky.

Other people are there already – two women in hijabs, smiling as they take selfies, two bikies in sleeveless leather jackets leaning against a fence, and a redheaded man setting up a time-lapse camera on a tripod. Nobody speaks. Solomon motions for Scarlett to leave and she stares at him.

'We just got here.'

'Relax. Come 'ere. Supposed to be an adventure, isn't it? My second in a week, actually.' He smiles mischievously.

She follows him back down the track. He jumps a fence. She looks at the no trespassing sign for a second then shrugs. They walk through the bush, watching for snakes, taking their time. Scarlett rubs her hands over the subtle bodies of eucalypts as she passes and breathes the aromatic air. When they arrive at water, they follow it and are soon at the lip of the waterfall. They can see the couples below them, and the valley where the creek runs. Solomon stands dangerously close to the edge of the waterfall, arms outstretched. He looks like he is going to dive off but instead he sits. She joins him.

The summer heat has dried the moss on the rocks into white rosettes. A bearded lizard dances past them and over the edge of the rock into space. Solomon pours two cups of coffee from the thermos and sets them down. He takes Scarlett's left hand and places it in a groove in the rock. 'Feel that?' he says.

She nods, feeling the smoothness of it, the depth. 'What is it?'

'An axe-grinding groove. This is where the blackfellas came to teach their boys customs and to make axes out of stone. Grind the stone, wash it in the water as you worked, bind it, fix it with gum. They liked to use diorite. It's a type of green stone.' Scarlett looks at him sideways, surprised, but says nothing and continues to rub the groove with her thumb. 'And see down there? Those caves? That's where bogong moths hang. Millions of em. Someone once told me when they leave the caves and fill the sky, it goes black, that's how many there are. And hundreds

of blackfellas would come up every year and feast on em. Imagine that.
This country, right here, this feeling – must've been what it was like
everywhere. So much beauty, so much loss. The land has a soul. You can
feel it, right? A memory. I guess like all of us it wants to forget, but it
can't.' He looks shy and splashes his hand in the water. 'I dunno. What
the fuck do I know?'

She places her hand on his and points with the other. 'Are there cave
paintings down there?'

'Nah. Well, there might be. Doubt it. Not many in this part of the
country.'

'Too bad. Still, it's cool you guys learn about this stuff at school. My
ex told me that Aussies barely teach any Aboriginal history.'

'They don't.'

'Where'd you learn then?'

Solomon doesn't speak. It is as if he hadn't heard. The waterfall roars
and cockatoos screech high up in the leaves. Then he says, 'Jimmy's dad.
He taught me.'

'Jimmy's dad?'

'Yeh. After my old man died, Jimmy's dad appeared. He just kept
hanging around. He'd visit Mum when we were at school and mostly
she'd tell him to fuck off; but sometimes she'd give in and he'd stay for
a cuppa and have a yarn. There was something she couldn't resist, even
after all the shit he put her through.'

'He beat her?'

Solomon shakes his head vigorously. 'Nah, nah. I don't think so.
There might have been the threat of that, but I don't reckon it ever
happened. More like a constant torment, she said. Jealousy. Saying she'd
lived the life of a whore before him. He used to take her credit card and
buy and buy and buy. A closest full of unworn clothes. A hoarder. Mum
told me once that he grew up real poor, so she kinda forgave him for all
of it, you know? Until my dad came along and said enough was enough.'

'Your dad knew him?'

'Hell, yeah. They were best mates. When Dad first got here from
Samoa, they worked in the same kitchen. He even gave Jimmy's dad the

nickname The Prince, because he said he was descended from royalty. At first it was affectionate, then it became a bit of a gibe. Then Dad started to notice how his stories weren't consistent, how manipulative he was, how he treated Mum. The cunt wasn't even by her side when Jimmy was born. So Dad began to console her, like, just as friends. The rest is history.' He smiles, looking away.

'But when did he tell you about the waterfalls?'

'So one day, after Dad died, The Prince comes around and he's real excited. He tells us there are these waterfalls just out of town, only a forty-minute drive. He said he'd take us there. We'd never heard of any waterfall near the Town, thought it was another bullshit story of his; but for some reason Mum says we should go with him, so that was it. When we got here, he could name every plant, every bird. He told us as an Aboriginal man it was important to know the language of your forefathers, even if everyone said it was dead. Flowers – *gambarra*. Ironbark – *thirriwirri*. Stone – *gurrubang*. He showed us these axe-grinding grooves.'

'So Jimmy's dad's Aboriginal?'

'Doubt it. He said he was at the time, but.'

'What do you mean?'

'Aw, man.' Solomon exhales and speaks slowly. 'Jimmy's dad . . . is a mystery. Nobody knows what his background is. Sometimes I wonder if he even knows. A born liar, like I said. He changes his story all the time. The next time I met him he said he was Pakistani. When we were kids, he said Greek. Once the story was even that he was Irish.'

'Pretty different, aren't they?'

'Totally, but his looks are ambiguous – he could pass for anything. A chameleon.'

'Like Jimmy,' Scarlett nods.

'Exactly. The weird thing, though, was that all the shit he said about the land, the names of trees, this place, I looked it up and he was spot on. And later with Islam – he knew it all. I still don't get it. But back then, to me, it was kind of a novelty. I never liked him, but I realised I could learn shit from him if I just listened.'

'And Jimmy?'

Solomon laughs, but it sounds like a snort. 'I can't begin to tell you about the hatred Jimmy has for his old man. The *shame.* It consumes him. Always has. A lifelong obsession. To find out what his ethnic background really is.'

'He can just do a DNA test, surely.'

'That's what I say. But to him, it's more than that. He wants to hear it from his dad's mouth. And Mum could never understand why; why wasn't he content just to know her race, why did he have to know his dad's? But Jimmy couldn't let it go. Not knowing what he is has become what he is.'

'Wow. That's a paradox. Like your only home being homelessness.'

'Exactly.'

24

Jimmy is thinking of every movie he's seen about prison and wonders if anyone has escaped from this one. The security guard can't stop yawning. The jail smells freshly painted and the overwhelming feel, beneath the boredom and mundaneness, is of fear. Jimmy passes through security and is told to remove his belt. He gets thumb-printed and searched. He wonders if someone might check up his arse. Do they actually do that in jail? He hopes he wiped properly. The security guard pulls the two photos out of his pocket and examines them, suddenly attentive. One of the photos he hands back, the other he holds up. 'What's this?'

'Um. Art.'

'Did you get a permit for this?'

'Yes.' Jimmy tries to hold the guard's eyes but can feel himself wavering.

The security guard examines it again and then bends it back and forth, back and forth. Jimmy wants to snatch it from the cunt.

'It's a present . . . A special present for my friend.'

'Looks like graffiti to me. Graffiti's illegal, mate. Not allowed in here, I'm afraid.' The man smiles.

'But I —'

'Sorry.'

Jimmy looks away so the man can't see that he's on the verge of tears. He drags his feet as walks into the meeting area, shoulders slumped, but smiles when he sees Aleks.

There's glass between them.

'What's going on, mate?' Jimmy shifts in his seat uneasily.

'Same shit.'

'Been doing anything fun?'

'Fun?' Aleks smiles. 'Nah, just trying to sort shit out. Bloody lawyer finally came through. Ten thousand bucks later. He'll get me out of this mess, but.'

'Dope.' Silence. Two other men are talking with low voices. Jimmy grins crookedly, then quotes one of their favourite lines from *Chopper*. 'Well, ya really landed on ya knees, didn't ya, mate?'

They both laugh so hard they're nearly crying. The security guard comes over and quiets them. Rubbing tears from his eyes, Aleks says, 'So, what 'bout you?'

Jimmy raises his eyebrows, grins and produces the remaining photo.

'Bullshit! Fuck, that looks nice, bro. Muscle car! Dodge Coronet?'

'Yep.'

'Fark. Where'd you get the cash?'

'Saved up. Drove it here even. Goes like a dream.' Jimmy's never looked so proud.

'Fark me dead. Good on ya, cuz.' They sit grinning.

'Solomon loves it.'

Aleks stops smiling. Silence, then, 'Any good music coming out?'

'Heaps. Young gun from Melbourne called Dr Flea. Raven. Prime. Bunch of gangsta shit from Sydney.'

'Gangsta shit, huh?' Aleks looks away.

'Yeah. And there's heaps of tours happening. You gonna be out for the Sin One show?'

'Should be.'

'Me and Solomon gonna try go but he's always with his new missus.'

'How's Solomon?' Aleks is still looking away, seemingly distracted by something on the wall.

'Good. He's trying to start this youth basketball team. Dunno. Never seen him like this before.'

'Good for him.' Aleks looks back and Jimmy can see that he's hurt.

'He wanted to come, bro. Serious.'

'Yeh.' Silence again.

'So. Made any mates in here?' Jimmy asks, at last.

Aleks is about to snort but then he looks thoughtful. 'Actually. My cellmate. Sudanese bloke. Tried to top himself a while back. He wouldn't stop crying, bro, for hours. Eventually calmed him down, got the story out of him. Walked all the way across Sudan, in and out of reffo camps. Poor bastard swallowed ten condoms of heroin in exchange for a plane ticket. Got caught in Sydney airport, shat the bubbles out. They gave him a bunch of time, then they're probably just gonna deport him.'

'Jesus. No wonder the poor cunt tried to top himself.'

'Tell me about it. Been talking to him every night, telling him everything will be all right. He's good to talk to, brother. Good listener.'

Jimmy doesn't know if this is a dig at him and Solomon, so he doesn't reply. They both sit thinking, then Jimmy smiles. 'We did a piece for ya. Security guard confiscated it.'

'Cunt.'

'I know, ay?' Jimmy shakes his head. 'Was gonna be a surprise.'

'All good, brother. Cheer up. Where?'

'You know that place on the edge of town? Fuel depot?'

'Ooooh, good spot. Killer,' says Aleks.

Jimmy, with his right fingertip, draws the piece on the glass, going through the process, explaining the colours, the fight with the seccas. Aleks lets the piece appear in his mind's eye. It is radiant, shining outwards like a multicoloured sun.

* * *

'One bottle down, another bottle down, GO!'
        Tornts' aggressive voice is bursting from his headphones.

Jimmy is sitting by himself
        at a bar in the City,
a glowing metropolis
        of empty glasses and bottles
        in front of him.
He thinks it looks like something
        from a sci-fi movie.

He stands up
        and shakily goes to a table
        of people who went to school with Solomon.
They're all dressed in suits,
having been to a wedding.
He hovers at the edge of the group
        until one of them recognises him
        and waves him into the group.
The man is gym-built,
the tux fitting like cloth pinned over blocks of stone,
        smoothing down a merlot tie.
'This is Amosa's brother!
Amosa was the best basketball player ever, remember?
So athletic he could've been in the 1st XV.
A Samoan who doesn't play footy.
First time for everything, ay?'
The man raises a beer to the light,
                drains it,
                        and the rest follow.
He continues,
        'Yeah, he was always going on about all that culture stuff.'
'Where is Solomon?' someone else asks.
'Fuck Solomon,' says Jimmy.

He means it as a joke but it comes out harsh.
    Mutter, mutter, mutter.
Jimmy is watching a leggy, tanned brunette
    in a saffron dress,
holding a glass of red wine
    with three fingers and thumb.
A creature from a world Jimmy has no passport to.

The clean-cut bloke whispers out the side of his mouth:
    'She's a newsreader in Sydney now, mate.
    Looks good, ay? Talk to her. Seriously,
    she likes tall guys.'
Jimmy scrolls through his phone then stumbles over.
    'Hello.'
    'Hi.'
It takes her half a second
    to scan him and figure out
    all she needs to know.
She asks anyway, 'What school did you go to?'
Jimmy replies and she nods,
before turning her head,
    ever   so   slightly,
    away.
He looks puzzled,
    and asks in a loud, clear voice
    'Do you like cars?'
holding out a picture of the Dodge on his phone
in one hand like a child cupping a butterfly.

She continues to stare away,
    at a point somewhere far in the distance –
    something of intense interest there.

He puts the phone back in his pocket

and stumbles away,
    hearing laughter in the background.

He feels someone run up next to him.
    It's the clean-cut guy,
    who drops a hand on his shoulder.
    'Sorry about that, mate. She's a snob.
    No hard feelings, ay? Say hi to Solomon for me.'
Jimmy shrugs the hand away.

The game's wired,
    just like Dialect said in his song.

But Jimmy strides ahead with one purpose in mind.

He goes down a set of stairs
    with a single halogen globe swinging
    and he's in a small club.
The beat
    of ScHoolboy Q 'Man of the Year'
    uncoils beneath him like a serpent,
    then wraps him up,
    swallowing him.
    He is drenched in wave after wave of frosty synth,
    bouncing, running his hand along the skittering drum pattern,
    falling headlong into the bloodstream.

'I'm the man of the year!' he yells.

* * *

Jimmy's in line for burritos
    behind an enormous figure,

whose head is nearly at the height
>   of a light fitting.
Jimmy's eyes are closing,
>   tiredness and liquor
>   taking hold,
>   and he trips into the man,
who turns sharply
>   and catches him beneath the armpits.

Jimmy is suddenly looking into a pair
>   of surreal, bright eyes,
>   so green they could be Ironlak Cameleon.

Sin One.

Before he realises it,
he's shaking the man's hand,
reeling off his favourite moments from Sin One's career.
Instead of freaking out,
the enormous man smiles kindly,
'Wanna sit down, bro?'
Jimmy nods.
'What's your name?'
'Jimmy. Well, James.'

They begin to talk.

Sin One tells Jimmy
he can see pain in him,
but resilience too,
that he has to work hard
and leap the hurdles in front of him.
Sin One tells him of his own struggles in America,
where people treated him like an idiot or second-class citizen,

reminding him constantly that the US
was the mecca of hip hop.
Jimmy tells him about his troubles with his father,
about buying the car.
He scrambles in his pockets for headphones,
and plays one of his beats for Sin One,
who bobs his head.
Sin One tells Jimmy that he is true hip hop,
someone who has made something from nothing,
made beauty from the bricks.
Jimmy grabs a napkin,
a perfect white square with a cactus logo on it,
and hands it to Sin One.
Sin One signs it with a flourish,
and the ink soaks into the paper,
        but the tag is still visible.

SIN ONE

On the way home,
Jimmy can't help smiling
and keeps reaching into his pocket
to touch the napkin.

He tries to remember
the reason Sin One named himself that –
it wasn't a graff thing,
even though it sounded like one.

It was something about the original sin of Australia.

In the morning,
        dozens of hellish belltowers
        are clanging in Jimmy's head.

Then he remembers the signed napkin
      and smiles.

It isn't on his bedside.
He leaps up,
unsteady, still a bit drunk,
and begins to turn his room upside down looking for it.

Eventually,
he finds a similar napkin
      a perfect square with a cactus on it,
         but it isn't signed.

25

The night before he dies, Ulysses dreams of a great vaʻa, *a huge dugout canoe full of men carving moonlit iridescent waves led by a navigator on the prow. Ulysses is one of the oarsmen, his muscles full of their previous strength, hauling a massive wooden paddle. Jimmy and Solomon huddled at his feet. He hears the navigator yell that there are no clouds to guide by, that he is searching for the perfect channel but can't seem to find it. Ulysses is sweating, sweating so much that he thinks he will pass out. It is inexplicably hot. He looks up and sees that where there should be ocean there is only fire.*

26

A biro sketch

When she hands it to me,
her eyes are green flags –
      fear? love? warning?

It's me
on a black sand beach,
clouds roiling,
the whole drawing black and white,
red paint drips on the border.

No chick's ever done something like this for me,
besides a sickly R&B song
      a girl made in high school
      called 'Big Brown Boy'.

Jimmy says it looks nothing like me.

Can't let him get me down, but.
Not today.
I've got a plan,
a present for the kids
        for their hard work.

I fold up the picture neatly.

Scarlett and I have never been to the beach together.

Dead bees

The streets are covered in them.
No one knows why.
Jimmy says that madness is a snowball.

My lungs are growing

Tar and nicotine out,
the world in,
        the summer sky and all the good that's in it.

My bro reckons I'm walking different, talking different.
I wouldn't eat Oporto's with him yesterday
        cos of my diet
and he almost tried to fight me.

The kids are practising layups
and I'm kicking pegs out of the earth
on the sideline.
        What are these things?

Toby's not here much.
When he is,
he shoots the ball like shit on purpose,
looks at his feet when he runs.

Today,
he is facing the road,
cross-legged,
pinching the heads off daisies and dandelions.

He looks back at the court
and our eyes meet.

That look.
    Like Jimmy.

The next day,
he doesn't come.

Or the day after that.

But Amosa's All-Stars are booming.
Sponsored by a local kebab shop,
we have red jerseys now.
    Slick as,
logo designed by a graff writer I know.

My palace,
  my kingdom.

I am not just fluid,
    I am fluidity.
I am not just immortal,
    I am immortality.

27

'Good day?' from bottom bunk to top, Gabe directs his question to Aleks's reflection in the stainless steel mirror. The television is on. With an Australian flag behind him, Crawford announces that he will contest for a seat at the next election, if he gets the backing of his party. Aleks changes the channel and a white comedian in blackface comes on.

'Good? Dunno about that, brother. Busy, but. Been on the phone most of it.' Aleks vaults down off the bunk and squats on the floor excitedly, using a stiff index finger to draw imaginary lines. 'Here, brother. Here's where I could plant the vines. And here, I could build a workshop to process the grapes.'

'Have you ever been a farmer?'

'Nah, but my granddad was. I'd learn fast enough. As long as you take pride in hard work, the rest follows, brother. What did you do, back home?'

'I was a teacher. A poet, too.'

Aleks is too lost in his own thoughts to register Gabe's words. He spreads his arms out as if to balance himself then stands up, gymnast-like, before leaning against the bunk. 'I wonder. I wonder.'

'I'll see my own homeland soon enough. Once I finish my sentence.' Gabe looks away and coughs into his hand; then, with a teacherly, inquisitive tone, asks, 'Sorry for my ignorance, but what is a Macedonian? I only know Alexander the Great.'

'Good start.' Aleks smiles then scratches his temple. 'Ah, brother. It depends who you ask. The Balkans is no easy place to get your head around. Ask an Albanian, a Maco, a Bulgarian and a Greek and they'll all tell you different shit.' His voice becomes fervent. 'People have tried to fuck us over again and again, whitewash our history, steal our land.'

'Like the Aborigines?'

Aleks wrinkles his nose. 'Dunno. Never thought about it like that . . . Nah.'

They sit in silence, but it's comfortable now. Somebody is yelling, far away and behind that is the sound of a high wind, a great river of turbulent air. Aleks thinks of Torture Terry, that now he is on the outside, somewhere, wreaking havoc on the population.

Aleks draws the bead from its hiding place in his sock. He rolls it between his palms as if it is a piece of dough, and he imagines it becoming larger and larger, as big as the planet Earth itself. Gabe observes him.

'What is that bead? It's very beautiful.'

Aleks looks up sharply. 'It's . . . something I've had for a long time, brother.' He turns it and the gold flecks throw little speckles of light on his knees. 'I done something very bad to get this bead.'

He thinks of the day he first saw it. A woman named Stephanie had moved into the flats above Aleks and below Jimmy and Solomon. She had a little daughter with her named Juliet who Jana Janeski got along with very well. Stephanie was from Sarawak, and was Malaysian-Chinese. When she was cooking with *belacan* (prawn paste), Aleks' family was making pickles and the Korean family next door to them were making kimchi, Grace would hold her nose in mock disgust and say, to each of them, 'I can't believe you can eat that stuff!' But she got along enormously well with Stephanie; in fact, everyone did. She was famously resourceful and would take broken tables and chairs from skips and make them brand new. And she was a storyteller:

'This is an ancient bead. It was made in Venice, nearly a thousand years ago. Back then beads were traded across continents – Africa, Asia, Europe. They were beautiful, durable, easy to transport. Something's worth is not just its monetary value. It's what it means to its owner. But it is beautiful, no? See the gold flecks inside the blue. This bead was in a chest that had taken a long journey and it was the only one that survived. You can hold it if you want to. When they first got to my country, the land of my birth, Borneo, the tribes people coveted them. To the tribes people, the beads meant wealth, standing and power. The most valued were named *lukut sekala* amongst the headhunting tribes. These ones were worth the same as a man's life.' *The same as a man's life.* Aleks' eyes widened as she said that and the bead fell into his palm.

She said that she was going to give it to Juliet on her sixteenth birthday. Juliet, who would one day become Jana's lover, who Aleks would strike again and again out of shame, from whose neck Aleks would seize the bead. The sounds of beatings were common in the flats then, punctuating the night like horn stabs on a beat, but this one was different. Aleks' first true transgression.

'We have all done bad things in this life. Sometimes, they can't be helped,' says Gabe.

'I wonder. This one, brother, this one could've been. But there was something pushing me towards it. It's like something was holding my hand when I did what I did. But once I got my hands on that bead, I couldn't let it go, like it holds all my badness, like *magic*.'

Gabe runs his right thumb over a thin scar that passes from the centre of his forehead, around an eyebrow and down to his chin, level with his lips. 'When I was on the plane here, it was like hell. My first plane trip ever. But then, as the plane got lower, I saw trees and flowers and green squares and blue rectangles. I later found out they were swimming pools. Sydney summer – the air, the sky. For a second, I thought that my life had been transformed. Then a man in uniform appeared and said, "Come this way, sir. It'll only take a minute." That minute turned into ten years, like *magic.*'

A bird cries in the distance, though it could be a hinge.

'Do you think people can change?' says Aleks.

'It depends.'

'On what?'

'On whether life lets them.'

28

Church

Fresh slacks,
     black-mirror shoes,
        scratchy collar,
           shaved neck.

    Patience.

I sit in a pew at the back.

The service is in Samoan
so I can't follow,
but the hymns are lovely.

No greater pressure
on a Samoan than to be religious, ay?

Someone slides in next to me

and begins to translate the service
into my ear.

It is Viliamu,
a distant cousin.
Most of the Samoan fam
went to Brisbane and Liverpool,
but there's a few in the Town
and he was always my favourite.
He doesn't look surprised to see me,
even after all these years.
A little heavier set but still
good looking and fresh skinned.

That's what no drink, ciggies or drugs does, ay?

I knew I'd find him here.

My palms are sweaty
and I can't stop thinking
of the way American rappers say 'chuuuuuch!'

The sermon:

'Even the wilderness and desert will be glad in those days.
    The wasteland will rejoice and blossom with spring crocuses.
Yes, there will be an abundance of flowers
    and singing and joy!
The deserts will become as green as the mountains of Lebanon,
    as lovely as Mount Carmel or the plain of Sharon.
There the LORD will display his glory,
    the splendour of our God.'

There is thunder and lilt in the Reverend's voice,
a rapper-like flow that builds and builds.

'With this news, strengthen those who have tired hands,
    and encourage those who have weak knees.
Say to those with fearful hearts,
    "Be strong, and do not fear,
for your God is coming to destroy your enemies.
    He is coming to save you."
And when he comes, he will open the eyes of the blind
    and unplug the ears of the deaf.
The lame will leap like deer,
    and those who cannot speak will sing for joy!
Springs will gush forth in the wilderness,
    and streams will water the wasteland.'

Sunday lunch

The Reverend Timothy Kevesi
has hands as dry as blotting paper,
wrinkled in the forks.

I tried to excuse myself
but he insisted I eat.

His wife mentions
'Jesus' and 'The Lord'
at least ten times
over the delicious array of foods
donated by the congregation.
She and Viliamu
do most of the talking.

I listen quietly,
but catch the Reverend looking at me.

His voice rich and steady:

'You look so much like your father, Solomona.
Not just the face, the spirit.
It's uncanny.'

I pounce in the carpark

'Cuz, I need your help.'

A quizzical look from Viliamu.
          'Course, *uso*. Anything.'

I begin to explain about
          Amosa's All-Stars,
          the kids,
          how I want to reward them with an *'umu*
but I have nowhere to do a ground oven.

That I don't know how to do it.

'Pssh. That all? Thought you were coming to me with a moral question.
Too easy, cuz.' Then playfully. '*Tsk tsk*, a Samoan who doesn't know
how to do an *'umu*. Shame.'
I grin. 'Tell me about it. Had to come to my best man. Thanks, *uce*.'
He hops into his car. 'See you next Sunday, then?'
I crack my thumb knuckles.
'To be honest, this ain't my buzz, bro. I just . . . never got that feel, ay.
Never had that fire like you.'

He gives me a strange look
and I start to apologise
but instead he smiles.
'Each to his own. Lucky you're in Aus, though.
Wouldn't get away with that in Samoa.'

'Yeh, I know.'

His car throws up a ghost-shaped
          plume of dust
that dances away into the summer.

29

Clint and Aleks are watching the movements of birds across a hellish sky. Men around them are playing cards and chess; others just pace the yard, anything to relieve the boredom. A man walks past with a Bible quote tatted along a shank wound.

'Dunno, bro. It sounds good. We'll see.' Aleks is biting his bottom lip. 'Might be time to go straight.' He is distracted, having been composing a letter to his sister in his head. He is set to get out soon, and feels himself tilting every which way, like an egg running over a pan.

'Fair nuff. Remember this number then, just in case.'

Aleks stares at Clint as he recites the number, and then silently repeats it several times. He won't forget it.

30

The ʻumu

A pyramid of hot stones
        tumble
    into a thick layer.

Dense, stinging smoke
and Viliamu barking orders
    at five church mates.

A pig,
eyes closed and mouth bloodied,
stuffed with leaves and hot stones,
sits almost patiently,
    wrapped in wire mesh.

The men place thick discs of taro
    directly onto the stones
        around it,

then *palusami* wrapped in foil.

'Sorry, *uso*! If we were back home,
would've used the real thing,
not coconut cream from a can!'

I smile.

Dad used to say that.

Before the end,
he used to reminisce more and more,
about *limu*,
grape-like seaweed you could pick by the bunch in the reefs,
about *pone*,
the angel fish that could be eaten raw with seawater,
its flesh bitten off the bone,
stripped there and then when the fisherman came in.

Viliamu has marinated
some chicken and fish
and he smiles at Muhammad's dad,
nodding to show that he is cooking it
separately from the pig.

Muhammad's dad
doesn't seem to care
and is sipping on a beer.

The kids lean in to watch.

I've cut my dreds short
with a nice fade up the side.
The square basslines and live instruments

of 'The 'Umu' by Koolism
bouncing from the speakers.
Seems appropriate,
even if Hau is Tongan.

Scarlett sips a beer,
speaking rudimentary Samoan to some of the aunties,
who look well chuffed.
She learnt some at school,
she reckons.
      Amazing.

Soon someone has a guitar out
and is shouting, 'Turn that rap crap off.'
The sky is darkening,
being played into night
with each strum.
      Several voices harmonise straightaway.
Mum sways and sings along,
smiling serenely,
wrinkles appearing at the corners of her mouth,
and it occurs to me
that she is entirely heroic –
      her whole life an act of balancing, outlasting,
        of living out her name.

A hand on my shoulder.
      Viliamu.

'This is a good thing you're doing, *uso*.'
'Ah, it's just ball. A bit of fun.'
'No. *Tautua*. Service. It's important, it's who we are. *O le ala o le pule, o
le tautua*. The way to leadership is in serving.'
'Yeh. Dad used to say that.'

An auntie is dancing now,
twisting and unfurling her hands,
her big frame controlled and delicate.

'He'd be proud of you right now. He was a good man. Used to send a
lot back to the village.'
I feel guilty. 'Do you send any?'
Viliamu nods slowly. 'Yeh. Yeh, I do. Wonder about it sometimes
though, cuz, ay.'

We are all music
and smoke and night and now.

The world

The world is opening up and stretching out,
being sketched in biro
        and coloured in.

My skin, too.

The needle goes in –
I register it,
        accept it.

Scarlett is tattooing a kite on the back of my arm.

Each puncture
is beauty and sadness,
is fear of falling back into bad habits,
is furious freedom,
is knowledge I can change,

that I have changed.

Beneath our feet,
tectonic plates are gliding,
        shifting.

31

It is Aleks' last day in prison.

He wants to wish Gabe good luck, although he knows the man needs much more than that. He thinks of giving him the cross or a hug, but instead he speaks. The words a cascade.

'Violence.

'Anyone can do it, brother. Just depends on the village you grew up in. And chance. Dunno . . . When I first got to Australia, I used my fists because no one could understand me, because they used to point at me and say, "Wog! wog! wog! wog!"

'It became power, but I was powerless to control it. Figure that fucken riddle out. But that doesn't explain everything. I've always had it. It starts as a feeling in your neck, in your spine, tingles all the way up and then it burns, uncontrollable, and it has to get out somehow.

'All of a sudden you're bashing some cunt and, if there was no reason to, you make one up; you can't stop, you don't want to. And when you're finished, brother, your hands are bloody, your dick is hard. The closest I've ever got to poetry.

'But that's changed in me now, brother.

'I won't sell my soul for no one again. Not my wife, not my daughter.

Before, my soul was out for rent. If it was for my family it didn't matter how bloody my hands got. Hell exists here. I've burned on earth, many times. And I won't do it again.'

He looks up at Gabe and his eyes are grief-filled. His voice lifts.

'No more, brother. Cos there's only three types on this earth – the winners, the losers and the dead.'

32

I'm walking up the street,
ball against my hip,
watching an African woman
carry her washing on her head.

Daniel Merriweather in my headphones.
What happened to that dude,
so soulful with all his angel-headed devils?

Scarlett just told me some news.

'I've been offered a full art scholarship in Perth.'
'What are you gonna do?'
'I'm gonna take it. But what are you gonna do?'

Fuck, man.

Cherry-blooded summer,
maybe the perfect time for a new start.

A sheer wall –
the whole year
     faces it.
Do you climb it and peek over?
Graff every inch of it?
Knock it the fuck down?

The court will give me an answer.

All I have to do
     is breathe and run,
turn my limbs into a Kevin Durant-style
lava-hot slingshot,
and hurl shooting stars at the basket.

The smile drops off my face.

A bloke is hammering a sign
into the earth.

'Development Notice.'

'What the fuck's this?'
He looks at me like an idiot. 'We've been surveying it for months,
mate.'
'What's it for?'
'Block of flats.'
'Why here?' My voice high-pitched.
'Not my decision, mate. It's business.'

I haven't cried in years,
not since Dad died,
but there it is.
I turn away, head down,

and I feel like a shuddering prow,
and I can hear him back at work,
then laughing into his phone
as if I'm not even there,
and I'm walking away, away
and I hear him yell at me from afar:

'It's just a bloody basketball court, mate.'

33

Jimmy is lying in bed, imagining that he's a swinging door between a room lit by a blinking red light and a garden filled with limbless, headless statues. His phone rings and he answers it with eyes closed.

It is the voice. 'James?'

'The fuck do you want?' Jimmy's voice is slow, not yet awake.

'Are you hungry? Are you hungry, James?'

Jimmy touches his belly. As if by magic, he is overwhelmed by hunger, a massive expanding balloon in his gut. He nods.

'I thought so,' the voice says. 'What do you have in the fridge?'

'Nothin.'

'Well, get up. I told you I would teach you how to make curry. Do you like curry, James?'

Jimmy wants to hang up but the hunger is unbearable, so instead he nods. He gets up in his sweaty clothes and puts on shoes. He walks to the supermarket and it's open but empty. Despite the bright colours, it reminds him of a desert. The voice directs him down the aisles and orders him to buy vegetables and spices. Jimmy pays for it all at a self-service register. As he walks away, he realises he didn't see another person in there.

* * *

'I want you to put the rice on, James.'

'I've never cooked rice before.'

'Never cooked rice?' The voice is horrified, but turns jovial. 'No worries. It's a piece of cake, as long as you cook with love.'

Jimmy moves robotically, taking orders, pouring the rice into a pot, adding hot water, turning on the stove. His movements are sedate but precise, as if he is popping and locking in slow motion. The voice continues: 'Now usually I'd trim the meat, but with the fat it tastes better, and this is a special occasion. So, cut the beef into cubes. After that slice the onions – rough is fine. Got it? Then, mince the garlic and ginger, really fine. It's important to bring out the flavours.'

Jimmy carefully starts cutting the meat, surprised at how easily the knife goes through it. He cuts the larger potatoes into equal quarters, the smaller ones in half, places them in a bowl.

'I learned this when I was a kid growing up in India,' says the voice.

Jimmy doesn't reply, his mouth too dry to conjure words.

'If you know how to make a basic curry, it'll serve you well throughout your life. My mother told me that.'

'I thought you said you grew up in Mexico,' Jimmy manages to say.

The voice grows faint. 'I've been around.'

Jimmy keeps cutting.

'Now. Heat the oil. Fry the onions until they are not quite golden. Leave them a bit pale. Add the ginger and garlic after that, then all the spices. Turmeric, garam masala, coriander seeds, cloves, cardamom. Now, leave them to fry. Put on some music in the meantime, maybe. You can keep these spices now, see? Build up a nice spice rack – annoying at first but worth it. Remember this recipe for later so you can impress your lady friends. You got any lady friends?'

'A few things on the boil,' mumbles Jimmy. The curry smells delicious and his mouth fills with saliva.

'You know they usedta have greyhound jockeys?' Suddenly the voice is fleshed out, human, colloquial.

'What? What's that?'

'Monkeys that ride greyhounds. Here, in Australia.'

'Bullshit.'

'Seriously. They had water and hurdles, too.'

'I don't believe it,' says Jimmy, stirring the curry.

'How could I make that up?' the voice laughs.

'Well, where can we see em?'

'Ah, they stopped doing it in the fifties. The monkeys had a strike cos they weren't being paid enough.'

Jimmy laughs, despite himself. Then he grows serious. 'Tell me the truth. Where are you from? Who are you?'

There's a click, silence and when the voice returns, it's distant and urbane again.

'Check your rice. It should be almost ready to eat.'

The line goes dead.

Jimmy wants to call back but it's a private number. With both hands, he pats down his body, as if looking for his wallet. He can feel his ribs, and his skin is gross. He wonders if he can touch his spine through his belly button. When he starts eating, he can't stop. It is a demonic hunger. He has cooked enough for four people, but he eats and eats until there's not a single grain of rice or spot of curry. Resting the cutlery on the plate, he looks around then jumps up, food swinging in his gut, and runs to the door.

The night has turned incredibly cold. Mercury Fire is shivering in the back yard, freezing or terrified or both. Jimmy hugs him close then brings him inside and feeds him. The dog eats fiendishly, as if he too is fuelled by the same hunger. Once satisfied, the dog looks at him with its shining eye, kind and hopeless. Jimmy pats him and whispers, 'Hello, little dog. Hello, little dog, my friend.' He brushes him with the cat brush and pats his flanks. Mercury Fire curls up at his feet. Is this the only real love possible? The dumb love of an animal? He looks into Mercury's eye and swears he can hear a voice saying, 'Don't worry, Jimmy, you are going to make it. Even if there's no one else, *I* am here with you.'

Jimmy smiles weakly and falls asleep.

PART THREE

'What was I saying? Oh yeah. So . . . years ago, a spaceman came to our hometown. Landed right on the outskirts. Wearing a massive round helmet, he walks straight to a pack of feral dogs sitting under a tree, bro. He speaks in their language, and teaches em how to dig up bones. Then he leads em to a kink in the river and tells em to start digging. They do it, and what they unearth are the graves of blackfullas. A massacre. The dogs dig em all up – femurs, skulls, ribs – and begin dragging em to the doorstep of the mayor and the town councillors at night. These old white cunts, right, they wake up to get their morning paper, or milk, and what do they find? Blackened old bones piled on their doormats, bro. They wonder, where did they come from? But this mayor, he's a sharp one. He knows. He tells em, "Don't whisper a word to anyone about this or by God you'll be doing the air dance in no time." So they get some other blackfullas from the outskirts of town and force them to bury the bones far away, down in the gorge. But the spaceman? He'd taught those dogs well. They found the bones again, dug em up and brought em back to the doorsteps of the town. This went on for two whole weeks, mate, till eventually the mayor gave an order: shoot every dog in sight, cremate them on a pyre with the blackfullas' bones and crush the whole fucken lot to powder.

'As he watched the pyre burning, the mayor's eyes turned into two black opals in his face. That fire burned so bright that you could see redness in the sky all the way down on the south coast.'

1

Midday

A redblood sky.

Here I fucken am, ay?

Booze on booze,
every cell liquor-filled,
the sun crushing me like a can,
pavement so hot
my sneakers leave sticky tread marks.

I call Scarlett.

'I love you, baby. You know I do.'

Slurring.
     Steady now.
Laughter.

Is that her or someone else?
Battery. Dead.

The Leagues Club.
Cricket. Who's playing?
Fuck cricket.
Schooner on schooner.
A bar chick.
I wink but she turns away.

The basketball court,
        no more.

Bulldozer teeth.
Blacktop skinned.
Tears,
hot as napalm.

Another court maybe?
        It won't feel the same.

Fuck the court. Fuck the kids.
And fuck Scarlett if she doesn't wanna call back.

Maybe she'd stay if I got her pregnant . . .

'Oi. When's the boxing on?'
'We're not showing it.'
'What? It's the bloody world championship.'
'Well, yeah. Nothing I can do. Sorry, mate.'
'A pub's gotta show the boxing. If it doesn't —'
'Look, I've got work to do.'

On the balcony,

looking over the river.

First ciggie in ages.

Fuck I've missed you.

The river roaring.

A little girl drowned in there,

remember?

A day later a boy was bitten by a tiger snake.

They find bodies in there sometimes.

Dangerous, snakey river.

But I love it.

The river doesn't change.

The river goes on and on and on.

I scrape together shrappers,

only a few gold coins in there now.

Let the liquor carry me.

No drugs today.

No, no, no, just little golden clouds,

my limbs are treacle.

What'll those kids have left?

And me?

Something. There's always something, ay.

That something is change.

Perth?

A couple,

down by the river,

hand in hand.

Georgie!
With a new man.
They are in love, for sure.
I'm happy for you, Georgie,
I really am.

I'm sorry.

They don't see me.

Eyes closed.
Many women,
faces melting,
then it's just Scarlett there,
sunlight and Scarlett.

Yes I can love,
I know that now,
but can I hold onto her,
I don't know, I don't know,
some things aren't meant to be,   .
but fuck it,

it's all love,
all love that I'm thinking of,
the fury of, the triumph of,
the madness of,
          love.

I wake up in the old graveyard
          against a tombstone.

How the fuck did I get here?
My head is ballooning with pain

and the sun has dried me out.
Skull full of moths.
My phone charged, somehow.
I can see a call to Scarlett
that went for thirty minutes.
What did we talk about?

Maybe I could head to the court?

No more.
Maybe I can use the other one.
        Maybe Perth, maybe something.

I just stare at the sun
        until everything turns white.

2

Aleks stares at a bowl of glossy green apples for a long time, arms resting on the marble kitchen top. In his bedroom, all of his clothes are folded and clean. He holds a shirt to his face and closes his eyes, wiggling his toes on carpet so soft and thick he could sink into it like quicksand. In the basement, he looks at the crates of empty spraycans. A few are un-used, but not enough for a whole piece. He spies a length of yellow rope, which he picks up, loops around his neck, thinking of Gabe's suicide attempt. Holding it in one hand from above, he leans forward slightly, feeling the rope bite into his neck.

He hears the doorbell, distantly. Aleks takes the rope off, folds it up and climbs the stairs. Through the frosted glass, he recognises the silhouettes of his parents. He opens the door and they're holding shopping bags full of groceries. He swears they look smaller and older than he remembers, even though it's only been a couple of months. He tries to usher them in but his father hugs him in the doorway. They stand, holding each other on the threshold. Finally, Aleks says, '*Aide, tat,*' and guides them in. They head to the kitchen immediately.

Sonya comes out of the shower with a towel wrapped around her hair and Aleks kisses her briefly in the hallway. She has just got a new job working in a medical clinic. Her eyes are different, he can see that now. Something of loss, something of tenacity. A long way to go, yet.

When he comes back into the kitchen, a culinary operation is underway. Petar pushes a tulip-shaped glass of yellow *rakia* into his hand and they drink. Biljana is fussing over the stove. He can see they are preparing many of his favourite dishes – *tavche gravche* (beans in a skillet), *polneti piperki* (capsicum stuffed with rice and meat), and a variety of meats ready for grilling.

He tries half-heartedly to help them but they wave him away, moving as a team. He recognises for the first time that his mother's face is inscribed with something like a timeless pain, which is perhaps contained within every Maco, every person from the Balkans, who at some point has just had to cop it, again and again. The lines on her face like infinitesimal divisions and subdivisions of anger, trauma, loss – a tumbling alphabet within the DNA. When Aleks and Jana were children, Petar sometimes recited lyrics that were taken from a song called 'The Orphan' by Konstantin Miladinov of Struga. The last lines come to Aleks now:

'And I feel a pain in my heart
Which reduces all to dust and ashes,
It's as if I had only winter before me,
As if I were always walking in a dark fog.'

Aleks looks outs the window but it is still summer, clear as diamond.

Mila gets off school early and isn't as inquisitive as usual, just overjoyed to see him. Sonya had told him on the phone that Mila had taken to hugging his work overalls to her body in his absence. Aleks takes her by the chin, kisses her, then presents her with a brand new iPad and soon she is watching Beyoncé and Rihanna film clips on it. As he and his parents eat, they discuss Jana's imminent return from Brisbane. Whereas previously the thought of her filled him with a sickening nervousness, he is now calm. The fact that she agreed to come to New Year's is a good sign. She will see him changed, cleansed, ready to face the future – against all odds. People drop in throughout the day. Nicko. The local Orthodox priest, who, wearing purple, holds him by the shoulders and smiles benignly. 'May God be with you.'

'And with you, father.'

'I hope one day to see you in Ohrid. I am going back there soon.'

'God willing.'

Each one of his visitors keeps stealing elegiac looks at him and he wants to yell, 'It's not like I died or anything, for Christ's sake.'

But instead, he pours another *rakia*, and thinks that what he would love most of all is to go for a paint. Then he silently recites the number Clint gave him.

* * *

He's preparing to go to the paint shop when he has a final, unexpected guest. Grace is standing between the twin plaster lions at the top of the stairs, fidgeting. When he sees who it is, he breaks into a big grin and gives her a hug. He busies himself making coffee and hunting through the pantry for cakes, but Grace insists he needn't bother. She looks at his big hands holding the coffee cup.

'Long time no see, Aleks.'

'Too long, too long. Cake?'

'Sure.'

The conversation starts with Jimmy and Solomon, and moves onto how quickly the Town is changing, then it draws to the inevitable, the reason she has come.

Grace begins to tell a story, breathlessly, of how she has been having trouble with a pair of neighbours. One of them, a truck driver, has taken to teaching people how to drive trucks in the carpark behind the flats from as early as seven a.m. on a Saturday. One day, after a long shift, Grace had had enough, and approached them to tell them off. The response had been swift and vituperative. They told her she was an ugly old slut, a coconut fucker, and mocked her for still living in the flats. There are tears in her eyes as she finishes the tale. Aleks looks at her with his head cocked like a bird. A dog barks down the street. He takes a neat sip of the coffee and says, 'Which house is it?'

'The big one. The old one with the lemon trees.'

Aleks knows it. It's the most beautiful house on the street, directly across from the flats, like something designed to taunt them. A Nazi had lived there years ago, hung himself in the attic and now his ghost haunts the place, or so the story went. Nowadays a gunmetal-grey Porsche sneers from the driveway next to two trucks. Aleks nods to himself then stands up and hugs Grace. 'All right; sorry to be rude, but I better get going, Grace. Gotta make the paint store before it closes.'

'But what about —' she starts.

'I heard what you said. I listened. I'll fix it, all right?' He replies in a short but kind voice.

'Thanks, Aleks,' she says guiltily.

* * *

Aleks stands looking at the legal wall, rubbing his hands together. He quickly identifies the piece he is going to paint over. 'Poor bastard, even after all these years his pieces are so toy,' says Aleks. Solomon nods, dazed. It'd taken Aleks ages to get onto Solomon and when he finally had, he told Solomon to bring his new girlfriend along, intrigued. However, when he picked them up they were sullen and quiet. Solomon was drunk already and they'd clearly been fighting.

To Aleks' surprise, Scarlett has brought her own paints. She shakes a tin of MTN 94 and eyes the wall, saying to no one in particular, 'I love how these smell. Kinda like bubblegum.'

Aleks grins. 'You must be crazy. Smells as bad as every other paint.' He's bought the new Ironlak Sugars and is giving them a burl. Particles of paint float in the air. It's hot but a cool breeze is coming through, and soon Solomon is up and at it as well. He puts Spit Syndicate's 'Sunday Gentlemen' on the speakers. Aleks props himself on the tips of his fingers as he paints, relishing the sun. He has no plan, but he writes JAKEL freehand in his tight, interlocking script. He has always been the best writer of the boys, a natural instinct to conceive a whole piece in his mind and execute it to perfection. He had re-arranged some letters in his surname to create that tag. He smiles to himself, thinking of his very first tag, KBAB, when he was just getting accustomed to Australia, and the ridicule he got for it.

The piece is starting to take shape, with a light blue to navy chroming effect in the middle, then black, then yellow. He's sunburnt within an hour.

He gets a message on his phone from an unknown number. It is a photo of a hand with a finger stitched to it, dark blue and scabbed around the stitches. The message below simply reads, 'No hard feelings, ay?' He grimaces and deletes it, then keeps painting. The colours are really popping now and he uses a see-through paint, a black techie, to get a shadow effect on the letters so that they look 3D.

Scarlett, meanwhile, is painting a figure, a woman who is half bird, half human. Solomon is helping her and the wings are a vibrant yellow-to-white fade, like a sulphur-crested cockatoo. Aleks thinks that it's definitely got an art-school vibe but is dope nonetheless. He is surprised to see them share a gentle, conciliatory kiss. *Love and hip hop, ay?* he thinks.

Once finished, they stand back from their pieces. They look so alive they could pop from the concrete and fly through the air.

* * *

Aleks stands in the garden of the house across from the flats. There is a fountain, terracotta tiles and four perfectly manicured lemon trees: a chiaroscuro in blue-black and white. A few fallen fruit on the ground. Holding something downwards in his right hand, he is rolling the blue bead with his left. He pockets the bead, steps forward and picks up a lemon with his free hand, weighs it, sniffs it, then places it carefully back on the ground. As he stoops to do so, the backdoor swings open and the owner of the house appears holding a garbage bag. The thin sound of laughter from a television inside.

Aleks steps silently back into the shadows against the fence; hidden in a darkness so pure it could be an extract of the outer reaches of space. The cricket bat in his right hand feels incredibly heavy, as if it could sink with him into the core of the earth.

The man is well put together, wearing a collared linen shirt tucked into his jeans. He has a military-style haircut. He reaches into his mouth, pulls out a piece of gum and throws it into the garbage bin. Everything he does is purposeful and his face is set severely. Aleks thinks of Grace and his hand tightens on the cricket bat handle, his palms sweaty. He swallows saliva and the man looks up, squinting towards the fence. Aleks doesn't move.

The man steps forward into the moonlight, leaning out as if looking for land from a prow. Aleks stays in shadow, shapeless. His breathing and heartbeat has slowed right down to this moment. Too easy – jump out, three quick steps, then swing the cricket bat right into the man's head. The weapon, the wolf, the victim, the piñata skull, each linked in a chain leading back to the bloody birth of the world. Each illuminated by a caustic falling of stars and well aware of the game's rules – sacrifice, loneliness and violence. *Who chooses their choice?* he thinks.

Aleks spies something at the man's feet. It is a child's tricycle with a basket attached to the handlebars, lying on its side. Aleks had bought one just like it for Mila for Christmas a few years back. Aleks remembers the way she waggled her little toes as he guided her sandalled feet onto the pedals. He relaxes his grip on the cricket bat.

The man, content he hasn't seen anything, turns and goes back into the house. Aleks leans his whole weight against the fence and exhales.

He drives away, parks on the edge of the river, and sees that the water is moving deceptively fast behind bending reeds. Often it roars, a guttural moan like a beast or a plane taking off. But tonight it is quiet and black, reflecting an almighty white swathe of stars. He looks up, squinting hard, and decides he will forget the phone number Clint gave him, he will let each number float from his mind like smoke rings.

He looks around. There is no one there. He reaches into his pocket, takes the blue bead out and pitches it into the water.

3

Jimmy is at the wheel.

The red bonnet is reflecting the murderous sun, throwing up vertical spears of light. The fan is not working. He hasn't eaten since the curry four days ago and is unsure if he is awake or asleep. He feels faint as he listens to the voice on the other end. The voice – robotic, metallic – is unmistakably his father's.

'Magic is faith, James. You don't trust me, I know that, but sometimes there is nothing to lose. And everything is contained in nothingness. You are on a road that is long and straight, no?'

Jimmy nods, even though he is alone in the car.

'I want you to close your eyes and drive. You can open your eyes any time you want. Just trust. If you trust me and drive, and turn when I say, I will tell you everything you need; no, everything you *want* to know.'

Jimmy has the urge to hang up, to tell him to fuck off, but instead he listens and stares straight at the febrile sun, then closes his eyes to blot it out.

'You're on a straight road. Now drive and listen. Listen.' Jimmy, eyes still closed, turns on the engine and begins to drive, with the phone on speaker. 'James, all you need to know is contained in what I say. One. You come from a line of kings. They were a people who lived on the richest land on earth. They had once been wealthy, but they became poor. These people were cast from gold. Their skin, their bones were gold, even their voices. They were each other's gods, each to each. It was a land of mirrors they lived in, everything they saw was gold. But their land, which was once abundant, was now a land of drought – desert, where there should have been water, famine, where there should have been fruit. So the golden people, they began to walk. They walked over the deserts, treetops, over oceans. Turn left now.'

Jimmy does as the voice says. He's parched, and when he speaks, it sounds like he has a mouth full of dead bees. 'The golden people. What were they called?'

The voice doesn't answer, and all Jimmy can hear is the engine and the wind before the voice speaks again. 'The thing is, James, the golden people kept walking and along the way the elements tugged at them, their skin, their golden muscles, their bones. And they resisted. For a time. But they were hungry, and knew a thirst you and I hope never to feel. They began to sell pieces of themselves, bit by bit. First it was an eye, then an ear, then a tongue, a heart. Soon it was a free for all. Within no time, all that was left were golden voices on the wind. Turn right.'

Jimmy follows orders, sharply. There is silence and he drives onwards and onwards. The sweat drips down his nose and onto his lips. He hits something, hard, but doesn't open his eyes. Instead, he keeps the wheel steady. The voice speaks again.

'The second thing you must know is the most important: the truth is not real. Sometimes all we have are questions and no answers. So we make up the answers.'

'Stop talking to me in riddles. If you are who you say you are, then why can't we meet in person, face to face?'

'Because I had an accident.'

'What kind?'

The voice coughs. 'I was burned.'

'How?'

There is a long pause and Jimmy waits patiently before the voice finally speaks again. 'I was living in an abandoned car, somewhere on the coast, could've been Port Macquarie, or maybe further north. It doesn't matter. It was an old Holden, cleaned out by rust and scavengers looking for parts. Two side windows were shattered but somehow the driver's side windows were intact, as were the seats and roof. During the day, I would walk along the beach. I would get high up on the cliffs and look for changes in the horizon. I saw schools of dolphins. One day I even saw a whale, although it could have been a submarine. Mostly, I just watched the restless sea. I soon began to notice the smallest variations in its moods. It's the same with music, isn't it? To a trained ear, the wrong snare on a beat becomes as obvious as the carcass of a dead elephant on a suburban street.'

'What did you eat?'

'I caught fish and prized shellfish off the rocks. I ate them raw with seawater. At night, I huddled in a blanket and listened to the thin fingers of rain drumming away on the roof. The rain would wiggle down the window in patterns, throwing shadows, like moving scripture, onto my lap. I swear I could read messages in them.'

'Like what?'

'Turn right.' Jimmy does as he is ordered. The voice continues, as if it hasn't heard the question. 'On the dashboard, someone had pinned the photo of a young boy. He was skinny and wearing a Mickey Mouse jumper, staring straight at the camera. The boy seemed so full of longing my heart felt fit to burst. He looked like you, James. Since I had no photos of you, I began to imagine he was. I would tell him jokes, teach him recipes, tell him about my travels, my childhood. I apologised to him, James, I apologised for not being there. I told him I was ashamed.'

Jimmy can feel a bodily presence next to him in the car now. He can smell the sweat and breath of a man. The car is excruciatingly hot and he resists the urge to open his eyes or reach out to touch the man in the passenger seat, whose voice is now only half a metre from his ear. Instead, he drops the phone and takes his foot off the accelerator. The voice keeps talking, alive, present, close.

'One night, when I was sleeping, I heard voices. I smelled petrol, I saw flames. There were men dancing around the car, laughing, shouting. I nearly died, James. They left me for dead. I don't know how I got out of the car, but I did. I have burns on most of my body. I look like a fruit that has been peeled and left to harden. That kind of pain is . . . unbearable. My eyes don't work, my legs. I am so ugly that I am glad I have no eyes to see. Nowadays, I just lie in bed and dream of rain. Not a light sprinkle, but something heavy and sweet and soulful, silver droplets, fat as coins or bullets. I raise my face and imagine the rain hitting me side on, from above, from below, turning this skin into thick mud that flowers can grow from. But it is a long, long time since any of us have seen rain, isn't it?'

Jimmy can feel the car slowly coming to a halt.

'So. That is the *how*. But you surprise me. You didn't ask the most important question.'

'Which is?'

'*Why?*'

Jimmy clears his throat. 'Why?'

The voice doesn't reply. Jimmy lets the car stop. When he opens his eyes, he is facing the lake. He is alone in the car. The bonnet is steaming, as if it just passed through fresh rain.

* * *

He wakes up in hospital, a drip connected to his arm.

'You're badly dehydrated, mate. You should stay overnight,' says a nurse.

'Nah, nah, I can't.'

'You have to.'

'I gotta feed my dog.'

'Can you get someone else to do it?'

'Nah. I have to. I have to. Please.'

She smiles softly. 'I understand, mate. I can't live without my dog for more than a couple of hours.' She pats him on the hand. 'You're a nice bloke.'

At the bus interchange, Jimmy comes across a crime scene. The cops are pulling a tarp over a bloke and a woman is crying. A hand is stuck out from underneath the tarp and the cops are shooing people away. One of the younger cops looks scared. Jimmy watches from across the street. He's never seen a dead person before, besides Ulysses Amosa, waxen and well dressed at the funeral. The arm that sticks out, resting palm up on the concrete, has a tattoo of a swallow on the wrist.

The evening goes from pink to purple to black as he walks home, the night full of shapes and shadows. Jimmy can smell tinder and see the moon through the powerlines, blind and lost. He stumbles forward, as if drunk. When he gets home, he'll sleep for ages. Tomorrow. Tomorrow he'll go shopping. Stock the fridge.

In the light of a streetlamp, objects begin to appear: a car, a shopping trolley, a sofa, a jumble of sticks and leaves. He moves forward, as if through a fog, although he's walked this street so many times before, too many. The Town is a maze, with a beast at its heart, like that ancient Greek story Ulysses Amosa used to read to the boys. Or maybe the Town is a thousand-roomed madhouse, built by a psycho, and somehow he's meant to find his way out.

A final shape appears in front of him, magically, in the gutter. He runs to it.

He's crouched in the gutter at first, patting the fine fur. He traces his right hand over the hound's muscled legs, touches his paws, rubs his thumb on its nose – dry already. His hand rests on Mercury Fire's belly, which is still vaguely warm, though it could be the sweat from his palm. He shifts his weight and his knees crack like buckshot. He cradles Mercury Fire in his lap then holds him to his chest. The body is almost completely stiff. Lights come threading through the darkness. He's aware of car horns, and maybe even a person talking to him, but he doesn't reply. At a certain point, he lies next to the dog, still holding him. Eventually he stands and carries him to his house. The door is open.

He gently places Mercury Fire on the couch and begins to brush him. He sniffs his fur, which is mostly odourless, but now has a tinge of dust. He tries to feed him some water, but it dribbles onto the couch, a spreading stain. He sends signals with his brain, messages of love, but there is no reply now.

He talks to him the whole night.

At dawn, he showers, dresses as if for church, and then takes the hound in a blanket down to the river. He has a shovel. He covers him with dirt, beneath a willow tree. In the morning light he sees a crow land nearby. He shoos the crows away, again and again. Jimmy cries for a long time.

4

Jimmy is awake, the mattress beneath him warm with sweat, the dark room compressed. He is eleven. Pinstripes of light on his upturned face from the closed venetian blinds. His lips tremble. He cannot breathe; he almost moans at the heat. Jimmy rises and looks through a chink in the blinds. An owl sits on the branch of a plum tree. Hello, owl, *he says in his mind.* Hello, little owl, my friend.*

The owl swoops away in a bellying trajectory, surreal.

Jimmy eases the door open and goes into the kitchen, walking on tiptoe. Scale disappears in the darkness but he knows his way instinctively. He feels around inside a cupboard. He touches a screwdriver, a hammer and a light bulb before his hand lands on what he's looking for.

He goes down the stairs, past the potted flowers on the landing – freesias, geraniums, irises, all colourless in the moonlight – past the second floor that has no pot plants just pools of water, past the first floor (leaving wet footprints now) with its jam jar full of ciggie butts, then onto ground level, the concrete cool on his bare soles. He almost considers throwing some rocks at Aleks' window but is afraid of his father. He army-crawls under the stairs and through a space that leads into the carpark underneath the flats. There is a 4WD and a busted Datsun, covered in spiderwebs and drawings in its dusty windows. He goes deeper into the carpark, feeling his way along the brick wall when it gets too dark to see, until he is in the corner. He squats on his haunches.

When the first match lights, it flares in front of his face, lighting it up like an animated mask, the contours of cheek and chin, eyes glistening like a Kathakali dancer, until it burns to his fingertips and submits him back to blackness.

The second match he examines, turning it, watching how the feminine flame drips upwards, ancient gold, so steadfastly committing to wood and oxygen. He looks at it from beneath and from above before it dies. 'Hello, flame. Hello, little flame, my friend.'

He lights ten more matches before he thinks he needs something to set aflame. Gathering dry leaves into a mound, he grins at how quickly they burst into flame, sending smoke into his face. As the flames grow, an emptiness fills momentarily. A question is answered. He stares and stares and the fire pushes outwards in a circle like the iris of a glowing eye.

Jimmy strikes match after match and flicks them onto the dry leaves. Each match his own private explosion, his own handheld Hiroshima, a mini sun, consigning the leaves to the nothingness of things forgotten. Here in these new flames, the most ancient, an atavistic energy that absolves him of all sin, all recent memory, all he feels and is, all he knows and is never to know. Jimmy sees himself within them, trying his best to mirror the flames' forgetfulness and, for a moment, succeeding. As the flames lower to a lambent murmur, he wonders how it might burn with petrol on it.

He looks up, feeling the sensation that someone is watching him. Anger spikes within him that he has been robbed of this moment. It morphs to fear, realising that nobody is there. He stamps out the fire and goes upstairs. Everybody is still asleep. He tucks himself into bed and drifts into slumber, fingers still humming from where the matches burned them.

5

'Move with me to Perth, Solomon.'
'And live with all those sandgropers?' I try to smile.
'I'm being serious. Make up your mind.'

I don't answer.
I just stare at a cat-shaped
        water stain on Scarlett's ceiling.
'Kush and Corinthians' by Kendrick Lamar coming from the speakers.

'You want it to be easy, don't you?' she says at last.
'I don't know what I want.'
'You do. You want it uncomplicated. But it doesn't come like that – it
only comes rough and broken and weird.'

I'm lying on my side now,
        fingers in her messy hair.
We're face to face. 'This place is all I know, Scarlett.'
She is almost pleading. 'You said it yourself. The Town is changing.
There are Toby's in Perth; there are basketball courts in Perth.'

'But if I don't come to terms with this, I won't come to terms with anything, with the whole lot. Just give me some time, Scarlett. Stay.' I muster the courage then add, 'I checked out a space today. I'm thinking of renting it. Maybe turn Amosa's All-Stars into a drop-in centre for kids.'

She doesn't reply,
        just nods,
        the look
        on her face
                unreadable.

I can hear a lawnmower passing outside.

This was not the Australia
        Scarlett had wanted to escape to.

She had dreamed of an endless road,
        a ribbon through rainforest and desert.
She had dreamed of the red heart,
        coral reefs and perfect beaches.
The Town,
        to her,
is small and mediocre.

But it's mine
and fuck it,
sometimes you don't have to move outwards,
you can burrow down and plant roots.

She nods again as if she's read my mind,
then kisses me,
on the corner of my mouth,
        so gently,

and when she draws away,
there's a faint smile on her lips.

Now I understand.

To her I'm fading –
a memory, a ghost already.

6

'Happy New Year, ya mad cunt.'

'You too, bro.' Aleks and Solomon clink glasses and drink down to the ice.

'And welcome home,' says Solomon in a lower voice.

From Aleks' balcony, they have a panoramic view of the whole Town. Rosettes of blue, white and orange pop and sizzle in the blackness, revealing a strange and blanched suburban geometry. Inside, behind a glass sliding door, a party is in full swing, the sound of laughter, cutlery, glasses and music. Frank Ocean's 'Pyramids' is playing. They watch Jimmy swig straight from a Jim Beam bottle, wipe his lips and then drink again.

'Remember that storm we saw from here?' says Aleks.

Solomon nods. A year ago the storm had rolled in, its body like an enormous shark rolling and thrashing across the sky, summoning other phantom monsters from the depths, revenant creatures playing between forks of pure light. As soon as the lightning grounded on the far hills, they saw thick columns of blue-grey smoke rising from the bushland.

'Solomona. Why didn't you come visit?'

'Man . . . I didn't have the time . . . '

'Tell me the truth.' Aleks' eyes steady.

Solomon looks into his glass as if more liquor will magically appear. He speaks tentatively. 'I was scared, *Atse*. All that shit you were going through was like . . . poison. I didn't want it to touch me. I'm sorry, *uce*.'

Solomon puts his hand on Aleks' shoulder. Aleks looks down and shakes his head. More fireworks explode, a long chain scribbling love heart shapes in the air. Aleks puts a hand in the air in front of him, palm outwards, as if pushing open a door. 'Nah. You did the right thing. Everyone wants to change.'

'I just needed a break from it all. Needed time to think, to handle shit on my own,' says Solomon. Aleks looks back inside. Jana Janeski has arrived. She is dressed in a cream blouse and her hair is drawn back tightly. She seems poised and confident. Aleks finds it hard to reconcile his memories of her as a child with this woman. His stomach lurches and he is surprised to feel that even talking to her will require great courage. Solomon doesn't notice and keeps speaking. 'It wasn't easy to do, cos we been through so much shit together. You can't just leave all that behind. History, bloody history.'

Aleks turns back to Solomon and clears his throat before speaking again. 'You know, there's a rock that looks like a runway, just below the Church of St Clement. You can see most of Lake Ohrid from there, brother, the most beautiful lake in Europe, the pearl of the Balkans. That church is where St Clement taught his disciples the Cyrillic script for the first time. Stand there on the rock and you can see all the way to Albania, wood smoke over the villages, mountains, fluro crosses, clouds like . . . purple angels. There's three hundred and sixty-five churches around the lake, one for every day of the year, and crosses so you don't ever forget God, understand? Look down from the rock and you can see right to the bottom. A million coloured rocks and light, so much light.

'And everyone is loud and hysterical. All your mates egging you on and you're shouting back *I'm gonna do it, I'm gonna do it!* But fuck me dead, you're scared as shit. You take a run up along the rock, sprint hard and jump out as far as you can – there's only a bit of leeway cos there's two rocks just under the water on either side. If you misjudge, you'll crack your leg or your head. My mate Vladko saved a man's life down there. The bloke knocked himself out on a rock – Vladko had to swim down till he nearly drowned himself and carry the bugger to the surface. You've got all that in your head and the noise and the beauty and then you jump. You fall for three seconds, joy and fear and oxygen and your heart going *da doom.*' Aleks pounds his fist on his chest. 'Then you hit the water, it slaps you right on your rib meat, and it's cold, all bubbles, cold, the weight of water right on you, your heart about to burst. And you've never felt so good in your fucken life, swear to God, brother.

'We've all been falling. And who knows where the fuck we'll land.' He drinks. 'When I first got inside, I thought it was a test. Not just for me, to see if I could get through it, but to you, as a mate. And I lay awake every time you didn't visit, thinking that you'd failed the test.' Solomon goes to protest, but Aleks holds up a hand. 'But maybe it was what we needed, brother. Both. All.'

The last of the fireworks fade, revealing the Town's pulsing catch of lights, driven by more than electricity, by some raw and essential turbine, a galaxy within each window. Even from this far away they can see the smoke drift and hear faint cheers.

* * *

As soon as they go back into the room, the music hits them.

'Bloody boiling in here!' says Aleks, and busies himself hauling another fan into the room.

The evening is edging towards the countdown. Aleks' Pakistani neighbour, Amjad, is nibbling a chicken wing, admiring an icon of St Clement that Petar Janeski has finished. Sonya and Biljana bring in more and more food, every surface covered by pizzas, smoked fish, pickles, chicken. Aleks has never felt so blessed, so lucky. Jana is picking at a salad and Aleks walks up to her, but he doesn't know what to say. All he can muster is, 'You look beautiful.' With tears in his eyes, he hugs her and feels her stiffen. When he pulls away, her eyes are bright but her mouth is still set and severe. It is then he realises that certain things loom larger than forgiveness and reconciliation: memory, for one, and history, bloody history.

He is about to say so, when all of the room comes alive with cheering and the clinking of glasses. 'To Aleks!' they yell. Solomon is sitting on the lounge, eyes shining, laughing with Scarlett on his knee. 'Aleks! Come here, come here, bro,' he slurs. Aleks pinballs between people, accepting kisses and hugs and punches on the shoulder. There is a pop rap song on, the bass bleeding. He sits down next to Solomon and Scarlett. Sonya sets food in front of him. He tears a piece of skin from the chicken breast and chews it slowly, the grease shining on his lips. His daughter jumps on his lap and kisses him. She smells like berry cordial and she, too, has grease on her lips. 'Hey, sweetheart.' She smiles, staring, searching his face like a puzzle. He cannot bear her eyes. He looks away and sees Jimmy, alone in the corner, watching him. Jimmy nods slightly, his eyes full of some kind of longing.

The hip hop beat changes and there is silence. Then, as if by magic or design, a *gajda*, the Macedonian bagpipe, wails an ancient note. A moment later, a heavy bass drum kicks in. The song is a traditional *oro*, somehow mournful and jubilant at the same time. The partygoers are in a trance. Aleks rises to his feet; all eyes are on him. He slowly shuffles side to side, raises his arms and begins to dance. His feet are clumsy at first but the music is moving like clouds beneath him, buffeting, carrying him. The note was birthed far, far away, in a resonant goatskin. The note expands and in it are mountains and crosses and boats full of countrymen, navigating their souls to places unknown. It holds the bones of soldiers and sailors, Ancient, heaped on the floor of Lake Ohrid and the Aegean. It contains their strange, small town, the bushland surrounding it, each and every one of them. His eyes close.

As he dances, he thinks of lost dogs, who snarl and pant in alleyways; those that race and are put to death; of all the pretty birds that fly so fast but never fast enough; of dignity born from suffering, only to be translated into madness and bone; of endurance; of sad fires lost in space, flapping like tattered flags.

The flutes kick in and then the tempo begins to speed up, insistent. For a man of his size, Aleks is nimble, he is moving, he is dancing, he is moving, a frenzy. He opens his eyes and sees that everyone has joined in, they too with closed or joyous eyes. He is with his family, blood and chosen, and he has made his choice. He will leave Australia.

The countdown begins.

7

The day after Ulysses Amosa's funeral, Jimmy walks to the river and sets fire to a patch of grass. The flames rush outwards, catching on every dried blade and burr. The sound of cicadas is soon smothered by the snicker of flames. It blows low towards the river where a stand of poplars rises, opposite the old graveyard. He kneels before the flames to watch them shear across the grass. They move out evenly, an expanding diadem of flames. Then he lies down, watching the flames rise like the points of a moving crown, fluid, completely consuming all thought and concern. The flames grow more mesmerising the larger they become, beating an awesome rhythm, the perfectly malleable and self-creating edge of flame. The sun bears silent witness, watching a distant relative washing its thousands of hands over and over and over. It is quite a fire.

In the flame haze he can see his stepfather's funeral, the Samoan community singing, their hymns binding into something utterly ethereal. He can see Grace crying, Petar weeping for the first time in anyone's memory, Solomon expressionless, Aleks full of impotent fury. And maybe it is a trick of the light or his blurry eyes, but he thinks he can see his father standing in a suit, slightly removed, with a crooked smile, escaping the blinding heat under a tree. He can see his own skinny, shaking hands, aching to strike a match.

As he lies on the ground and watches the flames, he begins to smile and he isn't sure why. There are tears in his eyes, but there is some sort of release and connection between his tormented heart and the rippling flames. He is hauled up by his collar, so hard that his neck twists and his knee is wrenched. It is the man who lives in a ramshackle house near the river. He drags Jimmy away while his wife dumps buckets of water on the fire. They sit him in their lounge room. The woman calls the cops while the man drinks port wine and watches Jimmy until Grace and the cops come. Grace's eyes make Jimmy cry; but in the years to follow, Jimmy will be locked up four times for graffiti and firestarting. Something unstoppable has come alive in him.

8

You, Jimmy Amosa,
walk down the path,
grass, twigs and stones,
a million fibres scattered
        by flood,
            clay drought-cracked.
There are wild oats,
blonde and bending to your right,
            the ochre of barbed wire,
and lower in the valley some green beneath the muted tones.
The black of previous fires,
the warp and arch of trees,
ragged branches and strange shapes that hang like lanterns.
The bluestone path abraded to reveal the dirt beneath,
the jacaranda purple and brilliant.

You splash petrol on the ground   from a jerry can
            and lead it in a thin trail back up the track.
Methodically you dry your hands,   every crease in the knuckles

where the petrol could hide,   in between the fingers.
You take a ciggie out of your pocket and light it,
hesitant, scared the flame will catch on some hidden fuel.

You smoke and you are very calm.

You are a king who is about to set in motion
a choreography of dancers   and jesters.
You toss the ciggie on a patch of leaves that shimmer with fuel.
They take the ember
and spit some flames into the air.
You dance back,
the flames spread their fingers through the grass.
A shudder goes through you and   you look around.

You are completely alone.

You climb for twenty minutes
until you reach the ridge that overlooks the gorge.
You turn around and can see
the Town on the other side of the hill.
On the ridge,
you look down at the fire,
amazed that it has grown so fast.
The heat reaches you,
even this high up.
Sweat on your forehead,
your fringe damp.
You unzip and pull down your jeans.
Your cock is harder than it's ever been.
You reach down and begin to stroke it,
smudging it with fuel and grit.
You can feel the heat of the fire –
the heat, the summer, the smoke and, at last,   the power.

Soon you are masturbating ferociously,
sweat drops running down your back, arse and legs.
You stare at your creation below
and when you come,
a scribble of semen spurts
onto the shale at your feet
and sizzles.

Are you awake or asleep?
Are you laughing or crying?

The bushfire,
that frenzied heart,
bursts.

Alleycat flames dance,
backs arching and teeth
grinning, snarling, unravelling,
gibbering waves that leap and cascade onto fresh tinder,
swallowing gumnuts, dry twigs, timber rich with oil,
grass, sacrificing shrubbery to their holy wrath.

The wind lifts a single burning leaf
and it alone
holds the furious sorcery
waiting to inscribe itself on the world.

Trees explode.
          Like.
                    That.

Animals next,
galloping and loping, barging and shouldering,
that shiver, somehow, then shrivel,

whirling, backflipping in anguish,
screaming weeping pirouetting shuddering and finally falling.

The bushfire is an ignorant brute,
racing up hills
        with determined and muscular movement.

Koalas are immolated in trees/
        spraycans explode/
                Horses scream against fences,
                        teeth lathered and skin bubbling/
                                a cow's milk curdles in its udder.
                                A woman poached in her swimming pool.

Now a dog screams from the scrub, his fire fiercer.
                                It is coming indeed.

Your heart leaps,
because at first you think it is Mercury Fire.
But it's not.
It's a feral dog aflame –
                        a satellite of monstrosity.

You see it all now.

In the flames there are scriptures and mazes,
        a labyrinth of tinted moving mirrors.
There is a whole population
        treading down the corridors of flames,
                thousands of people,
                        men, women, children,
the pretty ones, the ugly ones, the young, the lost,
        the Damien Crawford's who never die,
        those who submit, those who endure,

those who burn within or drown without,   arms linked, in lines,
moving forward,   a legion facing the greatest horror of all,
their eyes reflective, their skin spangling with blisters then charring,
but they walk on, their skin peels, muscle falls from their bones
and they are a great phalanx
                              of reeking,
                                          clattering skeletons.

And each skeleton now raises an awful finger
and points to the sky
to where the other planets are,
who have disowned Earth for its beauty and follies.

You see it all,
Jimmy Amosa,
our origins and ends,
           our ruin, our rejuvenation.

A monstrous, deranged chaos prevails.

A cardiogram of the nation is written into the rumbling flames. From
the Eyre Peninsula to Gippsland to the Blue Mountains, horizons shimmer and bend. The needle on the fire-danger sign points to *catastrophic*
and *code red*. Life and Death are both staunch in their will to survive.
The large and small clash against one another – wind, land, water,
fire and man embroiled in a tussle with no resolution except that it
must happen again. Sobbing and screaming. Sirens. Black clouds cauli-
flower. Rubber is scribbled on asphalt as trucks swerve through the
firewall. Animals seek refuge on highways, mammals and reptiles next
to each other, stunned by fear, arranged as if by design on tar so hot a
man's foot can sink in it. Power generators break down and dams are
filled with a turbid mixture of ash and silt. In two days, a fire truck is
burned to its spine, ten people lose their lives and hundreds of houses

are destroyed. Rumours of looting. Abandoned cars showed their ribs to the sky.

After the fire has moved on, people pick through the carnage of their houses like rag and bone men, with tears streaking clear lines down their masks of soot. A woman clutches a photo album to her chest while her husband sifts through bricks and broken pottery and misshapen blobs that were once glass bottles. He stoops, picks up a diamond ring and holds it to the red sun.

Sympathy and charity flow and a school hall is turned into a makeshift camp for the displaced. People who have never met sleep side by side on donated mattresses and many ask why it took a catastrophe of this magnitude to finally bring forth compassion in Australians.

The simmering whispers now.

How did it start? Lightning in the mountains? A firefighter, a glory seeker, a wannabe hero (and indeed an off-duty fireman did arrive at the blaze a little too quickly)? Some say it was live ordnance practice at the army facility that kicked it off. Some say it was the emergency services department's fault for being tardy and underprepared. The emergency services department points out that a pine forest too close to the suburbs had been allowed to grow uncontrolled for too long. Was it further proof of global warming? The prime minister replies that global warming is a fallacy and that bushfires had been a part of Australian life for as long as anyone can remember. He poses next to the firefighters for pictures before his PA ushers him back into the chauffer-driven car.

An old woman, sitting on her verandah, notes to her daughter that the Ancients had long used fire to shape the land, to create abundance, to allow flora to flourish that needed fire to release its seeds, to control the wilderness and to prevent bushfires through back-burning.

And indeed, soon, the rejuvenation will begin. Little bluebells will appear from cracks in the earth, tiny stark eyes that observe the world as it remakes itself. The immense gallery of black trees will grow new leaves and stand on grass as level and green as felt on a pool table.

But for now, the fire, with its millions of beating hearts, understands, and will understand, all.

9

I'm there early,
     watching the support act
          with Scarlett.

He is obviously nervous
and keeps yelling,
     'Putcha fucken hands UP!'

The room has five people in it.

Scarlett orders two gin and tonics.
The barman hands her change
     over with a smile.

It's a five-dollar note.
     Queen Elizabeth wears a crown of thorns
          and there's a timebomb on her shoulder.

Scarlett crushes it into her pocket.

. . . And here come the lads

Charged up and gnashing their pearlies,
kebab-fed thoroughbreds and mongrels
single file down the club stairs like
mercenaries,
stamps drying on their wrists.

The show is about to start.

Sin One at first seems more phantom than flesh.

He emerges from the darkness at the back of the stage,
         slowly.
He is wearing an oversized hoodie, face full of shadows.
Then we see the jagged nose and cheekbones lit red by gelled spotlights.
He moves towards centrestage
like a latter-day monk or prophet.
Jimmy nudges me,
 and his teeth glow neon in the blacklights.
DJ Exit is spinning now, an industrial beat.
                      Dirty, bassy.
His face is rendered masklike by the lights
but his eyes are feral,
dancing from the decks to Sin One to the crowd
then back to Sin One,
who posits himself at the front of the stage
and stands rock still.

He is enormous.

He pauses,
then raises his left arm.

The room is only half full,
but responds
with a terrifying, guttural roar like a
beast in a bear pit.

The bassline is a deep drone
but DJ Exit is scratching on top of it now,
rapier precise.

Aleks leans over and whispers to Jimmy,
who nods and takes something from him at thigh level,
 slips it into his mouth with a jerky movement
then takes a swig of vodka, lime and soda.
Aleks smiles at him and nods,
his lips pursed almost flirtatiously.
Jimmy whispers to me
but I shake my head.

Jimmy has a look of absolute concentration
on his face,
        that could be excitement or terror.

DJ Exit's eyes are closed,
in a trance.
Sin One has been perfectly still,
but then his right arm lifts to his face,
creating a ninety-degree angle.

At first his flow is a whisper.
People crane and stretch to hear him.
Then he begins to snarl and yelp into the mic –
fast, complex, wordy.

Despite his speed,
the crowd is yelling every word.
He is their god.
They are moving up and down
with their arms around each other's shoulders,
like a bedsheet billowing.

There is something in his performance
that seems significant,
like all the anger and futility and tenderness
within in him are rising and capsizing in his sea of words,
bobbing between him and his audience.
The maimed captain of a shipwrecked generation,
roaring against certain death.
His words are respite from the pain,
futile,
but respite nonetheless.

Scarlett turns to the crowd,
with all their parched lips
and upturned faces.
Some people are laughing,
some are intently focused,
some are shaking their heads in wonder.

I must look disturbed,
because Scarlett asks, 'What's wrong?'
'Nothing. This is dope. He's different to what I remember. He
looks . . . old.'
'Well, it does happen, Solomon. Even to you, baby.'

I grimace.

Sin One

I approach him and he's arguing
with the promoter.
'Bro, I didn't see a single poster around town.'
'There were heaps. And we did online promo.'

Sin One turns and gives me a tired smile.

'Bro, I'm a massive fan.
Any chance you can sign this?'
I say, holding out my ticket.

'Sure. Actually, I'll do one better than that.'

He fumbles in his pocket
and pulls out a crumbled piece of paper.
'What's your name?'
'Solomon.'
He scribbles on the page and passes it to me.

It is his set list.

At the bottom,
in surprisingly neat handwriting –
'Solomon. Thanks and peace. Sin One.'

The paper is damp with sweat.

I look at him and know
that I'll never see this man again.

The end

The clubbers emerge in a daze
not wholly induced by drugs and drink.

The dawn sky is black –
the rising sun is lipstick red.
'I'd forgotten about the fire!'
says Scarlett.

Her arm is linked with mine
and we look up at the firefighting helicopters
sniggering overhead.

Jimmy is laughing, head far back,
and we smile at him.
The strange look he had is gone
and replaced with something
      jubilant.
Aleks' eyes are dull with drink –
a piece of pizza in each hand,
head moving from one to the other.
We walk past the late-night
watering holes and bloodhouses
that haemorrhage noise and people.

Scarlett is watching me.

I catch her eye
and I can see the end.
We smile at each other regardless,
      broad and pure.

We kiss.

This will end soon, my darling.
This beautiful, dumb love –
this will end.

My Scarlett.

I look beyond her shoulder
and begin laughing and pointing,
eyes full of wonder.

'What's so funny?'

Soon she is the same, though,
our eyes upwards –
pointing and laughing
like farmers seeing the first rain
in years.

But it is not rain.

It is ash,
the finest black powder
falling onto our collars and shoulders,
drifting around us, falling down
     like soot from the grate of heaven.

ACKNOWLEDGEMENTS

In memory of Andrew McMillan, Hunter MC, Ollie MC, Auntie Marj and Grandma.

Above all, I must thank my mother, Helen, for everything.

Thanks to my father, Musa bin Masran, and my family in Malaysia. Special thanks to my editors Ben Ball, Caro Cooper and Michael Nolan for their insight, patience and sharpness. Extra special thanks to Sophie Cunningham, who lit a fire under me to write this thing in the first place. Thanks to the brilliant Penguin team of Anyez Lindop, Rebecca Bauert, Alex Ross, Adam Laszczuk, Laura Thomas, Andre Sawenko, Rhian Davies, Clementine Edwards, Cate Blake, Nicola Redhouse and Heidi McCourt. Thanks to The New Press team, including Maury Botton, Julie McCarroll, Michelle Blankenship, Ben Woodward and Carl Bromley. Thanks to Fatima Bhutto. Thanks to my agent Tara Wynne at Curtis Brown. Thanks to Cole Bennetts, Kadi Hughes, Simon Cobbold, Sof Ridwan, Karolina Kilian, Kilifoti Eteuati, Sisilia Eteuati, Will Small,

David Celeski, Aleksandar Celeski, James Rush, Tristan Gaven, Antony Loewenstein, Joshua King, Bibi Jol, Leanne Pattison, John Mazur, Lamaroc, Tornts, Brad Strut, The Tongue, The Australia Council, Hau Latukefu, Daniel Merriweather, Horrorshow, Mantra, Tom Thum, Newsense, Mohsin Hamid, Christos Tsiolkas, Nam Le, Sarah Tooth, Stephen Atkinson, Luka Lesson, L-Fresh the Lion, Rob Lancaster, Daniel Guinness, Mighty Joe, Sean M Whelan, Raph Dixon, Marksman Lloyd, Big Village, Gary Dryza, Joelistics, Thundamentals, Maxine Beneba Clarke, Emilie Zoey Baker, Polly Hemming, Kate Shelton at Benedict House, and Ali Cobby Eckermann at the Aboriginal Writers Centre: all great advisors, readers and friends.

Finally, much love and many thanks to you, the reader.

Omar Musa, Queanbeyan, 2015

CREDITS

Lyrics from 'Life is . . . ' by David Dallas (2011), Dirty Records, Dawn Raid Entertainment and Duck Down Records. Courtesy of the artist.

Lyrics from 'Listen Close' by Horrorshow (2013), Elefant Traks. Courtesy of the artist.

Lyrics from 'Animal Kingdom' by Trem (2011), Unkut Recordings. Courtesy of the artist.

Lyrics from 'Face the Fire' by Jimblah (2011), Elefant Traks. Courtesy of the artist.

Lyrics from 'Poison' by Tornts (2013), Broken Tooth Entertainment. Courtesy of the artist.

On page 325, the line 'Now a dog screams from the scrub, his fire fiercer. It is coming indeed' is an interpolation of a line from the bushfire scene in *Tree of Man*, Patrick White (1955).

Please note that every effort has been made to contact copyright holders. Anyone with an outstanding claim should contact the Penguin Group (Australia).

Publishing in the Public Interest

Thank you for reading this book published by The New Press. The New Press is a nonprofit, public interest publisher. New Press books and authors play a crucial role in sparking conversations about the key political and social issues of our day.

We hope you enjoyed this book and that you will stay in touch with The New Press. Here are a few ways to stay up to date with our books, events, and the issues we cover:

- Sign up at www.thenewpress.com/subscribe to receive updates on New Press authors and issues and to be notified about local events
- Like us on Facebook: www.facebook.com/ newpressbooks
- Follow us on Twitter: www.twitter.com/thenewpress

Please consider buying New Press books for yourself; for friends and family; or to donate to schools, libraries, community centers, prison libraries, and other organizations involved with the issues our authors write about.

The New Press is a 501(c)(3) nonprofit organization. You can also support our work with a tax-deductible gift by visiting www.thenewpress.com/donate.